DESERT
STAR

AVEN JAYCE

Mirror Call Press

DESERT STAR

Copyright © 2014 by Aven Jayce
New Edition, Fall 2017
A&M Michigan Editing
Cover and Book Design by Triple J Marketing
Published by Mirror Call Press

ISBN-10: 099140498X
ISBN-13: 978–0991404988

www.facebook.com/AvenJayceAuthor

DEC   2018

For AK

The NOVA trilogy is intended for mature audiences due to explicit sex scenes, strong language, and abusive situations. It contains subject matter that may be disturbing for some readers.

One

"I TOLD THE KID to wait upstairs, Paul. I did my best to calm him down, but he took a swing at me, and he's crying."

"Did you get the take?"

"Yeah, I did." Doron pauses. He searches for regret in Paul's face, but sees only a smirk of pleasure. "Who the hell will be turned on when they watch shit like this?" He exhales. "It's obvious in the take that he didn't want to do it. Everyone's gonna see that. I don't know about you, but I couldn't jerk off to it."

"I can't believe you'd fucking question one of the best business decisions I've ever made. You know how many clients asked for this? Just wait. If they like what they see and want more, our bank accounts will be overflowing in a few months."

"Well... Leondra's gonna kick your ass. Fuck, Paul. I might have to kick your ass. This feels wrong. My head hurts just thinking about it. You better be careful, this kid's messed up right now. What's the plan to calm him down? What if he goes to the cops?" Doron asks, pacing next to the kitchen table, watching Paul drop a needle through the grip of a tattoo machine. "Why do you have two of those?"

"One's a liner and the other's a shader," Paul says, ignoring Doron's other questions. "Maybe you should head home. *I don't need you for anything else. Besides, your wife will be on your case again if you're late. I can handle our young Star on my own.*"

Doron stops and grips the back of Paul's chair. He peers over his shoulder at the machine, shaking his head in disbelief. "*So, you're really gonna do this?*"

"*What? Scare the shit out of him so he knows not to cross me? Yeah, I am. It's part of the game. He'll know he's mine every time he looks down at his chest. This is only step one. Trust me, the kid won't go to the cops. He's a momma's boy, and I have a surprise for him.*"

Doron sighs. "*I'll stay. I won't be able to sleep tonight with the image of him in tears stuck in my head. I need some sort of closure to what we did this afternoon.*" He walks to the stairwell and listens for Cove. "*It's quiet up there. Do you think I should check on him?*"

"*No need, I'm ready. Follow me.*"

"*Alright, did Natalie leave?*"

"*She took off when you were still upstairs. She has two video shoots for us tomorrow, so I told her to go home and get some rest. You know, she's become one of the top requested girls by our clients. People love that small pussy and tight ass.*"

"*You must've paid her a fortune to do this shit.*" Doron groans as he follows Paul to the second floor.

"*Yeah, just like I'm paying you. Now shut the fuck up. I'm tired of the way you moan like a bitch.*"

Paul opens the door to an empty room. "*Where'd that fucker go? Look in the closet and I'll head over to the other bedroom. He's around here somewhere.*"

"*Not in the closet. I'll check the bathroom,*" Doron says.

Paul walks down the hall and stops, turning back toward

Doron. "Wait, I hear sniffling. Listen."

There's silence for a moment, then a weep and a rustle in the hallway. "I think he's next to you in that linen closet."

Doron opens the door and sees Cove huddled on the floor. Cove lets out a fierce kick and strikes his foot against Doron's shin. Paul pushes Doron out of the way and drags him out.

"Aaew!" Cove howls. He punches Paul in the leg and screams. "My father's going to kill you, Paul. Just wait. My mother's going to sue your ass."

Paul lifts him up by the neck. His feet dangle and his face turns red. "Knock it off!" Paul yells, inches from Cove's face. He instantly complies, unable to escape the two men who are three times his size.

Paul looks into his eyes and holds his neck and chin so he can't turn away. In a low threatening voice, he lets him know who's in charge. "Do you want to die today, my little Star? It'd be easy to tie a concrete block around your foot and toss you into the Mississippi. How long can you hold your breath?"

Cove raises his knee and makes contact with Paul's balls. Paul glares into Cove's eyes and shakes his head with a grin. "If I didn't need that face in pristine condition, I'd have your teeth in the palm of my hand. You're a fighter little one, but you're not a man. No man would knee another man in the nuts. Still, there's something about you that I like. That's why you're my Star. My NOVA." Paul drops him to the ground.

Cove holds his hands to his neck as tears well in his eyes. He gasps and chokes for air.

"I wonder how far I can take you? How much money the two of us can make together?" Paul says, walking to the stairs. "Bring him down, Doron. We have some business to take care of. I'll be in the living room."

Doron holds his hand out to Cove. "Come on, I'm gonna

3

take you home soon. *The faster you move down those stairs, the faster I can make that happen.*"

"*Don't touch me, you prick,*" Cove says, rising on his own, refusing to touch Doron. "*You're going to jail just like Paul, unless my father kills the two of you first.*"

"*Don't tell me you didn't enjoy being with Natalie.*"

"*Shut up.*"

"*No one would believe you if you told them about it anyway. You have no proof,*" Doron says in a frantic voice. "*Do you think some cop is gonna listen to a teenager complain that a woman did that to him? Think about your description of her to the police. 'Yeah officer, she was beautiful with long brown hair and giant tits.' The looks they'd give you and the humiliation you'd feel... it isn't worth it. And do you really want your mother to know about this? You'd break her heart. Your father's too.*"

"*I'm not stupid,*" Cove murmurs, heading down the stairs.

"*Neither is Paul. Don't ever forget that. Now take a seat on the recliner.*"

Cove sees the tattoo machine on the coffee table as he sits in the faux leather chair. He swallows hard with wide eyes. His hands shake as he looks around the room for Paul. It's dark. The curtains are closed and there's only one table lamp on in the space.

"*Worried? You're starting to look a little peaked. Would you like to repeat what you just said to me?*"

"*Repeat what?*" Paul asks, entering the room with a bottle and three shot glasses in his hands. "*Is our Star still acting out?*"

"*I think he might be coming around, although he did mention that his father might kill us soon.*"

"*Is that right?*" Paul says. He places the glasses on the coffee *table next to the machine, filling each one to the brim. "Take a shot, Cove, you'll need it," he says, handing him the drink.*

Paul downs his with a smile. Doron follows with a shake of his head and a squint in his eyes as it goes down.

"Ooooh baby, that's good," Doron squeals. "I need one more of those. It's been a long day."

Paul pours two more and Doron quickly reaches for his, only to have a firm hand seize his wrist. He looks at Paul and puts it down, waiting for permission.

"Our guest still needs to drink before we have our second round," Paul says, turning toward Cove. "Drink up. You'll feel better."

Cove swirls the liquor around the glass and spills some on his jeans. He sniffs it, scrunches his nose, and places the shot back down on the table.

"Hold your nose and drink it, you'll regret it if you don't. I wouldn't want someone giving me a tat while I was sober."

Cove picks the shot back up, looking at Paul in disgust. "Do you really think I'll be able to hide a tattoo on my body from my parents?"

"Where I'm going to put it, yes. Unless you want them to see it."

"Well then, I guess I'll have my proof."

Doron disregards Paul's request to wait and downs his shot. He stands and paces, then takes off his Yankees hat and throws it across the room. "Let's wash him up and take him back. I'm tired of all this shit. The money's not worth going to prison. Jesus, we have our whole lives ahead of us, we're only in our mid-thirties, and I just got married."

"No, Doron, let Paul do it," Cove says with a smile. "I can handle a tattoo. Can you handle getting butt-fucked in

prison?"

Paul whispers to Doron to leave the room. "Go have a cigarette and come back in five. I have some things to show our friend." Doron nods, puts his hat back on, and flips a cigarette into his mouth as he leaves.

Paul turns to Cove with a grin. He takes his laptop out of his bag and rests it on Cove's lap. He opens a video and clicks pause, then takes a seat on the sofa next to the recliner. "You know, I make a lot of videos. I have been for a few years now and it's served me well. I have a nice home in Vegas and a few rental properties where we film, like this one." He waves his hand around the space. "But I want more, and you can help me get there. You're a handsome little fucker. I showed your photo from the Rosens' reunion party to a few of my clients. They told me what they wanted and what they would pay in order to get it. I have to say, Cove, if you can do this for me for a few years, you'll make a bundle yourself. Wouldn't you like to buy your mother nice things?"

Cove's silent.

"Cove. I know you love your parents. How about you click play and have a look at how much your father loves your mother."

He's a statue, detached, not moving a muscle. Paul lifts the screen up to the level of Cove's face and selects play.

"Watch it."

The video shows his father with Natalie, the woman who was just here. She undresses and dances in front of him, and his father clearly enjoys the show. She sits on his lap and they start to kiss. Cove closes his eyes, unable to watch what happens next.

"Like father, like son, I always say." Paul laughs, closing the video. "This would be great for your mother to see, it would do wonders for her marriage. Of course, the one of you might

interest her more. What would she think to see you and your father with the same woman? She'd assume he must've had something to do with this, wouldn't you say? Hmm, Star? But then again, maybe you and I could keep this our little secret."

He winks, opening a second video. This time the screen displays a meeting room at his father's office. Dayne and Doron Rosen and Cove's father are pondering NOVA. Cove listens as his father discusses what the move into this territory will mean for everyone financially, and the best means of security for the sites.

"Our safety is our top priority. This is dangerous ground, we all know it, but I think I have the site secure and all the bugs worked out," Cove's father says. "We can bring in some eighteen-year-olds. We already have a handful in the business that look to be around thirteen. But we need to be careful and make sure everyone on this project is doing the correct checks on these employees. We recently had two sixteen-year-olds slip into the system. The men also need to look young, very young. Our clients for this line are mostly women. Rich, lonely women, and we all know the other group requesting it aren't the safest clientele to have, but they'll pay us a fortune for any video with young boys, real or not."

Paul closes the screen and puts the laptop away.

"Sounds like your father is in charge of a lot of this. I wonder what the police would think after seeing everything I just showed you." He slides the shot across the table, moving it closer to Cove.

Cove swallows the drink, slams the glass down, and lets out a cough.

"Good boy."

"Why do you have to do this to me? To us? Don't you have any kids? Don't you feel bad? I don't understand. Is it all just about money?"

"You have a lot to learn, little Star. Everything is about money. Everything."

Doron walks back in and slumps on the sofa, his body smelling of smoke. He places his feet onto the coffee table, more relaxed than when he left. "Let's do this shit so we can get the fuck out of here."

"Sit on him, I'll get the ink. It will just be an outline so it won't take long."

Doron kneels onto the recliner, places his knees to each side of Cove's legs, straddling his hips.

"I don't want to do this. Take me home. I won't talk, I promise. Just let me go!" Cove pleads in a high-pitched voice as he struggles to move the 220-pound body off his legs. "You fuck, let me go." He pounds Doron in the chest, but Doron grips his hands and holds them above his head.

"I'm not gonna argue with Paul, you're his project. His baby. Close your eyes and relax."

"Give him another shot," Paul says, returning to the room. He pours alcohol in the glass for Cove. "Here, you need it."

Doron releases Cove's hands and takes the shot from Paul. "Drink it," Doron demands.

He gulps the drink without hesitation, handing the empty glass back to him with a shaky hand. Doron places it on the side table, noticing the paleness in Cove's face.

"Scared?"

Paul adds the ink to the container and plugs the machine into the wall. He steps on the pedal to check the movement of the needle. "Perfect. Take off his sweater."

"No wait!" Cove yells. "Where are you putting it?" He pushes against Doron's arms in an aggressive fight to be free. "Please!"

Doron pulls the bottom of the sweater up. Cove tenses, his face strained, his eyes frantic and full of fear. He shudders, and with one quick jerk forward, vomits down the front of himself.

Doron steps away, looking down at the mess. "Fuck, Paul."

"Just take his sweater off, he'll have to clean himself up later."

Cove's bottom lip trembles and tears fill his eyes. "Paul, please," he whispers.

"Doron... leave."

"What?" Doron turns, not sure he heard Paul correctly.

"Go home. You're done. Go take care of your family. I'll finish this myself."

"Are you kidding?"

Paul puts the tattoo machine down, sits back on the couch, and places his hands in his lap.

"You're eerily calm about all this. Lifeless. Insensitive. I can't stand it," Doron says.

He clenches his teeth, looking into Doron's eyes. "Leave."

Doron straightens his hat and looks down at Cove quivering in the chair, vomit on his chin, tears streaming down his cheeks. "Paul... the kid looks bad. Are you sure you know what you're doing?"

"Get out, Doron. Now!"

He leaves the room and a moment later Cove jumps at the sound of the back door slamming shut. He's alone with Paul.

"So my little Star. Let's do another shot together. I have some things to discuss with you while you're getting inked, and I need you to be as relaxed as possible. The more you drink, the less you'll feel, and the easier all of this will be." He pours two shots, slides one over to Cove, then raises his glass and waits for *his new employee to imitate the gesture. Cove submits and Paul gives him a wink... "To NOVA."*

• • •

I'm cold. Snow falls and sticks to my wet sweater that's now frozen to my skin. Paul forced me to shower, made me wash the puke off my clothes, then sent me out into the winter darkness. My hair is stiff. The ends have become icicles.

Six more blocks to warmth and safety.

It must be around five. Dad will be home from work soon. I want to hide. I have to run away. Where can I go? Mom is out on a photo shoot. Maybe I can go to her studio. No one will think to look for me there.

My feet are frozen. Paul kept my socks, t-shirt, and underwear. He's sick. That fucker is sick.

My stomach turns from the liquor. What did he make me drink? I think it was vodka. I've had beer with my friends and mom allows me to have a glass of wine at holiday dinners, but this was different. It burned my throat. I'm still queasy from it.

I fucking hate Paul.

Four more blocks to warmth and safety.

I will remember this day. Natalie and I together as Doron filmed us. Paul said people want to see it, that they'd pay money to watch it. Why? Will they laugh at me? Did I do it right?

How can I hide this from my parents? If Dad is part of NOVA, won't he see my video? And why is Paul in St. Louis? Did he come out here just to do this to me? I know he plans to talk to my dad... maybe I should tell my dad myself.

Two more blocks to warmth and safety.

My chest hurts. The tattoo throbs. I should have puked in Paul's face. That monster. He said he'd see me soon. How can I get away? Maybe I can stay in my bedroom for a while. Stay home from school. Pretend I have a cold and not go outside. If I go out, he'll grab me and take me back to that house. I don't want to go back there. Ever.

I shiver. I need to get this frozen sweater off. My fingers and toes tingle. It's the first week of March and we shouldn't have this much snow. It's never this cold so late in the season. In another week, there should be buds on the trees. This has to be the last snowfall.

The steps are shoveled. Dad must be home. He'll be angry that I didn't get that done for him and he had to do it himself. He hates walking up the path to our home in deep snow. It gets inside his expensive oxfords.

I open the door and the warm air encases me like a hug from one of my parents. I want my mom to place her arms around me, yet I can't imagine I'll ever enjoy the touch of a woman again. Not even her. I can't tell her what happened. Not after what Paul said when he dropped me off. I don't want to die. I don't want my parents to go to prison for what they're involved in.

The rug in my bedroom feels soft under my bare feet. I stand for a moment, staring into the full-length mirror that's attached to my closet door. I look like a raccoon, with dark circles under my eyes and a deep shade of purple in the tips of my fingers and toes. I pull my sweater off and see the NOVA tattoo for the first time. The words are swollen and my skin is red. Paul taped plastic wrap over it. He told me not to get it wet for a few days.

Bastard.

I vomit again. It drips down my chest. I look at my

stomach and think back to Natalie with her hands on me. I wish Doron hadn't been in the room. I don't want a man to watch me do those things. And Paul...

My stomach knots and I begin to cry. I cower in the corner of my closet next to a pile of dirty laundry. Dad... I hear him... he's coming up the stairs. He calls my name. I'm silent, searching for comfort in a fetal position.

"Cove, why didn't you shovel for me today?"

The door to my room opens and he walks in.

"Cove?"

Silence.

"Dear God, Cove?" I hear him next to me. His hand is warm on my skin, but I jolt from the contact. "Hey, are you okay? What's wrong?"

Silence.

"What happened? Are you sick?"

I turn my head so he can see my face, vomit fresh on my lips.

"Oh son, do you have the flu? Let's get you off the floor and into bed." He places a hand under my body and begins to lift.

"Aaew!"

"What the hell's wrong with you? Are you hurt?" he asks, setting me down. He rubs my arms and legs, feels my body then places the back of his hand on my forehead.

"Jesus, you're frozen. And you smell like a bar. Were you and your friends drinking at Pagoda Lake again? I told you not to go over there. Did they push you in?" He touches my feet and quickly walks over to my dresser for a pair of socks. "Your feet are ice cold, get out of the closet and put these on. If you're not sick now, you will be if we don't get you warmed up. Here."

I don't move.

"COVE," he yells. "If you're drunk, fine, we'll talk about that later, but get your ass out of the closet."

The strain in his voice forces me to rise. I lift my upper body but keep my head down, too embarrassed to look at his face.

"Oh, fuck," he says, horrified. "No, no, no, no, no, Cove? Fuck! Paul, you shit!" I jump when his hand breaks through my bedroom wall. He pounds into it, again and again. "Fuck!"

I keep my head down. I tremble from head to toe. My body jerks and I curl back into the corner of my closet.

I hear him take out his cell, his breathing's heavy and fast. He strides around my room while he frantically waits for Paul to pick up the call.

"You fuck!" he screams. "How could you do this to my son? You piece of shit! My son! I'm going to the police. You won't get away with this. Any of this. Not this time you fucker... no, you listen to me. My son's curled up like an abused animal in the corner of his closet. What the fuck did you do to him?"

There's another loud crack against the wall and I wrap my arms around my ankles, rocking back and forth.

"No! I am going to the cops... no, you fuck... I can. I don't care what happens to me, you're not doing this to Cove. Don't come near him, don't touch him, don't even think about him... Paul." The room goes silent except for Dad's heavy breathing. He curses a few times before sitting next to me, resting his hand on my chest. "Paul," his voice quivers in a low, defeated tone.

I wait... he listens.

"Doron? No." His hand travels around to my back as he lies next to me, trying to warm my body. I shake. "Paul... no. I won't. Don't do this. I'm begging you... I can't live like this. I

won't have my family be a part of this."

He places his head against mine and kisses my forehead. A tear rolls down my cheek, and I can hear Paul's voice ending the call.

"You really don't get it do you? There's no discussion after this point, nothing to think about or talk about. Get your shit together, get your son's shit together, and enjoy the benefits. I'll have a check to you tomorrow."

"I don't want it," Dad responds dryly.

"Give it to our Star."

"Don't call him that. He's not part of this."

"Did you hear what I said to you? You're fucked if you think you can change this. They want him."

I hear the front door open. Mom. She's home from work.

"Fuck, Leondra's home."

"Take care of things over there. I'll be over tomorrow afternoon."

He throws his phone, then places kisses on my head, shoulder, and cheek. I feel smothered as he holds me close. "I'm sorry, Cove. I'm so sorry. Please be okay, please. I didn't know."

I hear Mom walk up the stairs.

"Fuck, stay here," he whispers.

"Where are my two handsome men? Cove the second and my adorable young Cove the third? Come give me a hug. I've missed you guys today," Mom calls out. I don't want her to see me like this. Don't come in here.

Dad stops her in the hallway as she approaches my room. They kiss.

"Hey beautiful. How was your photo shoot?" he asks.

"It was fabulous... are you okay? You look fatigued. Tough day at work?"

"Yeah, but I'm fine. I just have a few things to work out with Paul."

"Well, Paul gave me a huge bonus for being there today on such short notice. We should celebrate. How about we eat at Rucker's tonight? They have such wonderful food. I'd like to treat my boys to something special. Where is Cove, anyway?"

"Honey..."

"What? What is it? Did he get in trouble at school?"

"No. He's drunk. He must've been out with his friends again."

"What? Cove," she calls out. *"Get your bottom out here right now, we need to talk."*

"Leondra, wait," he says. *"I'll talk to him. Let me finish this conversation, just father and son before we come down for dinner. And I think we should stay home tonight, considering his condition, but let me take care of this. He threw up all over himself and he's not in the best condition to go out. Give him time to sober up."*

"No, I really do need to see him."

"Leondra, I'm serious. This one is man to man. Trust me. I'm not going easy on him and it would be best if I help him clean up. He's at that age in his life where he doesn't want his mother to see him naked."

There's a sigh and I hear my name.

"Cove?"

I clear my throat, not sure if I can speak without a crack in my voice.

"Cove, answer your mother," Dad calls into my room.

"Yeah," I respond, trying to sound tougher than I feel.

"You okay?"

"Fine, leave me alone," I grumble.

"Cove, I want you downstairs in an hour for dinner, whether you feel like it or not," she says in a strict tone.

"Fine."

He speaks quickly, trying to keep her out of the room. "He's fine, just grumpy and nauseous. Give me a few minutes then I'll be down to help you cook."

I hear a kiss and Mom descends the stairs. My door closes and I'm engulfed in Dad's arms. Warmth.

"Cove, how sick are you? Can you clean yourself up and put on some warm clothes? Or do you need my help?"

I don't want to move. I have no energy.

He pulls away and my arms shake as I try to push off the floor. I waver, reaching out for support. "I need to go to the bathroom."

"How much did Paul give you to drink?"

"Four shots."

He places his arms around me and holds the back of my head against his chest. "When?" he whispers.

"About an hour ago."

"Who was there besides Doron?" He kisses the top of my head after each question, his voice hushed and calm.

"Natalie."

"Natalie?" He sighs. "She's only eighteen. Did anyone hurt you, son?"

"Paul showed me the video of the two of you." I swallow hard.

"Cove, it's not what you think. That was Doron's bachelor party. It's not an excuse, but you have to believe me that I love your mother. It was a mistake..." He sighs. "What else happened?"

I take a step back and he releases me. My head tilts as I

look into his eyes. "I heard you talk about NOVA."

"How?"

"Paul has a video of you in your office with Dayne and Doron Rosen."

He puts the back of his hand to his mouth and looks past me. If Mom wasn't home, I think he'd punch the wall again. He runs a hand through his hair and turns away, taking clean clothes out of my dresser. "I'm assuming Paul made you shower, but I'd like you to take another one. Warm your body and I'll place some clothes in the bathroom for you. Keep the tattoo covered from both the water and your mother," he requests in a quiet voice.

He didn't know about the video. I wonder what else Paul has on him.

"Go use the bathroom son, I'll be in there in a moment after I get your clothes together."

"Dad?"

"Yes?"

"Don't go to the cops, okay? I don't want to lose you."

He slumps to his knees and places his hands over his face. "Oh, Cove," he says. His head is down, shaking. "I'm so sorry."

"Paul said this is what people do and I know that's true. I'm not a little kid anymore. And he told me what Mom does, and if the police found out, I would be taken away and never see you two again."

He stands and races across the room and pulls my face up to look into his. With eyes full of pain and sorrow, he shakes his head. "Don't you ever believe a word that comes out of Paul Jameson's mouth, do you hear me?"

I nod.

"That will never happen. Your mother and I are good

people and we love you. We'd never hurt you. Don't allow Paul to control your mind. What your mother does is legal. Only one person she photographed was underage and she didn't know it at the time. Don't believe what you see and hear in those videos either. Fight him as much as you can. You understand?"

I nod again.

He holds me steady as I teeter from the alcohol. My body is wrecked, cold, and sore, but my mind is clear. I can comprehend his words, even after four shots, but I can't get my body to work with my brain.

Dad wipes the tears off my cheeks and helps me to the bathroom. He runs the water in the tub, testing it with his hand.

"Give it a while to warm up. I'll get your clothes."

"Do you love Natalie?" I ask, not satisfied with how our conversation just ended.

He hesitates and closes the bathroom door, locking us in. "I don't. No. I love your mother," he responds in a low voice. "I'm sorry you had to see that. People make mistakes sometimes. I regret what I did."

"Am I supposed to love her?"

"No. Absolutely not." He takes a seat on the edge of the tub as I lift the lid to the toilet. "Are you hurt? Do you need to see a doctor? Do you want to talk about what happened?"

"I need to pee, I think."

I haven't pissed with him in the room since I was a toddler. He looks at me and I know he's worried about my body.

"Did Natalie have a condom, Cove?" he asks in a quiet voice.

"No."

I notice his fists are clenched as he tries to hold in his anger.

"I thought people needed those if they came inside a woman."

"Yeah, but you need them to protect yourself from diseases, not just pregnancy. That's not like Paul. Even though all of his employees are clean, they still use them. Maybe Natalie thought it was safe because you're so young. She didn't try to put one on you before you pushed inside her?"

"No. I wasn't inside her."

"You weren't inside her at any time, front or back?"

"Front or back?"

"Cove, did you put your penis inside any part of her body?"

"Only in her hand."

He exhales and leans against the wall. "Thank God."

"Paul said I'd have to do that again. I'll have to do it a lot by myself. I don't understand."

"I don't either son, but I'll speak to Paul tomorrow and we'll clear all of this up."

"Shh, I can't go when you're talking so much."

He gives me a moment to start my stream before he asks another question.

"Where's your underwear?"

"Paul kept it."

"Why?"

I shake my head that I don't know, focusing on the toilet. Dad's right, I'm more relaxed now that my bladder's empty. I flush then slide my jeans all the way off.

He stands and places his hands on the counter, gripping the sink. He leans toward the vanity mirror and I catch him watching my reflection. I step into the tub, leaving the curtain open to reassure him that I won't fall. I set my hands against the tile wall and steady myself as the water pelts my face. My eyes are closed as I enjoy the balmy steam that rises around my body.

"Cove?"

"Hmm?" I mumble.

"This isn't what people do. It doesn't matter what Paul said. He's wrong. I know you've seen some porn online and have looked at nudie magazines, many boys your age do. But what happened today... it isn't real. Having sex with a random person is different than making love. I hope you understand that someday. I hope you find someone special and you can forget about all of this. I don't want you to think that this is it. There's a lot more to it, and I hope you realize that once you find her."

Dad looks remorseful and defeated.

Two

"WHAT TOOK YOU so long, Babe?" I ask Cove.

"I had to wash up and I got lost in a daydream."

"About me, I hope?"

"Yes, in the end it was about you... the gorgeous woman who I just made love to. How did I get so lucky?"

Cove takes my hand and kisses the top of my fingers around to my palm. I melt at his eagerness to please me. Most men I've fucked fall asleep a few minutes after sex, or I leave so I don't have to deal with small talk. He's different.

"You doing okay?" he asks.

"I'm nervous about losing you. And I miss Mera."

"We're on our way to take care of things."

"It's time to tell me about your plan. What are you going to give my dad?"

"Whatever he wants."

"Not a good enough answer."

"A truthful answer. I have only one thing for him, and it probably won't be enough. So its whatever he wants."

"But you do have *something*?"

He nods. "What I have might piss him off. I won't know until I meet with him. If he accepts it, I think he'll release Mera. Then the two of you can head back to St. Louis, but he'll put me work to make him some money. I won't be able to come back with you. I know that for a fact. Paul's never satisfied. He'll always hate me."

"Because you wanted out?"

"Because I tried to get him arrested and it backfired. He'll make me pay for that for the rest of my life, or at least until he stops making a profit off my body. Then, he'll make me disappear."

"Okay, enough. I still can't believe this is my dad we're talking about. He's always been so sweet to me. Weren't the past seven years with him real? How could he put on a show for so long? He loves me. I know he does. I can work this out with him."

"Soph, I know the *real* Paul Jameson. Don't think he won't dispose of you and Mera if he knows what I've told you. He's good at covering up any illegal dealings in his company. My father sitting in prison is proof. My entire life is proof. All we can do is play his game and hope for the best."

"So you really don't have a plan?"

"I have a small plan, enough to take care of you and Mera. That's what's important."

"But I want you," I say quietly.

"I know." He squeezes my hand, turns away, and observes the passengers on the plane.

"Still think he has a guard on me?"

"If he does, it's a newbie, or someone who knows how to keep a low profile."

"That's hard to do on a plane."

"Yeah, we're probably off your father's radar until we land."

"Cove?"

"Yes?"

"You do exaggerate when you say that my dad would dispose of someone, right? You don't know that for sure. You've never seen him kill anyone, have you?"

"I've heard rumors. I know he's violent. When I was a teen, he put me in a few situations where I was afraid for my life. But most of the time people who cross him end up being ruined financially. I've witnessed some brutal force, though." He turns to remind me of the bruises on his face. "It's rare that he's directly involved in a beating, but I understand why it was him who needed to punish me the other day. Normally his bodyguard does all the real nasty work. If you haven't noticed, Paul always looks like he's a model for *GQ*. Perfectly styled hair, crisp shirts and suits, manicured fingernails. He doesn't like to get dirty himself, only if it's personal. With me, it's always personal."

"I see." I turn away and look out the window, admiring the dense clouds below the plane.

"By the way, when was the last time you were at his home in Vegas?" he asks.

I pull out my cell to show him a few photos. "This is Mera and me on the strip last May. My dad got us a room at one of his casinos for a weekend, but I've never been to his home. We also took a trip out together my freshman year of college, when I wanted him to meet Mera."

Cove flips through the images and smiles at our silly faces. "Mera has the body and the look that Paul loves. Small frame, long dark hair, blue eyes, and a large chest, but not fake large."

"Well, they're fake, but done well. She didn't overdo the procedure."

"Do you know anyone there besides your dad?"

"No. He would meet us by himself. Except one time he brought a friend with him. A guy around his age. Tall and muscular, short dark hair, wearing a sport jacket and jeans."

"Did he chain smoke?"

"Yes."

"That was Doron Rosen, Devery's brother."

"Really? I met Doron and didn't even know it? I thought my dad said his name was David, or something like that, but I was drunk, so he could've said Doron. He only sat with us for a few minutes before he had somewhere he needed to be."

Cove stops on a photo and his face turns pale, it's the shot of the three of us in front of a fountain on the strip. My dad has his arms around Mera and me. "This guy, way back here. Is that who you met?"

I take the phone and look into the background of the photo. It's Doron. I give Cove a look as if he's crazy. "I just said I met him, yes. Not on this day. I don't know why he's in the background of this shot. But yeah, that's the guy you just said was Doron Rosen."

"The guy you met smoked?" Cove asks.

"Yeah."

"That was Doron. The person in this photo is Dayne. They're twins. Dayne doesn't smoke. He must've been watching over Paul when the three of you were out that day, but he was hanging in the background."

"I don't understand."

"He's Paul's main bodyguard at the house. This was last May?"

"Yes, why? What's wrong?"

"I was right, Mera's the new house whore." Cove sighs.

"What?"

"Paul's had this plan for some time. Dayne was there to have a look at her. He lives in the north suite of Paul's home. He has just as much say about the women who move in as your father does. He was there to check her out. Paul's in charge, but he would still look for Dayne's approval in a situation like this. House whores can stay around for years if they're good. Paul takes his time to find the right one to make sure everyone involved is happy. He didn't take her because of us, he already had all of this figured out. What happened just made it easier. He made it seem like it was because of me."

"Fuck, Cove. Are you sure you're not paranoid again? This isn't just an overactive imagination taking hold of your brain, is it?"

"I know what I'm talking about."

"Does that mean your plan may not work?"

"It could change things. It depends on how attached they are to her, and if I can offer something better."

"What do you mean by that?"

"I mean, I might have to find someone better."

"Really? You would do that?"

"I would, but I'd do it in a different way than Paul. I'd find someone who's already used to that lifestyle and who wouldn't mind being in that house. I know a lot of people in the city, and if I put the word out, it wouldn't take long."

I look at my cell and touch Mera's cheek with my

finger. We look so happy. It reminds me of the photo Cove has on his phone of his parents. I close my photo App and place my phone back in my purse. "Hey, how did you know that was Dayne and not Doron? I understand that Doron smokes, but how could you tell by the photo?"

"I'm able to tell by the way that they stand. Doron slouches. He's always nervous, always scanning rooms, always pacing. He often puts his head down. But Dayne's body language exudes confidence. He stands with his chin up and his shoulders back. He looks you straight in the eye and he rarely smiles. Dayne's calm and Doron fidgets."

"And only Dayne lives with my dad?"

"Kind of. Doron's married and has two kids. He spends a lot of time at Paul's house, sometimes entire weekends, but he has a separate house with his wife."

"Oh, yeah," I say, remembering the photos on Devery's desk. "Devery has photos of his kids in her office."

"Really?"

"Yeah, why?"

"Well, just like Paul, the Rosens are pretty hush-hush about their families. Not very many people know that you exist, and that goes twofold for Doron's kids. He practically keeps them in a cell. I can't blame him after dealing with Paul for so many years. He wants to protect his family from the business. He saw what happened to my father."

"That reminds me, Devery sent me a text."

Cove turns swiftly. "When?"

"Last night... well, this morning while I was packing. She wrote that I should call her."

"Did you?"

"No, I don't trust her."

"I don't either, but I'm curious as to what she wanted, especially that early in the morning. She knows something. Or she needs information for Paul."

"That's what I thought. I don't want to call her."

"You should. Call her when we get to the room. Let's hear what she has to say."

"You think she knows about my dad and the business? I asked her once in one of my sessions and she only mentioned the casinos."

"She knows a little. She was close to my mother. The two of them were inseparable as kids; they even got their first tats together. But she's kept her distance after my father was arrested. I don't know if it's because she thinks he's guilty, or she knows her brothers are involved. Losing her friendship broke my mother's heart. It's tough. My mother's a Rosen, so I feel a connection to the family. And sometimes I think there's some good in Doron. We've been through a lot together, but other times I hate him just as much as I hate Paul."

"And Dayne?"

"Dayne's just a dick. I stay away from him as much as possible. Their parents are lawyers so they come from a respectable family, kind of... both lawyers, right?" He winks.

"Yeah, seedy."

"And it's awkward when Devery and Paul are together. They were friends in college, but there's definite tension between them. It's either sexual tension or a hatred for one another."

"You can't tell the difference?"

"Not with either one of them, no."

I think about all of my sessions with her and realize

Cove's right. She's hard to read. "I'll call her."

"Good." He smiles, taking my hand back in his. "So you've never been to Paul's house?"

"I think he was keeping his house whores a secret from me." I laugh.

"Probably."

"How many does he have at one time?"

"It depends. One, sometimes two if he wants a threesome."

"Oh, ugh. You *can* keep some things from me."

He laughs at my disgust. "Sorry. I've been in this for too long. What's normal to me is foreign to outsiders."

"So *you've* been to his house?"

"Many times."

"What for?"

"Business."

"You mean pleasure?"

"No, business. Parties, filming, press, private meetings, a few other reasons."

"You're not going to tell me what those are?"

"No, wouldn't you rather hear about the house?"

"I suppose. I've imagined it as a white mansion with a pool and servants."

"It's definitely a mansion, but not with a lot of staff. He has most of his food delivered, someone comes once a week to clean, and he hires the grounds to be taken care of. But other than that, it's quiet, unless there's a party."

"How often are those?"

"He throws a few big ones each month in the main living area. Friday night parties often last until Sunday."

"What else?"

"Dayne's suite is like a bachelor pad. Empty beer cans, big TV, unmade bed, the usual. There's also a nice pool out back and a trampoline."

"A trampoline?"

"Don't ask."

"Oh God, okay. I can only imagine."

"The house itself is brown stucco with a mission style clay roof, not white."

"What about Mera? Where will she be?"

"From what I've seen in the past, she'll be everywhere. Sometimes with Paul in his suite, with Dayne in his, with Doron when he comes over, in her own private room, or out by the pool working on her tan. Paul likes his employees to have some color. She may be lent out at parties for some of the top clients. It all depends on what kind of mood Paul's in."

"Oh." I look out the window and notice the clouds have disappeared. Only clear skies. We must be close to Nevada. The skies are bigger, more beautiful and open out west. "She'll be safe, right?" I whisper.

"What?"

I turn to him. "She'll be safe?"

"Yeah, she'll be fine."

"No, Cove. I mean sexually. She'll be safe? Both you and my dad have told me that he has a clean business, but tell me again."

"It's the only thing about Paul that I respect. He makes sure every one of his employees is clean. Yes, she'll be safe."

I massage his palm with my thumb. He closes his eyes and leans his head against the seat.

"That feels nice."

I love touching him. I've been so lost in our conversation that I nearly forgot what we just did in the bathroom. Cove making love to me was one of the most wonderful moments of my life. I hope he enjoyed it. I lift his hand to my mouth and kiss his wrist. It's soft and smells like soap.

"Even better," he says.

I place the tip of his index finger in my mouth and nibble. He exhales, leans in and whispers in my ear, "Just wait 'til I get you in that hotel room. You'll be begging me to stop."

I position my fingers on his pants and feel a slight erection growing under my hand.

"Sophia." He moans, placing my hand back into my lap. "Soon."

I smile and turn toward him, sliding my hand along his cheek. He leans in and presses his lips to mine. His tongue sneaks around and out.

"Soon, Sophia," he whispers, kissing my cheek.

I sit back with my arms on the armrests. The plane tilts and the pilot announces that passengers should remain in their seats until the plane lands. We'll be at our destination in ten minutes. I see land below. It's late morning and I'm exhausted. I wanted to take a nap on the plane, but my body got a second rush of energy after making love to Cove. Now, that surge is over. I'm exhausted. And I'm worried about him, too. About us. I have to remember to be careful. No matter how much I love this guy, I can't forget about my rules. It applies to all men, and we fucked up.

"Hey, you okay?" he asks.

"Yeah," I respond slowly.

"Say that again, but try to convince me this time."

"I..."

"What? Tell me."

How do I say it without hurting his feelings and without sounding like a slut?

"Sorry I want to wait until we get to the hotel," he says. "We don't have time to do anything here again."

"No, it's not that."

"Did I do something wrong?"

"No... well, yes. We both did."

His eyes show true confusion. "Say it," he commands.

I lean in and whisper in his ear. "You didn't use a condom."

"Oh, fuck," he calls out, his hands gripping the armrests. I cover his mouth and he turns his head to release my hand. He lowers to a whisper so that roving ears can't hear the rest of our conversation. "Aren't you on the pill?"

"Excuse me," an airline attendant says, obviously concerned by Cove's words. "Are the two of you okay?"

"Yes. My boyfriend was startled, but he's okay now."

"Sir? You alright?"

"Yes, I apologize for my language, we're fine."

"Okay, please keep in mind that there're other passengers on this plane. We'd appreciate it if you could refrain from using that type of language." We nod as she walks away.

Cove continues to grip the arm of the seat. "You *are* on the pill, right?" he whispers.

"No, I use condoms. The pill makes me fat," I whisper back.

"Why the fuck didn't you let me pull out?"

"Because you already shot into me, I could feel it. At that point, it was too late. And I couldn't think straight. I was in the middle of an orgasm and needed you inside me."

He runs his hand through his hair, something I realize he does when he's upset. "Sophia... God, I don't even know what to say. Talk to me, what's the issue here." He wiggles his fingers. "Are we okay or not?"

"I think I'm fine."

"You think? Or you know?"

"I don't know. I think so, but sometimes you never know."

I have to think back. My period was when I modeled with Monroe, the rubber band penis guy. That was the last time. I count back. "I was on my period about ten days ago."

"Is that good or bad? Wouldn't it be midway, like fourteen days? Or what?"

"Not necessarily. But I'm fine. I know when I'm ovulating. I get pimples. I'm also hypersensitive, aroused all the time. Plus my ovaries hurt for a day. It's not time yet, but it will be soon, so we need to be careful."

"You're sure?"

"Yes."

He forces out a quick breath and releases his grip. His head drops down into his lap.

"Cove, you look like one of the illustrations in the emergency pamphlet in front of us. You're going to scare people."

"What about me? I *am* scared. You just stopped my heart. It would be just my luck to get you pregnant the first time I ever had sex."

I laugh.

"It's really not funny."

I try to conceal my amusement, tightening my lips into a big grin. He lets out a smile and a small laugh as well.

"Okay, it's kind of funny." He grins. "But only because we're safe. I don't want to go through that again anytime soon. I promise to use a condom or pull out from now on. Why did you even mention it if everything's okay?"

"Cove?" I question his last comment. "Really?"

"What?"

"The issue isn't just about getting pregnant. I've had a rule for years that I always use a condom. That's why I asked about my dad's business. I know you weren't inside anyone, but you can get things other ways."

"I know, sorry. I'm clean."

"Well, this has to do with me too. How do you know that I am?"

He narrows his eyes, a look of worry on his face.

"I'm fine," I say to relieve his concern. "I've had this rule since I was a freshman in college. But we're still in the beginning stages of this relationship and I don't want to slip up. I've been down that road before and it isn't fun."

"You've... wait, what? What road?"

"I've been through a lot. The road to nowhere. I'd hate to think I haven't learned from my mistakes."

"What mistakes?"

"I gave myself to people. Anytime and anyplace."

"Shit. Is that why you went to Devery?"

I turn away not answering his question. Cove's silent. His foot taps as the plane begins its descent. I don't know how to explain.

"Sophia, tell me about some of your discussions with her. You said she told you to prepare for the worst when it came to falling in love?"

"She said be prepared for disappointment if it doesn't work out."

"And the conversation was about me?"

"It was after we were in your pool and my dad told me you were his business partner. I was upset. Very upset. She made me realize I had fallen in love with you."

"Did you tell her I was one of his partners?"

"Yes, and she insisted I didn't know the whole story, that I needed to talk to my dad before I talked to you. She made that very clear."

"I just can't figure her out. Did you tell her about the live cam?"

"No, I haven't seen her in over a week. I missed my last appointment the day Mera and I went out to The Dark Scarlett."

"Good."

"Good?"

"Yeah, I'm glad you didn't tell her I fucked your mouth. I don't want her to get the wrong idea about me."

I laugh at the absurdity of that comment. "You don't want someone to get the wrong idea that you stuck your dick inside someone's mouth? Think about that for a moment. No matter how you say it, it doesn't sound good."

"I know, which is why I don't want her to hear about it. If she thinks my father's guilty, and she found out what I did, that would confirm her belief about him. *Like father, like son,* as Paul always says."

"Well, I didn't tell her so you don't have to worry."

"Why did you start seeing her?"

"I had some things to work out about my childhood. Mainly issues with my mom, her physical and emotional abuse, but also worries about abandonment. I have a lot of anxiety about my past."

"Did she help you?" he asks in a soft voice, kissing my hand.

"Yes, I believe so. But she thinks I'm a whore."

Cove laughs, giving my hand a squeeze. "I doubt she thinks you're a whore. Devery's uptight. I bet words like that never even enter her mind."

"No, she sent me to a group for sex addicts."

"Why? I mean, wow... okay. I don't know how to respond to that. Really? How did that work out for you?" He grins.

I roll my eyes at his question. "Let's just say I was surrounded by felons and a woman obsessed with ass smoothies." He chuckles. "She *does* think I'm a whore, and maybe she's right. I told her I was too young to settle down and I was just having fun."

"Maybe she thinks your father is a bad influence and she wants to help you."

"Yeah, that could be. There was an incident in a parking garage recently that seemed to change things. My dad was furious. That's when Devery became alarmed."

"At Giorgio's?"

"Yeah, how did you know?" I turn to him, shocked.

"Paul was a mess that day. Everyone in the company worked for hours to clear that video off the Internet. It leaked out somehow. I didn't watch it, but... that was you?" Cove asks in a worried tone.

"Yes... sorry."

"Don't apologize, I just thought it was being shut down for an underage issue. I had no idea it was because Paul's daughter was involved. Then I had you on the live cam right after that. No wonder he pounded my face in." He places his index finger and thumb up to his mouth, gently outlining his lips. His eyes focus on the seat in front of him. There's a small curl to his mouth before he smiles. "Tomorrow will be very interesting."

"The expo?"

"Yes," he responds, snapping out of his daydream. "Paul has some choices to make and I might get to see him squirm. I've wanted this for years. Whatever he does to me, it'll be worth it. He's still upset about that live cam you know."

"You thought the garage was a child porn video?"

"Yeah, I did. That's when Paul freaks out the most. He's careful that those stay in the background and not on his main sites."

"He still has some?"

"I don't know. He might. I would assume so. When he had NOVA, it was underground. You can't have shit like that in the mainstream. The original sales, the first few years, were videos through direct meetings with distributors. Those distributors would then sell to their clients. Paul was careful not to have a direct hand in any of it. Then he had me do some other things online, but not on any of his main sites. Live cams. That's where all the money is these days. People pay to watch and interact. The original clients who bought the videos were the only ones who knew about it. No one else could access it."

"That's a big money maker?"

"Think of it this way. If you have 5000 people who are willing to pay a couple dollars a day to view a specific live cam porn star, you're gonna bring in quite a good amount of money just from that one site."

"Wow, I had no idea. But there's so much out there that's free. What's the draw to a specific person?"

"Why are you attracted to me? Why am I drawn to you? Looks are one reason. Some people become obsessed. Others are just loyal followers. They stay with the person they know. Feel a connection to them. Get used to that person in their life each day, or each week. They follow you to see what you're up to, how you've changed, grown... no pun intended. I've met some people at Paul's parties who think of me as a member of their family, even though the interaction doesn't really exist. It's scary at times. But yeah, a big money maker."

I'm quiet as I listen to how he spent his teenage years. Would I be as strong as he is today if I had gone through the same thing?

"There's also the dark web. If Paul is still into child porn, that's where it'll be. You need specific software to access it. It's a sleazy part of the digital world with contract killings, sites to buy guns and drugs, and tons of porn. If it's illegal, it's there."

"I guess I never looked that far into it. This is way more disturbing than anything I've ever talked to Devery about."

"Sophia, I know what's bad out there, and you're not it. I'm not snubbing your past, it sounds like it wrecked you, but what Devery says and tells you to do may not be the cure."

I smile. "So have you ever talked to anyone about this?

The live cams? Those sites?"

"My father. He knows. I've only told my mother a few things. She cries when I try to talk to her about Paul. It's better if she doesn't know the details of what happened. She has enough to worry about with my father in prison."

"Well, you can talk to me anytime. I don't know if I can help, but I can listen."

"I know... Sorry I got you involved."

"I'm not sorry. I'm glad you were forthcoming about my dad. Someone needed to be. I'm surprised by how much you've told me."

"How little, actually."

"Oh." I scrunch my nose. "Really?" He nods. "Well, the note and the phone message he left confirmed who he really is."

He leans in and places soft kisses on my lips. "I'm opening up because I trust you," he whispers. "And I love to talk to you and hear your voice, no matter what it's about. Even my mistake with the condom."

"Our mistake. There're two of us here. You don't have to take the blame."

The plane bounces as we touch the runway. I yawn and stretch my arms, looking forward to the hotel and a soft bed. I can't wait to undress this beautiful man.

He looks at me with a smile. "That was easy. Definitely the best plane ride I've ever had."

"Me too, Babe. You ready for an even better ride?"

Three

COVE LOCKS THE DOOR to the hotel room. His shoulder rests against the wall and his eyes burn into mine. He unzips his fly with a grin.

"Oh, fuck. That look, those eyes, your hard body. Tell me I can cum right now and I will."

He takes off his jacket and lets it fall behind him. His tie is next. I stare and wait as he unbuttons his shirt with one hand, enticing me with a tease of his flesh. Leisurely, he begins to expose his body. My insides throb as the shirt falls, joining the rest of his clothing on the floor. He takes one step forward, unfastens his belt, sliding it out of his jeans.

"I think I just—"

"Shh, my love. Let me pleasure you." He reaches out and wraps his belt around my waist, pulling me toward him. Our bodies meet. He's warm and his heart is racing. "I'm going to make love to you, but this time we can take it slow. I want to feel every inch of you. I want to put my mouth places where you've never been touched. I want you to cum over and over again because of me, because you're with me, and only me."

"Oh my God." I sigh. "I'm so turned on right now. Undress me. I want you to touch me," I plead.

We kiss, chasing one another's tongues. He rolls in warm and wet, then groans and pulls back out. "Where do you want me to touch you, Sweetness? Here?" he asks, and places his hand under my dress. "Here?" His hand rises up to my breast. "Or here?" he whispers, forcing his tongue back into my mouth. My legs wobble from extreme pleasure.

"Everywhere." I exhale.

He grips the bottom of my dress and pulls it over my head. My entire body is free for him to explore. I sit on the edge of the bed and he approaches me; the bulge in his pants targeted at eye level. I reach out to touch him, only to have my hand caught by his.

"Tsk-tsk. Be patient. I haven't even slid my tongue inside you yet. Lie back and spread your legs for me."

I fall heavily onto the bed with my hands above my head. "I surrender, be gentle." I smile.

His hands slide under my garter belt. "Do I have to?"

"No, but keep in mind that you're next," I say, looking down to see him grinning.

"That sounds more like a treat than a threat." He places tantalizing kisses around my stomach. My toes curl as he slides his tongue over my belly. "Hmm. I think that makes you happy."

I let out a quiet moan and drop my head onto the bed. His tongue swirls, his delicate lips brush across my stomach, lowering inch by inch until his mouth touches my outer lips.

"You smell wonderful," he says, kneeling on the floor, pulling my body to the edge of the bed. I shudder when his tongue finds its way inside. I whimper and clutch the sheets. My legs straighten, my body sent up and away from him. He laughs and grabs my legs. "Oh no, beautiful, you can't escape." He pulls me back and enjoys the fight.

"That's maddening. My head spins when you do that. It's too much." I moan.

"Take a deep breath and let yourself go. Enjoy my tongue and fingers inside you." He dives in then slides back out. His mouth travels up to my clit, races around and back down to taste my wetness. "That's better. Stay with me. Enjoy it before you have to beg me to stop."

He blows lightly on my lips. My body is covered in goose bumps and I can no longer open my eyes. In one swift move, he has two fingers inside, gliding in and out. I cry out his name as he encircles my engorged clit once more. His tongue flutters, licks, and sucks.

"I can't take this!" I yell, my legs closing around his head. "No... I can't... stop."

He pulls his fingers out and I instantly lose control. My hips thrust off the bed. "Oh my God, don't do this to me... you can't stop now, not now Cove, I need you." I place my fingers over my clit and quickly move them to finish my release. He pushes my hand away and I'm left squirming for more.

"Not yet, Baby," he whispers. "It's way too soon."

"Uh." I moan. "Yes, now... please," I whine and plead. My body shakes from head to toe. He climbs over me and holds my hands above my head. I rub against him, but he lifts his waist to forbid contact with his cock. "God, I'm still there, right on the edge. How long will this last? Just touch me. Set me free, Cove."

"I knew I could get you to beg," he says softly. "Sweetness... you know we just started. Do I turn you on that much that you can't control yourself?"

"Yes." I pant. "You do. Just put a finger down there and I'll cum."

"I won't let you give in just yet."

"My entire body tingles."

"Yes, that was my plan." He grins.

I exhale and finally allow my body to relax, taking deep breaths. In and out. Slowly. In... and out.

"Better?" he whispers.

I nod.

"Good, let's continue."

"What are you going to do to me?"

"Don't sound so defeated, you can take control anytime. No need to submit to me."

"Yeah, but I like it."

"I know," he says, kissing my neck. He skims one finger around my breast and grazes the nipple, then slithers around my abdomen in a snake-like motion. His finger circles my opening. "Here... this is where my dick will be in about a minute."

I sigh, opening my legs wide with approval. He bites and tugs at my bottom lip, his breathing faster with each passing second. I pull his pants down, exposing his stiff cock. We moan, our hands exploring one another's bodies.

"Make me cum, Cove. I want you," I whisper.

His lips touch my chest then move to my clit. He places his entire mouth over it, letting his breath warm the area. His tongue unleashes across my girlish erection, making me whimper with each quick encounter.

"More," I mumble, my inner thighs rocking into his chest. He grabs my waist and with one quick flip, I'm on my stomach.

"Give me your hand," he demands.

I place it behind my back and he puts my index finger inside his mouth, moistening it from base to tip.

"Position it over your clit, but don't move it. Keep it still over the area like you're lying on my dick."

I slide my extended finger in front of my aroused area, keeping it still. Cove caresses my ass, parting my cheeks.

I wait patiently, feeling a drop of saliva on my skin, his thumb rubbing it around. He gently pushes a fingertip inside... I hold my breath and tighten around it.

"Relax, Sophia." He pulls the tip away and kisses the spot. I jerk with anticipation. His finger slides slowly inside. I set my forehead on the bed, opening my mouth in a gasp of elation. "Oh, fuck."

"Try not to move. I know you want to rub yourself, but stay still."

"I want to cum."

"I know, Baby. You will. Give me a minute and you will." His finger moves slowly in and out. I've never felt so aroused in my life.

"Babe!" I cry out. "Make me cum, I'm ready."

"Move slowly, gently onto your finger. Don't lose control, keep with my rhythm."

With each slip inside of his finger, I push onto mine. As he slides his finger out, I lift. I grip at the bed with my free hand as my orgasm builds.

"Faster."

"No. Keep it slow. Feel it," he whispers. "Let me make love to you."

I whine with each penetration. My finger ridged against my clit, my insides tense. I climb, my legs and body shake.

"I'm gonna cum!" I wail, my finger pressing hard, pulsations shooting through my body. Cove pulls his finger out and pushes deep inside my pussy with his cock. He stops and holds himself, resting his hand on my forehead to support my head.

"Cum, you sweet thing. Cum."

"Oh, Cove!" I scream. Lost. Quivering. Out of control.

He holds me close. My head and arms restrained. "Give it, Sophia," he demands. "Let go." He pushes as far in as my body will allow, keeping still until my throbbing muscles come to rest.

I pant and sigh, unable to speak. He slowly frees my head, brushes my hair from my ear, and places a soft kiss on my earlobe.

"I can't believe I have myself inside you. My heart can't take the love I feel right now. Here... on top of you... my dick surrounded by your warm, wet, flesh," he says quietly. "I can't believe it."

I moan, at a loss for words. My head tucked deep into the bed as I feel his cock twitching inside me, craving more.

"Sophia," he whispers. "Turn over and look at me." He slides out and waits for me to respond.

I'm exhausted, but I don't want to sleep. That would mean I'd lose the precious moments I have left with him. I need to stay awake. I won't let him out of my sight. Not until the time comes.

I feel a tear form in the corner of my eye, then another. My lip quivers. I try to regain control, taking in a deep panicky breath. No luck. I let out a small cry then irregularly inhale, quickly coming undone in front of him.

I turn and wrap my arms around him, burrowing my head into his chest. I weep, unable to control or understand the feelings that are somersaulting out.

He kisses the top of my head and rubs my back, trying desperately to comfort me. "Tell me what's wrong."

"I-I don't kn-know," I say, as sporadic words tumble out of my mouth. "I t-think I'm happy."

He laughs and kisses the tears on my face. "Thank God."

"No. Th-this is bad," I stammer, unable to breathe. I start to hyperventilate and my body feels like it's on fire. *Control yourself, Sophia. Everything is okay. Calm down. Breathe.*

Cove rolls off me and sits on the edge of the bed. He kneels and wraps me in his arms. "Calm down... shh. Take a deep breath," he says, kissing my forehead, cheeks, lips, and ending with the warm brush of his lips over my eyes. My tears wane as he holds me tight. He presses his mouth against mine. He won't allow any further cries to escape. "Why do you feel this way? Talk to me."

"You're n-not staying here, Cove." I wipe my face with my hands and fall back onto the bed, my arm stretched across my forehead. I stare at the ceiling, taking deep breaths. "Not in Vegas. I'm not leaving without you."

"Sophia," he whispers. "I don't know what to do." He rubs my thighs then places his head on my belly, sliding his hands under my back. We lie in silence. I can feel his heart beating. I place my hand in his hair, gently massaging his head.

I wonder if I'm the one who needs a plan and not him. I'm relying on Cove to fix this, but maybe I need to step up. Mera is *my* friend, after all. But what can I do?

"Have you ever wanted to kill my dad?" I ask.

He stands quickly, looks down at me, his erection gone, his face troubled by my question. "No."

"I have, so you must've as well."

"No. I need Paul alive. If he dies then there's no hope for my father to be released from prison. Not until he's served his time. Paul has information about NOVA. I need it." He takes two bottles of Scotch from the mini bar and tosses one on the bed. "Sit up and do a shot with me."

"Cove, it's not even eleven in the morning."

"I know, and you're upset, and we're both tired. It will help."

We open the small bottles and fling our heads back. I shut my eyes as it goes down. He takes the empty plastic container from my hand and throws both in the trash.

"Another?" he asks.

"No."

I lie back as he takes a shot of whiskey from the bar and pitches it down in a second flat.

"Those are outrageously expensive, not to mention that's like your fifth shot in six hours."

"Fourth, I think. And I need it so that I don't break down like you just did."

"I got panicky."

"I know. I'm almost there as well."

"You still have hope that your dad will be released?"

Cove walks past me and pulls the pillows out from

under the covers, then tugs the blanket back. He places his hands under my armpits and gently slides my body up to the unmade spot. I rest my head on the soft pillow, watching him crawl over me to the other side. He wraps his arms and legs around me and sighs.

"Yes. I wouldn't be here today if I didn't have hope. He'll come home someday. Paul took him from me when I needed him the most."

"He'll do the same thing to us."

He's silent for a moment, swallowing hard. "It's bad karma to wish death onto people. I'm guilty of it. I've thought that way in the past. But believe me, it won't get you anywhere. My father and I used to discuss things like that when I was a kid. He has as much anger toward Paul as I do. He wanted to protect me and it destroyed him that he couldn't. We've always been strong for each other. It's best to get that thought about killing out of your head."

"It was only a question. I didn't mean you or I would kill him. I thought about it because you mentioned contract killing on the dark web. That stuck with me."

"God, Sophia. No. I'm totally repulsed by him, and sometimes I wish he could feel what I feel, but I've never thought about *really* killing him. I may have voiced it, but it's just the pent-up anger that's surfacing. I don't have it in me to kill another person, no matter how evil they are. Besides, I don't know what would be worse, to step into the underground world of the dark web and find someone to kill him, or to stay in the porn industry. Sorry I even mentioned it," he says with unease. "Let's not talk about Paul for a while."

I place my arm over his waist and pull him closer. "I say stupid things sometimes. I didn't mean to spoil the mood or upset you."

"I'm fine. I just don't know how to fix your heart. I've never had anyone cry over me before, other than my parents. I feel bad about that. I don't want to hurt you."

"You're not the one who's hurt me, Cove."

"I hope you still believe that tomorrow after we meet with your father."

"He's already told me that you're a monster. I'm sure he has more nasty things to say about you. I know it's coming. I'll be strong."

"Just remember, no matter what Paul and I say to one another, no matter what you hear... I love you." He brushes my hair off the side of my face and places it carefully over my shoulder. "Can you remember that for me?" he asks, looking into my eyes.

"Of course, Babe," I say with a smile. He closes his eyes and places his head on my chest. "How are we going to get close to him?" I ask.

"I'll send him a text this afternoon. I'll let him know that we're coming. I'm sure he already knows we're here, so he'll expect to hear from me today. If he doesn't get back to us himself, he'll have someone deliver a message. But honestly, I wish we didn't have to leave this bed. I'd like to just lie here and hold you for days," he whispers.

His cock grows back to its erect length and touches my leg. He kisses my breast, gliding his tongue across my nipple, while my hand caresses his shoulders and neck.

"That's nice," he says. "My body still hurts from the other day."

"I'm glad your bruises are starting to fade," I whisper. "So, what are we going to do the rest of the day?"

He slides closer to me, rests his head on my pillow. "We have to call Devery, contact Paul, and I have to check in with my mother. Sleep's also on the list."

"Yes, sleep."

"But right now..." He pushes my shoulder back and rolls on top of me; his beautiful dark eyes looking into mine, searching for approval. He lifts his waist and slides his tip over my opening, thrilled by my instant lubrication. I think about stopping him before he pushes inside, but he said he would pull out. He said he would. I trust him. God, he had better pull out. Maybe I should stop him. No, I trust him.

"Hey. Look at me. I know what you're thinking. I'll pull out long before I'm ready." He looks into my eyes again, waiting for me to relax. I smile so he knows I'm ready. With one quick thrust, he's inside. "Jesus." He gasps. His eyes close and his lips part. He holds steady for a few moments, enjoying the sensation.

He slides slowly back out, placing my legs over his thighs as he looks down. "I'm going to rock into you in the most gentle way, inching my way in and back out, bit by bit, until you cum."

"God, Cove." I squirm, placing my hands behind my head and under the pillow. "Who knew words would turn me on so much. This dirty talk thing is enough to make me cum."

He grins, definitely proud that he can get me off so easily. He pulls my knees to his chest and slides his shaft deep inside. I watch him bite his bottom lip as he begins to move in a slow, rhythmic motion. He puts just the right amount of pressure on my clit, causing me to roar in appreciation.

"Does that feel good, Baby?"

"Hmm-mmm." I moan, seeing the desire in his eyes. His tongue swipes his lips, leaving them suggestively wet. "You're so sexy," I say. "I need those lips on mine."

He falls against my chest and attacks my mouth with deep lunges of his tongue. We roll like fighting animals. I win. I'm on top. He takes my cheeks in his hands, panting hard, then flips me onto my back, inching back over me. His mouth possesses mine as he delivers an appreciative kiss. He looks into my eyes and runs his hand through my hair, shaking his head in disbelief.

"You amaze me," he whispers.

Our lips lock as he glides back inside. There's a grunt from deep in his throat, showing extreme affection with each gentle, delicate insertion. He loves it slow, and I can only imagine this kind of sex doesn't happen in the porn industry. But it's my turn to pleasure him. I've waited for this. He needs me to be relaxed and unhurried. I know what to do.

"Cove," I whisper. "Lift your waist just slightly so I have room to move my hips. Stay still for me, let me do all the work. All I want you to do is think about your cock as it slides in and out. Feel me. Enjoy me."

He groans, obeying my words. I position my legs between his. Slowly, I drop my hips. I move upward, gently, peacefully, until I feel him deep inside. Steadily I repeat the motion. With composure, I hold onto his waist, calmly gliding him in and out, his face tranquil, eyes glassy, unfocused.

"Stay with me," I whisper. "Look at me."

"Sophia." He moans.

"You made me cum. Feel how wet I am." I tighten my

pussy as I move, putting pressure on his cock.

"Fuck."

"Shh," I hush him. "Enjoy yourself. Let me fuck you," I say in my softest voice. "Watch me. Watch me fuck you."

"Nothing's ever felt this good." He takes in a deep breath. I reach down and massage his balls; they're huge in my hand. He's getting close.

"Pull out for me, Babe."

"Another minute. Let me feel you around my dick for as long as I can hold out," he pleads, sinking down to my ear and sucking on my lobe. I thrust and demand his body join mine. He succumbs and takes control of the movements, his entire body erect. He groans, and I release another explosion of lubrication.

"Oh, Sophia. Sophia. God." He moans, pulling out just in time. A quick burst of cum hits my stomach, then another. I grab his shaft and he moves into my hand, guiding his orgasm. "Yes, Baby. That's it... that's it."

His eyes are clenched as the final drop falls to my stomach. He releases an immense breath and collapses face down by my side, panting in pleasure.

I rub his back until his muscles relax. It takes us some time to quiet our bodies into a restful state. We face one another in silence, invading one another's hearts until our eyes become heavy.

I don't know which one of us said it—all I can remember are the words *sweet dreams, my love* before drifting off to sleep, feeling happy and safe next to him.

Four

THE ROOM IS DARK when I awake. I reach for Cove, only to find an empty bed. "You shithead. You left me again."

A surge of laughter comes from the opposite side of the room. I turn to see him in a chair with his laptop.

"I'm still here."

I lie flat on the bed, placing my arms above my head. It must be late afternoon.

"What are you working on?" I ask.

"Business. I sent Paul a text and I checked in with my mother, then I had some work to do."

"What kind of work?"

"Something for Paul. I need to clean up a situation."

"I thought he fired you?"

"He did, but I can still try to make him some money as an apology. I'd like to go back to St. Louis and be with you, so the faster I get some things together for him, the sooner he might let me go."

"How long do you think that will take?"

Cove closes his Mac and places it on the table. He sits back and folds his hands over his stomach, more relaxed than I've seen him in days.

"A long time, Sophia. I've done too many things wrong, but I can at least start to try to make him some money, that's what he wants more than anything."

I stand and give Cove a kiss before I head to the bathroom to freshen up. He goes back to his laptop when I walk away. He was smart to get a place so close to the strip. One of my dad's casinos is just a block away, and I believe that's where the adult expo will take place.

I look in the mirror while I wait for the bath water to warm. The reflection is of a happy young woman with rosy cheeks, someone who just got laid by the person she loves. I have the classic, ear-to-ear sex grin, and I can't see it disappearing from my face anytime soon.

I slide off my thigh-highs and step into the shower, washing the dried semen off my stomach. The hot water soothes my muscles, sore from two days of sex. I can't seem to pacify my craving for him. It's that face and those eyes, his body, hair, and clothes. The whole package makes me melt. And he's good in bed. No... fucking great in bed. I can't believe I'm with a porn star. I can see why he had so many followers.

I hope I satisfy him. I hope I can give him what he wants, what he needs, what he desires.

I turn off the shower and open the curtain, a bit startled to see him standing in front of me... fully erect.

"Wow."

He lifts me into his arms. I'm carried out of the bathroom and positioned on my knees in front of the bed. His chest is against my back, my head forced swiftly to the mattress. He holds my wrists, stretching my arms out in front of me. His knees part my legs and with one swift move, he's inside, both of us holding still, breathless.

"I need to fuck you, Sophia. Tell me that's okay," he whispers.

"I don't know why you need to ask. We've already done it today."

"No, I've made love to you. We've made love to one another. Now I want to *fuck* you. It's going to be quick and hard."

His words set me on fire. "Do it. Do anything you want."

He holds my wrists and slams further inside, his rigid cock stretching my flesh to meet his size. He pounds quickly, relentlessly, my cries turning him on, causing him to lose control.

"Fuck, take it from me. I'm gonna cum, Baby."

He pulls out and immediately prods at my ass. A burst of cum lubricates my behind, allowing him to push partway inside. I scream. He groans. He drives harder, trying to part me. He erupts, bursts of cum shooting inside. I try to crawl away, only to feel his grip tighten around my wrists.

"Cove!" I howl, trying frantically to catch my breath. I bury my head deep into the covers, biting down on the bed. My words are muffled until I come up for air, panting, as he slows and comes to rest.

He glides out and I feel a tremendous freedom. He rolls me over, kissing my lips in an apologetic way.

"Fuck, I was out of control. I just couldn't get you out of my head when you were in the shower. I kept picturing the water dripping down your gorgeous body."

"I want more."

"What?" He looks surprised.

"That was fucking bad-ass, in more ways than one. When can we do *that* again?"

He laughs and pulls me into a big hug. "Soon, but let's plan on us making love more often than having a quickie. I just needed to try it."

"You've never done that before?"

"No. I've felt it, but I've never done it. Not anal."

"Oh," I say softly, saddened by the thought of what that means. He gives me a kiss and takes my hands into his.

"Don't worry, Everything's good. What do you say we get dressed and I'll order us some food? You can call Devery."

Devery. I forgot to call her when we got here. I wonder what she wants. "Can you order me a chicken sandwich with French fries if they have it?"

"And if they don't?"

"A burger or a BLT will be fine."

"Coming right up." He picks up the hotel room phone and calls down to room service.

I pull my cell out of my purse and flip through my texts. There's a new one from Mera that I immediately open.

TABOH GHM NISM?

"What the fuck?" I mumble.

Cove sends an inquisitive look my way as he speaks to the kitchen staff. He walks over and looks at the message, shakes his head and shrugs. I send a text back as I wait for him to finish our order.

U OK? RU SOS?

"What's going on?" he asks, hanging up the phone.

"It's Mera. She's acting strange again."

"I don't text much. Tell me what all that means."

"Things are bigger out here... God help me."

"What's NISM?"

"I don't know."

Cove looks at the message again and tries to help me decipher it. "Not in... now I..."

"Need I say more," I reveal, realizing the reference is to more than just the Vegas skies and my dad's home. "She's with someone."

"She's with Dayne, I know it. He loves to fuck all the time."

"Well, so do we."

"Yeah, but it's different. It wouldn't bother him if twenty people were in the room, he'll fuck a woman anywhere in that house, no matter who's around. He can be rough, too, but women seem to like it."

"Yeah, Mera does like it that way. She's done some pretty crazy things."

"So you think she's happy?"

"Hard to tell, but she doesn't seem to be stressed or begging to leave."

"What did you write when you texted her back?"

"I asked her if she was okay or if she was in trouble." My phone beeps as her responding text comes through.

SFETE KITTY HPY!

"Smiling from ear to ear... her kitty's happy. She's fine. She's more than fine. Now what do we do?"

"She's not fine, not in that house. Not with Paul or Dayne."

"Well, I can't make her leave if she doesn't want to." I look down at my cell and send her one final text before I call Devery. I miss her shitloads.

MUSL

Cove lifts the suitcases onto the bed and we rummage through our clothing. I pull out my short, dark grey striped skirt and my grey hoodie with a t-shirt to wear underneath. "Is this too casual?" I ask.

"Not if this isn't," he says, holding a pair of blue jeans and a black hoodie in his hands.

"Ha, two hoodies, we'll match."

He slides into his boxer briefs and his jeans, leaving his shirt off for now. Does this man ever look bad?

"What?"

"Super model Cove Everton," I joke, giving him a quick flick of his nipple. He pulls away and covers his chest with a burst of laughter.

He bows with a smile and I laugh back. "Our food should be here in about twenty minutes. We should go for a drive after we eat. I'll take you past Paul's house."

"Okay, but just a drive by. I'm nervous after seeing that fight... I don't want him to hit you again. And I want to have more time with you."

"If he wanted to hurt me, or us, he would've already had people in this room. I know he knows where we are."

"True," I say, searching through my cell for the text from Devery. "I'll make that call now."

"Put it on speaker, I want to hear what she says."

She picks up on the first ring, like she's been waiting for my call.

"Sophia. I've been worried about you. I haven't heard

from you in over a week. Are you doing okay?"

"I'm fine. Sorry I missed my last appointment. I should've called."

"Where are you?"

"What do you mean?" I ask, wondering how she knows that I'm not at home.

"Can you come into my office today so we can talk? I know you're involved with the Evertons and we should probably have a discussion about them."

Cove shakes his head and rolls his eyes.

"Why didn't you tell me you know Cove and Leondra? You led me on... you lied to me."

"No. I couldn't. They're part of my family and I won't mention relatives in my sessions. That information is confidential."

"Have you talked to my dad recently?"

"Yes. He was worried about you and he wanted to know if I had heard from you. Can you come in today?"

"No. I'm not available today."

"Sophia, why don't you tell me what's going on. Perhaps I can help you. We can have a phone session if you'd like."

"Is that what this is?"

"Yes, is that alright with you? Do you have time now to sit down and talk to me? I won't charge you for this session."

I look over at Cove and he nods. I sigh so she can hear my aggravation, but continue on. "Yes, fine. We can talk. But I want to start."

"Very well."

"Why did you send me that text at four in the

morning? Why don't you tell me what you know and what's really going on with you and my dad."

Devery's silent. I look at Cove and he holds up his finger, signaling that I should give her a moment to respond.

"Are you alone, Sophia?"

"Answer my question."

Devery sighs and I can hear her chair swivel. She must be in her office.

"Sophia, have you been hurt by anyone recently or have you felt threatened?"

"Yes, my dad hurt me. He's an ass."

"I think your father looks out for you. What about Cove? Has he hurt you in any way?"

He tightens his fists. I rest a hand on his leg and rub gently to mollify his anger. "No, absolutely not. He's kind to me and he loves me. My dad's the dick, not Cove." He relaxes and smiles at my words, placing a soft kiss on my cheek.

"Do you know what his mother does for a living?" she asks.

"No, and it's none of my business."

"How about his father? Have you talked to Cove about him?"

He shakes his head in disgust, irritated by her questions. "Yes, I know about him, and again, even though we've had that conversation, it's really none of my business."

"Well, I think it is if you're involved with these people."

"Tell me Devery... do you know what my dad does for

a living?"

Cove takes a pen and notepad off the secretary desk and passes me a note. *Stay strong, Baby.* I smile and hold onto his hand.

"What your father is involved in is different than what the Evertons have done. He keeps his work clean and legal. Cove's father was involved in illegal activity."

"You're wrong. My dad plays you just like he plays everyone else. He set the Evertons up."

"What makes you say that? Did Cove tell you that?"

I look into his eyes and he throws his hands up in the air to gesture that it's my call as to where I want to take the conversation. "He's told me a few things, but I've experienced something first hand with my dad. I saw him beat Cove to a pulp and he took my friend. He's evil."

"Cove must have done something terribly wrong for your father to beat him. Think about that for a moment, Sophia. You've fallen for the wrong person."

He sits back and pulls his foot up, resting it on his thigh. He begins shaking it frantically, trying his best to stay quiet.

"Who's the right person?" I ask. "Did you even hear me, Devery? My dad took Mera."

"Did he? Or did your friend leave on her own?"

I feel like I'm in her office. She's in control, twisting my words. This is what she always does, she manipulates me until I surrender and see things her way.

Cove writes another note and passes it over. *Play her game. Bring up the twins.*

He's right. I don't have to always be nice to her. I can beat her this time.

"I'm sure your brother, probably both brothers, have fucked Mera."

I hear a click then silence. My brow furrows as I question the sound. I wonder if she hung up. "Devery?"

"Give me a moment," she says in a soft voice.

Cove passes another note. *She might be recording the conversation. Careful what you say.*

I wait, wondering if that's true... and legal. Is it even appropriate for us to speak to one another like this on the phone? I could probably get her license revoked, or at least suspended.

"Sophia. I'm sorry I called you." There's another click and she's gone.

"She hung up."

"Call her back."

I call but there's no answer. The phone goes to voicemail. I hang up without leaving a message.

"What just happened?"

"We found a weakness in Devery Rosen. Her brothers. Either she knows more than she lets on and didn't want their names recorded, or you just rocked her world. Now she has something to think about. Either way, you did great."

There's a knock at the door as I'm putting my cell away. Must be the food. "That was fast. I'm so hungry."

"Me too," he says, opening the door and wheeling the cart next to the table. "Voila!" He uncovers the lid and places the plates on the table. Two chicken sandwiches with French fries. He also ordered two cans of Coke and a large slice of cherry pie. The man knows the other way to my heart. Dessert.

"Looks great, let's eat then I'll let you take me on that drive. I'm curious as to where my dad lives. Maybe we'll even see Mera."

"I doubt it, if she goes outside at all, she'll only be allowed out back."

"Really?"

"Yep. Paul doesn't like anyone to see the number of women who drift in and out of his house. It's not good for the neighborhood. The less talk the better."

"I see." I take a bite of the sandwich and sink into the chair, in ecstasy over the flavors in my mouth. Melted Swiss and honey mustard. Perfect.

"You like?"

I nod and take another bite, relaxed and proud that I made the call to Devery. Everything she said was true. My dad hasn't incriminated himself, and he beat Cove because of the live cam. Plus, it does sound like Mera left on her own accord. I can see how someone on the outside would view me as a fool. I have to believe I'm not being conned by the Evertons. They wouldn't use me to get back at my dad. They're better than him. I have to believe that. I do.

• • •

"We're almost there. It'll be on your right."

"You sure he won't recognize the vehicle?"

"Sophia, really? It's a rental."

"But he won't see us in it, right?"

"No, he's at the expo. It's in full swing right now, there's no way he's home."

"Wait, isn't the expo thingy tomorrow?"

"It's a weekend event. Friday evening is a private party for Paul's biggest clients. Saturday evenings are open to everyone, but you don't normally see people from the general population there on that night. The tickets are pricey so it's more for wealthy businessmen and women. Those are the two days I usually attend. Sundays are more low-key. That's when we'll go. Paul tends to gear the first two events to sell his employees as products, by Sunday he's just focused on the sales from actual merchandise: posters, autographed photos, magazines, videos, toys, lingerie. It will be about twenty dollars to get in on that day, and we'll be able to enter with all the trash—as Paul calls them."

"Is that what *you* call them?"

"I don't know. I've seen a few lowlifes slip in on a Saturday night. They stand out like a sore thumb, wearing blue jeans and concert t-shirts, trying to get photos on their cells of some of the women. The other attendees on those nights are dressed in suits. They sip wine and never bother with any photos. They're classier; the employees are more relaxed around them. But I guess in the end they all want the same thing."

"That's true."

"The only difference is the wealthy can actually buy some of us, where the general population doesn't have a chance. They attend more for the fantasy aspect of it all."

"Jesus. So you've been sold?"

He nods. "One night, Paul auctioned off the four of us who were in NOVA. It was a long time ago."

"How much?"

"Huh?"

"How much did you sell for?"

"A lot. I was the face of NOVA. The others that night didn't do quite as well."

"So my dad made a shitload in an hour?"

"A few times."

"Oh, Cove. What did he do to you?"

"I got to keep a grand."

"Big fucking deal."

"Hey, it's not like I could've done anything about it. Besides, most of the people were nice to me. Kind of."

"Stop it! I would've killed him!"

He pulls over and looks me straight in the eye. "Look, I've been angry, punched walls, thought about suicide, I even took a gun once to Paul's house. I'm past all of that unless it involves you or my father."

"I'm sorry," I whisper.

He rubs his eyes with his thumb and forefinger, trying to clear his mind.

"What happened to the other people in NOVA?"

"Two died in a car accident. They were drunk. The other lives in Vegas. I haven't seen him in years. I heard he lives on the streets. He snorted his money away, what little money Paul gave him."

"That was it? There were four of you?"

"Yeah, that's it."

"What did you do with the money my dad gave you? How did you keep that a secret from your mom?"

"I always gave it to my father. He put it in an account for me. My mother took control of it after my father was arrested. We used some of it to open the Scarlett and for rent over the years. My mother makes a good amount from Paul, so she bought her penthouse on her own. That money didn't come from me."

"And your mom?" I ask gently.

"She's Paul's main photographer for his magazine and poster lines. The employees feel comfortable around her. She has that motherly personality that everyone seems to love. They trust her, and she puts the younger employees at ease."

"How did my dad keep you from having sex?"

"What do you mean?"

"I understand that you did what you were told in the videos and online sites, but how did he keep people, the ones who paid money for you, from having sex with you?"

"A few ways. Details aren't important."

"Well, if you don't want to tell me..."

"It's not that, Sophia. I'm just afraid that the more I say, the more you'll visualize me in those situations. If you view me that way in your head... what if I begin to repulse you? What if you're no longer turned on because all you can picture is my past?"

"I'm not like that. I'm not that type of person."

"Neither is my mother," he mumbles. "But it took her a year before she could even look at me after I told her a few things."

"I just thought I might be able to help if I learned more about what happened, but not if it makes you this uncomfortable. Maybe I'll ask another time." I take his hand and kiss his knuckle.

"I don't really ever want to talk about the specifics with anyone."

"Well, should we drive on?"

He points behind me, out the window. "Turn around.

We're here."

I turn slowly, in disbelief that we've been in front of my dad's house for a good five minutes.

My eyes follow vast steps that lead to a covered stucco entryway. There's a double entry door with black iron doorknockers. A row of four garage doors are to the far left of the house, and a set of two are on the opposite side. There's a second entrance next to the two garage doors, and I believe that must be Dayne's suite. The home rises up two stories, with rows of small windows spaced evenly along the top. It emanates wealth and seclusion.

"Wow." I gasp.

The exterior alternates between stone and stucco. Decorative iron bars cover some of the windows. Marble statues are set into niches along the first floor and balconies above. Expensive. Two small turrets with copper tops blend perfectly into the rest of the architecture. It's huge, the size of five houses in a well-to-do neighborhood.

"Wow," I repeat.

I'm in awe. The grounds have tall green palms and flowering cacti. I see a fireplace... or two... wait, there're three. Three fireplaces. Shit, there's another floor. That has to be a third floor up there.

"You okay?" he asks.

"Uh-huh." I nod, still speechless.

"That's Dayne's private area to the right, with the two garage doors."

"That's what I thought."

"The rest of the house is Paul's. He has a private bedroom suite and an office above the four-car garage, separate from his offices at the casinos. The third floor is off limits. I've never been up there," he says, pointing to the small windows that run along the top. There're a few private rooms... a massage room and other small rooms you don't need to know about."

"And the ground floor?"

"High-end kitchen, a large dining room that can seat twenty, that's all under Dayne's suite. The main area is open two stories. It's used for parties. There's also a theater room next to the garage, but he doesn't open that up very often."

"How long has he had this place?"

"Ten years. I was here when he first bought it. He threw a party and I flew out with my parents."

"Shit."

Cove nods. "Yeah, that's what I said when I first saw it."

"Okay, I feel ill sitting here. I've seen enough."

"So what now?"

"I want to go back to the room," I request in a dry voice.

"You don't want to see any other part of Vegas?"

"I've been here. I've seen it. I just want to go someplace safe. I feel vulnerable all of a sudden."

"Do you mind if we go to a safe place where there're other people?"

"I don't care, just as long as we're not parked in front of my dad's castle."

"I know just the place."

Five

COVE PARKS IN the driveway of a middle class cookie-cutter house in one of Las Vegas' many sprawling subdivisions. This development's called Coyote Prairie, and like all the other Elk Meadows, Eagle Mountains, and Owl Groves, I know we won't come across any coyotes.

"Who lives here?" I ask.

"Two wonderful people who I haven't seen for a while," he replies, locking the doors to the vehicle. Darkness has fallen and the house looks quiet, with only one dim light in the front window. Cove rings the doorbell, smiling at me. I hear steps to the door and a scream. The deadbolt is speedily unlatched.

"Cove! What are you doing here? Wayne... Wayne honey, Cove's here, and he brought a girl!"

A beautifully slim and tan woman in her fifties kisses Cove on the cheek, flashing a giant smile. Wealthy looking, wearing a grey sweater and black pants, her fingers covered in gold rings, and a thin gold chain around her neck. Her hair is full and dark with layers of bangs that frame her face.

She steps back and looks over his shoulder toward me.

"Cove, who is this gorgeous woman?"

"Aunt Lydia, this is Sophia."

"Oh, Sophia!" She pulls me into her arms and swings my body with hers. "Welcome to our home. Oh, I'm so happy to meet you." She kisses my cheeks and takes my hand, pulling me inside. "Wayne! Wayne, come out here."

Cove's smile is contagious and I find myself mirroring his joy.

"Leondra didn't mention you'd be in Vegas, I would've set up a room for you... and your friend."

"Girlfriend."

"Really?!" she screams, jumping up and down in delight. "WAYNE!"

"What, what, what, woman, hold your panties, I'm coming. It takes me a while to move in my old age. I just turned fifty ya know."

The man entering the room towers over us. He's in a black shirt tucked into a pair of brown pants. His hair is neatly trimmed and grey, with a short clipped grey beard. He's tidy, matching their neatly pruned exterior landscaping and immaculate interior furnishings. I can only assume that they've paid a bundle for an interior designer. Every piece of art on the wall has a rug to match or piece of furniture that's paired with it. The items in the home look perfectly spaced as if a ruler had been used to measure the exact distance between each object.

"Cove!" Wayne yells, sounding as boisterous and fun-loving as his wife. He shakes his hand and pats him on the shoulder. "How are you, my boy? How's that sister-in-law of mine doing back in the gateway to the west?"

"Wayne, Cove brought a young woman with him... a *girlfriend*."

"Holy smokes, you have a woman? My God, and she's a beaut. It's about time you got serious over someone. You know those little jigglers don't live in your balls forever. You got to get them out there, give them some exercise."

Lydia gasps. "Wayne, stop it. You'll scare them away."

"Not a chance," Cove says. "Sophia and I stopped by for a short visit and you can't get rid of us just by using the word *jigglers*, right Sophia?"

I laugh and feel ecstatic that Cove brought me here. He's introducing me to his family. That means a lot. "We can talk about jigglers all night if you'd like," I respond.

"Well alrighty then, she's a keeper," Wayne chuckles. "I like her, tell me where you picked her up and maybe there's one waiting there for me. Is she one of those fine ladies from behind the strip joints?"

"Uncle Wayne, I think you're good with Aunt Lydia," he jokes, relaxed in a way that I've never seen him before.

"I suppose you're right, besides it doesn't look like they made very many like her."

"True," he says, giving my hand a light kiss.

"Awww. Look at that Wayne, they're so cute together. Oh my God! I have to get my camera," she squeals. "Don't you dare move."

She races up the stairs and disappears around a corner. I hear a thump and a bang before she runs back down.

"Careful woman, I don't want to spend the night in the emergency room because you twisted your ankle on the stairs," Wayne says.

"Let me be, it's not very often my only nephew stops

by for a visit. Who can blame me if I'm excited." She raises the camera and Cove places his arm over my shoulder, pulling me close to his chest. We smile, waiting for her to take the photo. "Shoot, how does this thing work again? Wayne, fix it. Quick, it turned off on me."

"Maybe the battery is dead. When was the last time you charged it?" he asks.

"No, it can't be dead. I just charged it the other day, you remember, when we met the Andersons for card night. I wanted a photo of their new kitchen. Oh phooey, fix it," she demands.

"Try it again." He sighs. "You must be doing something wrong."

She points the camera at us and we smile. The lens closes and she stomps her foot in frustration.

"You've hit the on-off button. You have to push the shutter button for it to shoot."

"Well, here. You do it," she says.

"Sorry," Cove whispers through his teeth.

"Don't be, this is the most fun I've had in years. They're a trip."

"Okay, smile and say 'sugar foot'," Wayne requests.

"Sugar foot," we say in unison, my mouth in a circular shape when the flash goes off.

"Oh, Wayne, take another. They look like puffer fish."

We take a serious photo, then another, and another, until Lydia's finally happy with twenty.

"Why don't you two join us for the night?" Lydia asks. "We were just about to make some popcorn and watch a movie. It's Wayne's turn to pick, so I can't promise it will be a nice romantic comedy, but—"

"Yes it is," he says. "I want to watch *The Lone Ranger*."

"The one with Johnny Depp?" I ask.

"Yes."

"Yeah, that's a love story. I'll help make the popcorn," I say, breaking free from Cove's hand and following Lydia to the kitchen.

"Sophia, wait," he calls out to me, catching up before I disappear.

"Is this okay with you?" he whispers.

"This is incredible. It's a date night with two wonderfully fun people. I'm so happy right now. This is more than okay. I want to be able to hang out with you and do things like this. This is life."

"I love you Sophia Jameson," he says quietly into my ear.

I turn and walk toward the kitchen with a large grin. "Love you, too, Babe," I call back at him. A pan drops in the kitchen and Lydia screeches then runs toward us.

"Wayne! Did you hear that? They love each other. Isn't this exciting? We should have a party."

"Make sure you put extra butter on my popcorn," he responds. Cove and I laugh as I head for the kitchen.

"Oh honey, just humor me. Don't they remind you of us when we first got together?"

"No, they're much better looking."

Lydia shakes her head, still smiling. "He likes to joke around, that man. That's why I fell in love with him."

"So you're Leondra's sister?" I ask.

"Baby sister, yes. Although people always think I'm older because I've been in the sun my entire life. I have a lot more wrinkles than she ever will. She holes herself up in that art studio of hers all the time, never getting out to enjoy life. Have you met her?"

"Yes, she's actually my neighbor."

"Oh, you live in that old building in St. Louis? That's such a lovely space, how can a girl as young as you afford it?"

I pause, not knowing how much Cove's extended family knows about my dad. "My family has some money. My dad has been gracious enough to help me get a good start after I graduated from college."

"Ah, a college girl. Good for you. I've always hoped that Cove would attend somewhere. He's such a bright young man." She places a large bowl under the air popper and turns it on. The popcorn swirls as the machine roars. "So what sorority were you in?" she asks in a louder voice, speaking over the popper.

"I wasn't in a sorority."

"Really? I couldn't imagine those years without my sisters. I was president of mine."

Somehow, that doesn't surprise me. She's silly, bubbly, and hyper, the complete opposite of Leondra, who comes across as the depressed, artistic type. But what they do share is a loving personality, the one that I've always wanted from my mom.

"So you live right next to Cove? That's so convenient. Maybe the two of you should sell one of the places and move in together. It seems silly to have two penthouses for two people. You'd save a lot of money."

"Um, I'm not exactly sure we're at that point in our relationship. Maybe in a few months?"

"Well, don't wait too long. My nephew's a keeper. If

you don't snag him, someone else will." She gleams, taking four small bowls out of the cabinet. The popcorn pops and I help her melt the butter in the microwave. We make sure to pour extra onto Wayne's portion.

"Can I help the two of you carry this out?" Cove asks, walking into the kitchen, all smiles.

"Oh, Cove!" Lydia screeches, clapping her hands. "My favorite nephew, I'm just so happy for you." She pulls him into another hug and he laughs.

"*Only* nephew."

"And my favorite."

"So can I help you, or do you have it covered?"

"Yes, you can help" she responds. "Sit down on one of those barstools. I have a question for you before we start to watch the movie."

Cove obeys, and I can sense that he knows what she's about to ask.

"Cove, what happened to your face? I won't be able to enjoy the rest of the evening unless you tell me."

"I..." He hesitates, looking at me.

"Don't tell me Sophia beat you up. The way you're looking at her makes me feel like she had a hand in this."

"I was in a fight, with a business associate," he says. "And as you can see, I lost."

"I need more information than that, Cove. I'm a high school counselor and your uncle's a principal. You can't lie in this house. We'll know it. We deal with this kind of thing every day."

"Well, I'm not actually lying. I was pummeled by a business partner."

"Why?"

"Lydia. Leave the boy alone," Wayne says, walking into the room to pick up his bowl. "We haven't seen him since last Christmas. Let him be. Besides, I'm about to start the movie." He leaves the room and I pick up my bowl, following close behind. I hear her say one last thing to Cove as I walk out.

"Promise me you'll file charges if Paul Jameson's involved."

I sigh and wish again that my dad wasn't such a fucking ass. Cove doesn't respond, and in a split second after I hear her words, his hand is on the small of my back.

"Sorry," he whispers.

"They really care about you."

"I know. I just don't want to have this conversation again, especially tonight when I'm here with you." He places a kiss on my lips and opens the door to the back yard.

Wayne's spread out on one of the two outdoor futon loungers, waiting for his wife. I stop and gawk at the incredible space we're about to relax in. The two futons each have a plethora of pillows and a blanket. There's also a heat lamp between the loungers in case the blankets aren't enough. And on top of all of that, they have a beautiful fireplace with embers shooting into the night sky like fireworks. I'm in heaven.

"You coming?" Cove asks.

"Eventually, I just wanna enjoy this for a sec."

Lydia comes out and stands next to me. "Wayne set this up for me. Sometimes we just sit out here for hours and enjoy one another's company. We've slept out here many times too. He may sound burly to strangers, but he's actually a big cuddle bug."

"You're very lucky."

She looks at me with a sincere smile. "You are too."

I watch her join Cove and Wayne in the yard. She turns on a string of lights that illuminates a path for me. Three large palms line the area behind the loungers, functioning like a privacy fence from the neighbors. Lydia turns on a second string of lights that flow from tree to tree.

"Wow," I whisper.

Cove's already stretched out on one of the futons. He unfolds the blanket for us to snuggle under. I feel like a bride walking down the isle as I approach the outdoor theater. This can't be real. He looks at me and smiles, holding the blanket up. I crawl underneath with him, at ease in this moment.

"Let's start the show," Wayne says. Lydia claps her hands in excitement. He points a remote at the projector and the movie begins.

The large screen casts a warm yellow glow on our faces. There are chatters of *oohs* and *ahhs* throughout the evening, and Cove smiles every time I grip his chest during moments of suspense. I nuzzle against him, and he places his hand under my hoodie, gently circling my stomach.

Wayne starts to snore toward the end of the movie. And I smile when I notice Cove has drifted off to sleep as well. My arm is under his back, so I lie still, not wanting to rouse him until we have to leave.

Lydia turns off the projector and lights, gently nudging her husband awake. She places a finger over his lips to hush him. He slowly rises and places two logs in the fire for the night.

Lydia walks over to our futon and turns up the heat lamp, then lights two candles that are on the table next to us.

"Is Cove asleep?" she whispers in my ear.

I nod and yawn.

"You look tired yourself. Why don't you sleep for a while? The two of you can come inside if you get cold. I'll make you a nice breakfast in the morning."

I smile and she places the blanket under my chin, tucking me in like I'm her child. Wayne holds out his arm for her. She walks up to him, resting her head against the side of his chest. The two disappear up the path and into their home.

I look up at the desert stars. It's a clear night, very different from St. Louis when we left. The skies were grey and snow was falling. Now, I feel like I've stepped back to a cool summer night in August.

I think back to third grade, trying to remember some of the constellations that twinkle above. That's Ursa Minor, an easy one. That means Cassiopeia is right over... there. Next, there's Pegasus, and Pisces. Beautiful. I can't believe I remember these. And where's my favorite? I search the sky for Orion, finally finding his belt. Ah ha... you can't hide from me. Boy, when was the last time I noticed the stars? Really looked at them. Possibly a decade ago? How sad. That must be Gemini to the upper left of Orion. Hmm. I wonder what sign Cove is? I've never asked him about his birthday.

Ooh. A shooting star. I try to rise from the futon, but quickly remember my arm is trapped under Cove. I wish I could've said that out loud, I wish he could've seen it.

It's gone.

"What is it, Baby?" Cove whispers.

"You're awake?"

"Hmm-mmm."

"I saw a shooting star," I say in a soft voice.

"Make a wish."

"I just lived it."

He smiles and turns toward me, opening his eyes. "Make another."

I lean in and kiss him. He lets out a quiet moan and a heavy breath.

"God, Baby. I'm hard for you again," he speaks softly and nibbles at my ear.

I grab his hand and place it under my skirt. He moves my underwear to the side and pushes a finger inside, closes his eyes and shakes his head. "And I feel you're aroused too."

I nod with a smile.

"We need to be very quiet. Can you do that for me?"

I nod again, biting my bottom lip while I unbutton and unzip his jeans. He delicately sashays my underwear down to my knees. I pull my legs up, gliding them completely off with my feet. He massages my hips then pulls me closer to his body. Our tongues prance inside one another's mouths. His hoodie is soft and comfortable, but I'd rather huddle against his flesh. I reach down and begin to pull it off, only to have my hand captured.

"No, Sweetness. Remember where we are," he whispers. "I want this to be tender so that you feel my love, but I want to keep it between you and me. I don't want to put on a show for wandering eyes in the neighborhood."

"I adore you, Cove," I say softly.

He smiles as he takes off his jeans and boxers, leaving

them hidden under the blanket next to his feet. "Sophia," he whispers. "Lie back and look at those beautiful desert stars. Let me see the reflection of the night sky in your big brown eyes. You're just as radiant as they are."

"Cove."

"I'm gonna make love to you, Baby."

It's easy to submit to such passionate words. I lie back and look at the sky. I'm surprised to hear the crinkle of a condom wrapper, but decide not to ruin the mood with any questions. Cove's gentle as he slides on top of me. He holds the blanket tight to ensure privacy. His lips brush against mine, and with one quick sweep, both his tongue and cock are inside. We try our best not to release any moans. I keep my eyes open and look at the bright stars, watching his head move, his eyes staring into mine, while I peer into the night.

He places his head to the side of mine. His body methodically rises and falls in small thrusts. His dick grows, stretching my insides as our orgasms build. The pressure on my clit is precise. My arousal is quick, encased by the stars that glow overhead. We're hushed, our sounds imprisoned. I need to cry out, but stay silent as Cove struggles to stay in control, a low groan escaping his throat every few minutes.

I stretch my legs, my chest tightens, and my nails dig into his back. The stars blur and dance... then they're gone. I close my eyes, holding everything in. I fight to keep my words inside as he slows. My mouth opens. My body demands more. *Faster, Cove. Please. Fill me. Harder.*

His release starts as I near my end. He bites my shoulder, securing his cries. Deep, pulsating bursts throb inside me. His body is tight and trembles on top of mine. I hold him, as he exhales a large breath into the night.

"Dear God, that was incredible," he whispers.

He rolls onto his back, trying his best to keep his gasps low and discreet. I place my hand under his hoodie and trace his stomach, waiting for him to speak. He covers his face with his arm, shielding his eyes from view. I wonder if he's embarrassed or worse, upset.

"Hey, Babe," I whisper. "You okay?"

"Yeah," he says, his voice cracking.

"You sure? Look at me."

"No," he says.

I sit up and lean over him, moving his arm from his face. His eyes are filled with tears.

"Sophia..." He turns away.

"I'm right here for you, Cove. I always will be, unless you want me to leave."

"No, absolutely not," he says, turning swiftly. He runs his hand through my hair and kisses my forehead, holding his lips to mine. "I love you. I need you by my side... forever. I want you to be my wife."

I don't know how to respond. I look into his watery eyes and try to figure out if this is a proposal, if he's lost in the moment of passion, or if there's something else going on. "Cove, I don't understand. You want to get married?"

"Do you?"

"Well, eventually I'd like to marry someone."

He sighs. I watch him pull the condom off and toss it into the fire. He reaches for his jeans and slides his clothes back on. I grab his arm before he can escape, tugging him close to me. "Eventually, yes. But we need more time—"

"Stop."

"Let me finish," I whisper. He closes his eyes and listens to my soft words. "We haven't known each other long enough. We haven't even had a fight yet. Much of what we feel is love, but a lot of it is lust. We need to see how we feel after our honeymoon hormones calm down."

"We had a fight. In my mother's studio."

"Yeah, well we need more than one to know if this will work. Plus, the sex thing, I listened to you when you said there's more to a relationship than sex. Maybe we should spend tomorrow without touching one another, I mean besides kissing and holding hands. Nothing beyond the basics."

"Easy. I love being with you. Making out is a bonus, so yeah, I'm game."

"I mean it. It won't be as easy as you think, but we need to do other things besides fuck... or make love. And this isn't a game. I'm not going anywhere, but I'm also not hopping through some Vegas wedding chapel either."

"So, you don't feel what I feel," he mumbles.

"You're wrong, I think I do. I know I do. I'm in love, but since this is the first time I've experienced anything like this, I can't be a fool."

"Sophia?"

"What?"

"I didn't ask you to marry me," he says with a grin. "I'm just worried about tomorrow."

I brush his cheek with my hand, snuggling up against his chest. "What do you think's gonna happen?"

"With Paul? Maybe nothing. It's possible he'll just ignore us. Or he might have plans to send one more fist my way, but he'd have Dayne do it this time. But with you, I'm worried. Can you see us together forever, even if I upset you tomorrow?"

"Upset me how?"

"Maybe you should stay in the hotel room and I'll go to the expo on my own."

"Hell, no," I squeak in a raised voice. Cove covers my mouth and places a finger up to his lips to remind me to keep a low voice. I nod and he drops his hand. "I won't let you go there alone. I'll be right by your side," I whisper. "I need to show my dad that I'm strong and that I have feelings for you. And I want to be there to support you, no matter what you say to him, or what you have to do."

"Remember you said that. Okay?"

I sigh. "What are you really worried about?"

"You haven't seen me interact with Paul. You don't know... you may not like... let's just say I'm nervous. I'm not the same person around him as I am around you. I'm not an alpha male like he is."

I take his hand. "It will be okay," I say, nervous and frightened of the event myself.

"I said I wanted you to be my wife someday to distract my mind. If I have that in my head, if I know you're part of my future, I can focus on *that* tomorrow, instead of other things I need to do. Plus, yeah, I'm more than a little serious about the question."

"Yes."

"Yes what?"

"I can see us as husband and wife... someday. A long time from now."

He smiles, kissing me, his tongue moving in a happy dance. He exhales, closes his eyes and leaves an arm draped over me.

"Do you mind if we stay here tonight, or do you want

to go back to the hotel?"

"What time is it?"

"Probably close to midnight."

"Let's stay. It's comfortable. And I feel safe with your aunt and uncle close by."

He pulls the blanket up and tucks it under my chin, making sure I'm warm and cozy, just like Lydia did earlier. "Are you satisfied, Sophia?" he asks in a hushed tone.

"With what?"

"Am I giving you what you need when I make love to you? Or do you need more? Is what I do enough?"

"You're incredible, loving, sexy, considerate, sincere, rousing, erotic, stimulating, exciting... should I go on? Yes, I'm more than satisfied. I only hope I do the same for you."

"More than you know." He turns onto his back and I join him, his arm under my body. I rest my head on his shoulder and we gaze at the stars, drifting quietly to sleep.

"MMMPH!" COVE MUMBLES, his head held underwater by Paul.

"What the fuck were you doing outside of that police station, Cove? Dayne, get in here and hold this little fucker down," Paul shouts.

He releases the back of Cove's neck so Dayne can step in. Cove pulls his head out of the tub, quickly turning his face away from the water. He swings, striking Dayne's jaw.

Dayne laughs it off, pushing him back into the water. Cove continues to kick and swing, fighting back. He panics, his stomach clenches into a knot. Vomit burns his throat. He pukes, and Dayne pulls him out.

Cove slumps next to the tub, gagging and coughing water out of his lungs.

"You've gone too far this time, you little shit," Paul says, his teeth clenched.

"Please Paul." Cove gasps, trying to catch a breath. "It won't happen again."

"Damn right it won't," Dayne says. "Shoot him."

"No." Paul tosses a towel at Cove. "Tell us, Star. I want to hear what you were going to say when you walked into that station. Tell us your exact words. I know you had something planned. Talk to me like I'm a cop."

Cove looks up and shakes his head, letting out a short laugh in disgust.

In one quick thrust, Paul grabs his hair and drags his head to the floor. "You dumb fuck. Say it! Say the words, Cove."

He takes hold of Paul's wrists, trying to pry them away. "I'm not afraid of you, Paul Jameson. I already told you it wouldn't happen again, now let me go, you dick."

"Put him back in," Paul says.

"No!" Cove screams, flailing his arms as Dayne pushes him back into the tub. He cries out from under the water, places his hands on the bottom, trying in vain to push up. It's pointless. Dayne's a hundred pounds heavier.

Slowly, his arms relax. He can no longer hold his breath. His body craves oxygen. His head hurts. There's a sharp pain in his temple. His body reacts and sucks in water on a frantic search for air. He hears a muffled voice as he starts to fade into darkness.

Dayne hauls his body out. He inhales hard, coughs, and chokes in deep breaths.

"You afraid of me now?" Paul asks.

"He pissed himself," Dayne says, pointing at his pants.

Paul looks down and grins. "You terrified? Afraid of me, now?"

Cove is motionless, except for his heaving chest.

"I asked you a question," Paul says, taking Cove's chin into his hand.

"Yes," he says, voice hushed.

"What was that?"

"Yes, sir." This time louder, so Paul can hear his words. "You own me, Paul." He wheezes. "I promise... I won't do it again."

"No, Cove. You won't. Because next time, not only will you be punished, but I'll make sure your father is submerged as well. And it won't be in the tub."

Cove nods in defeat.

"Kneel for me, Star," Paul orders, standing in front of him. "Kneel and show me your face."

He kneels and looks into Paul's wicked eyes. He wants to tear them out of his head. He wants to place a knife in his heart and twist it. He wants Paul dead.

"Say it."

"You own me, sir."

"Say it again."

"You own me, Paul Jameson," he cries.

Paul grins, leans down and sweeps Cove's wet, dark hair away from his ear. He massages the skin on his lobe before tugging it lightly. "One more time, my pure Star."

"You own me, Paul..."

• • •

"Cove!" I shout, shaking his shoulder to startle him awake. "You have to stop saying that, please."

"What?"

"You were talking in your sleep... about my dad. What

the fuck?"

He pushes the blanket off and sits up, dropping his head into his hands. "What time is it?" he asks.

"Morning. Tell me what that dream was about."

"It doesn't matter, let's get up and go inside. I'm sure my aunt has breakfast for us." He stands and holds out his hand. I put my clothes on and stand next to him.

"I want to help you."

"My dreams are nothing you can help me with."

"Try me."

"Let's just say I learned to be your father's submissive little Star through a few coercive dunks in a tub."

"Oh, Jesus," I whisper as he folds the blanket and takes the path to the house. I watch him walk with his head down, conquered and lifeless.

A light's on in the kitchen and Lydia is by the window. She's in a white puffy robe that looks like a cuddly bunny. She sees me watching her and waves me inside. I catch up to Cove who's waiting by the back door.

"Sorry, Sophia," he says sadly, giving me a warm kiss as an apology. "Let's have a good day together before we go to the expo. I want to take you out to a few of my favorite spots, then we can have dinner before we get dressed for the night."

"Sounds great, Babe," I say, placing my hand in his as we walk into the house.

"Hooray! There're my two lovebirds. Get in here and sit down. I have coffee and scones ready," Lydia exclaims, way too loud for this time of the day. She takes the blanket from Cove and the two of us use the bathroom to freshen up. I wash my face and fix my hair before I join everyone at the table. The beautiful night restored my mind, and I'm hopeful that Mera, Cove, and I will be back in St. Louis shortly. I'm stronger than yesterday. Ready to go. *Bring it, Dad.*

Wayne's in plaid pajamas and lost behind a newspaper, while Lydia pours four coffees into yellow smiley-face mugs.

"Sophia, sit down. Let's chat," she says. I take a seat at the table next to Cove. "I've made cranberry scones this morning. I hope you're hungry."

"Always," I say, placing two on my plate. "I love your mugs."

Lydia rolls her eyes and Cove laughs. "Yes, a gift from my sister. She likes to send me the most colorful things."

"Well, I think they're cute," I say, taking a sip out of one in approval. Lydia has placed a small amount of caramel syrup in my coffee and my taste buds are grateful. "Mmmm, perfect. Just what I needed."

"Yeah, better than what we would've had at the hotel. Thanks, Aunt Lydia."

"You're welcome you two. Now, let's talk."

"Cove, did you use that thingy I gave you yesterday?" Wayne blurts out, his voice dominating the room. He sets his paper down and picks up a scone.

"Oh Wayne, that's not the conversation I was about to have. This isn't a sex talk with our nephew. He's too old for that." Lydia scolds her husband, shaking her head. "And why did you give him a condom?"

"Well, what if his father never talked to him about those things?"

Cove smiles and takes my hand. "My parents had the sex talk with me a long time ago. I'm careful. Now, can we change the subject?"

"Just wanted to make sure. I don't need that sister-in-law of mine to call here all panic-stricken that we allowed you to knock someone up in our back yard."

"Uncle Wayne, please."

"Yes, Wayne. That's enough," Lydia says.

"Well, don't say I never gave you anything. Latex gloves are the best gift an uncle can give."

"What the fuck?" Three sets of eyes look at me and I blush. "Damn it. Did I say that out loud?"

"Yeah." Cove laughs, squeezing my hand. "You did."

"Well then, 'what the fuck' is the phrase of the day," Wayne replies with a grin. "So Lydia, what the fuck do you want to talk about?"

Cove and I chuckle at Wayne's non-stop comedy routine, but Lydia sighs. I sense something's wrong.

"I wondered why you showed up at my door last night, so I called Leondra to make sure everything's okay."

Cove's about to take a bite of his scone, but stops and slowly puts it back on his plate. He brushes the crumbs off his fingers and sits back.

"She told me about the fight at the prison. She said you needed to get away on a little vacation, to relax somewhere outside of St. Louis. I'm so sorry to hear what happened. Are you doing okay?"

Thank God, she doesn't know everything. Cove's quiet and doesn't respond to her question. He nervously looks around the room. I can only assume he feels like my dad still has eyes on him.

"Oh, Cove. I'm sorry! I just realized that Sophia—"

"It's fine. She knows about my father," he says. "And

I'm fine too. I came out here for a few reasons. Getting away from what happened to my father isn't one of them. If anything, I'd rather be home and close to him when he's hurt."

He sounds aggravated that his mom explained things in such a way. I sip my coffee and try to remain a fly on the wall.

"Don't push it Lydia. Let him enjoy his time with this lovely woman by his side."

"Cove," she says.

"Lydia, I mean it," Wayne asserts. "Every time he comes here you push him into these conversations."

"I'm worried. I know what happened to his father must have something to do with those bruises on his face."

I look at Cove, happy to see that the marks are barely visible, and glad Lydia didn't see his face a few days ago.

"Sophia, if you haven't noticed, my wife is quite the snoop. Don't be surprised if she hasn't already looked you up online and has some questions for you. Though, I don't believe we've caught your last name yet," he says, with a hint for me to divulge more information. "My wife would make a good private eye. I feel as though I've spent half my life on the couch watching those CSI shows with her. I think she may have been a detective in her past life."

"Wayne, stop it. I'm just a concerned aunt who wants the best for her family... and some answers. My nephew doesn't just show up on my doorstep with a pretty woman at his side and a bruised face unless something's going on in that business. Sophia..." She turns and looks at me. "Do you work for Paul Jameson?"

Wayne's silent, staring at me, then at Cove. I look at the three of them and clear my throat, trying to break the silence. "Cove and I came out to find my best friend, she's in trouble, mixed up with the wrong—"

"Sophia," Cove stifles me. "Not another word."

"Let her speak, maybe we can—"

"Enough." He stands and nods for me to follow. "I appreciate the kindness you've shown us, but I think we need to go. We have a lot to do today."

"Cove, sit down," Wayne orders. "Both of you sit."

"I'm sorry," he says, taking my arm as he hurries us to the front door. "Sorry. I'm not going to discuss my business life with the two of you," he says, whisking me out front.

"I knew it, I knew Paul was involved. It was too much of a coincidence that you *and* your father were beat up at the same time!" Lydia yells. "Cove, don't you dare leave this house!"

Wayne races out the door behind us and takes hold of Cove's shoulder, stopping him in his tracks. "Don't get your girlfriend involved. Let us help you."

He releases my arm and places his hand on his uncle's, pauses for a moment before brushing it away. He walks to the car, as I look at Wayne, confused as to what to say or do. Maybe they *can* help us.

"Sophia," Wayne says. "Be careful around Paul Jameson. Make sure you're never alone with him. Stay close to Cove."

"He's my dad," I whisper.

Cove yanks my arm and pulls me away from his uncle. I watch as Lydia leans against the door to their home, Wayne standing aloof in their driveway. His eyes are blank, his mouth slightly open. He doesn't move, not an inch, as we pull onto the street and disappear down the road. I imagine he probably stood there until his wife dragged him into the house. I don't believe she heard who I am, nor will he tell her.

"Maybe they can—"

"No."

"Cove," I say, giving him a dirty look. "I just can't—"

He slams the brakes and jerks the parking brake up. In a split second, he's out of his seat and around the front of the car. He hits the hood then opens my door, pulling me out and pinning me between himself and the vehicle.

"Look at me," he says. "Look at my face." He takes my hair in his hands and pulls my head back, his eyes inches from mine. "You need to stop being so ignorant about Paul. I've been tortured by him, people have disappeared from his company, my father sits in prison because of him, and I'm not... let me repeat that," he says. "I'm *not* going to bring any more relatives into this shit."

Cove releases me and sighs when he sees a tear running down my cheek. He wipes it and looks up at the sky, wrapping his arms around me in a tight hug.

"Cove, I didn't mean to—"

"Shh. Don't," he whispers, kissing the top of my head. "I can't lose anyone else, Sophia. I can't. All I can think about right now is you. If this is going to work, I can't be distracted by my relatives." He steps back and frowns. "I'm under a lot of stress. I'm sorry I yelled."

I nod, sliding back into my seat. He closes the door and walks to the driver's side.

"Sorry," he whispers, getting back inside.

"You can only grab my hair and yell during sex," I joke, trying to lighten the mood.

"Where to now?" I ask.

"Hotel. I want to shower and change my clothes." He starts to drive.

"Me too."

"Remember, no sex today."

"I can control myself. How 'bout you?"

"No problem."

"Then what are we doing?"

"I'd like to go to the EHM." He watches my reaction out of the corner of his eye, but I haven't a clue as to what he just said. I shrug and he laughs. "It's the Erotic Heritage Museum."

"Ha, that sounds great."

"I want to have an old fashioned tourist kind of day with you. You know, museums, landmarks, whatever we come across that's interesting. I've always wanted to go to some of these places, but never wanted to go alone."

"Why?"

"It's not as much fun." He keeps one hand on the wheel and places the other on my leg, rubbing it gently. "I haven't had a vacation, a *real* vacation, since I was a kid. It would make my day if the two of us could just explore. You game?"

"Absolutely. It'll be like the educational trip I never had a chance to take with my family."

"Well, most parents wouldn't take their children to this museum, although your—"

"Don't say it."

We both laugh. I look ahead, noticing the streets are somewhat congested.

"I assume all these cars are headed to church? Do

people still do that on Sunday mornings? Maybe you can live stream it now instead of sitting on those hard pews. Have you ever gone?" I ask.

"Nope."

"Not once?"

"Nope."

"Have you ever been curious about it?"

"Nope."

"Well, okay then. Are you worried about going to hell?"

"No, are you?" he asks, obviously questioning the conversation.

"No. But I think all these people on the road right now are headed to church because they're worried."

"I'd say they're either on their way to work or on their way home after a long night at the casinos. Rush hour happens on the weekends too, you know. Vegas is a nonstop city."

"Maybe we should go to church."

"What? Really?" he says, shaking his head. "Why would you want to do that? When was the last time you went?"

I think back to my childhood. My mom used to drag my brother and me kicking and screaming to services, but not every week. I hated it, but I did go again on my own as a teenager.

"Quite a few years ago."

"By yourself?"

"Yeah, but for the wrong reason. I've never gone to church for the right reasons."

"I don't get it."

"We used to go when I was little, only my brother and I didn't understand it. We would talk to each other and play games and my mom would constantly hush us. She said we were supposed to ask for forgiveness for our sins, but I didn't think I had any sins, and I was probably right. I mean, come on, kids don't have sins. I was just too young to understand it. Church isn't for children."

"Is that a slogan? Church isn't for children?"

"It should be." I smirk.

"But you went when you weren't a kid?"

"I went again when I was around sixteen. I heard that if you pray, your prayers might be answered. I was having a rough time so I decided to sit through one of the services and repeat the same sentence in my head over and over for the entire hour. I didn't move or think of anything else, just that. I thought that if God were real, an hour of prayer would get me somewhere. Right?"

"So, what happened?"

"It didn't work. The whole thing is just a business."

"Well, duh. I guess you gave them some money too?"

"Yeah."

"And what did you repeat in your head when you were there for an hour?"

"Please God, please. Just bring John Miller back to me and I'll come to church every week. I promise. Just make him want to be my boyfriend."

Cove laughs, hard. I giggle myself at the absurdity of my request. I mean, John Miller? Who would want to be with that dope now?

"Are you serious? You actually did that?"

"Well, haven't you ever asked for anything?"

"Not for a John Miller, no." He continues to laugh. "You're not supposed to ask for things like that. I don't think church is the same concept as the North Pole. God and Jesus aren't like Santa. They won't just bring you presents."

"Well, they all have long white beards." I point out, jokingly.

"That's true. So you prayed to get a boyfriend back? That's fucked up. What made him so special?"

"I don't know, I guess he was just there. Like all of my relationships that lasted longer than a week, he was convenient, someone to pass the time with, someone who was good with his... well, let's just say he gave, and I took."

"So you were sixteen?"

"About, yes."

"So, you've been having sex for seven years?"

"Umm, longer than that."

"Oh," he says like a drone. He's silent for a moment, finding a parking spot in the garage of our hotel. He turns off the car and looks at me, wetting his lips with his tongue. He kisses me, his hand on my breast. I moan and pull away. I don't want to get too aroused.

"No hands today," I scold.

"I wanted one last grab. Fictional characters with long white beards really turn me on." He smiles.

"I'm glad I know when you're joking. Make sure you don't let anyone else hear what you just said about fictional characters. You'll piss off Santa lovers everywhere."

"Fair enough. So tell me why you want to go to church."

"I guess I don't. Like I said, I always went for the

wrong reasons, or I didn't understand it, and I still don't. I only thought it might offer us some comfort."

"It might."

"I thought we could ask for protection, for safety, including some for my dad," I say, waiting for a reaction to the last part. He says nothing, and I'm glad he let it slide. "I thought that if we stop by a church, we might have some kind of defense later on."

"You mean like a superhero? That kind of defense?"

"You know what I mean."

"I guess. You don't need to go to church for any of that. If you think you do, then all the pompous interior decorations those places purchase to impress people works. You're right. It's a business. If you'd like, I'll buy you some candles and a small ceramic Saint statue. Then I'll wear the hotel robe and splash some water on your face like you're being blessed. You can sit on the bed and pray for as long as you like, but I don't think you have to be in a specific place like a church to do so. That doesn't make any sense to me."

"Okay, I get it."

"Besides, if you're not actually religious, you may piss people off."

"People?"

"The higher powers that be."

"Yeah, I suppose if there is a God he wouldn't want me to come around every seven years with a request, then leave him high and dry, waiting for my utter devotion to him."

Cove laughs. "No, I don't think so."

"So it sounds like you know a little bit about religion, even though you've never been to church. Does that mean you believe in God?"

"No, and what I know I've read in books or learned from my parents. I was taught that I should be spiritual, but it was my choice as to how I wanted to decipher that. I meditate a lot, mostly late at night in my pool. It's always helped me to control my anger and deal with the loss of my father," he says, using his fingernail to nervously scratch at the steering wheel. "My mother went to the synagogue for a few years after he was sent to prison. She said she prays more now than she ever has, mostly for me. My father on the other hand was raised catholic, but I've never seen him attend church, and he doesn't like to talk about it either."

"I see. Well maybe that's what I need, to be spiritual."

"Yeah, you don't have to believe in God to do so."

"Umm, not according to Oprah."

"Well, Oprah doesn't know everything."

"Okay, you probably shouldn't let anyone hear you say *that* either."

He laughs, letting go of the steering wheel and taking my hand. "How did this conversation start again?"

"Sunday morning traffic."

"We just went through all that because there were cars on the road?"

"Yep."

"And that's why I love you."

His cell rings as he kisses my hand. He releases me, aggravated by the interruption. "I know who that's gonna be," he says, answering the call. "Hello, Mother."

She must have heard from Lydia. I can only imagine how that conversation went.

"No, I didn't tell them," he says. "I won't. I'm not going to get them involved. They don't need to know about the current situation." He glances at me, picking at the steering wheel again. "I wasn't going to tell them, I left that up to Sophia and it just slipped out in the end. What are they so worried about?" He's quiet and I wish I could hear her end of the call. "Tell them it's not like that."

They must've discussed the fact that I'm Paul's daughter.

"Well, tell them again. She's on our side." He sighs, placing his head against the headrest. "I know. But... no don't do that. I'm not going back there."

"Ask her how Lewis is," I request.

He holds his finger up for me to wait. "No, I'm not going to apologize... I have... no. Sophia wants to know how Lewis is doing."

He places his index finger and thumb over his closed eyes and rubs while he listens to her speak. He gives me a thumbs-up that all is well before he tries to end the conversation. "I wasn't changing the subject. I just said I wasn't going to apologize to him, leave it at that. Know that I... no. It's going to be fine. I won't let him separate us," he says, opening his eyes. "I'll call you after Paul's expo. Try to have some fun today." He hangs up and sighs. "My aunt knows who you are and she won't leave my mother alone."

"What do they know about my dad?"

"They know what my mother does for the company. And they know that my father's in prison because of what happened to me, and that your dad was the one who set him up, but they have no details, and they shouldn't. My mother told them years ago what she felt they needed to know. I guess I shouldn't have taken you over there."

"I'm glad that you did. And I know why you did. I want a normal life too."

"Well, let's work on that. How about a shower before we head out for the day?"

"Yeah, perfect. What are your mom's plans? I heard you tell her to try to have some fun."

"She found a box of trinkets that used to belong to her parents. She's going to photograph the objects today, probably out in the snow."

"Why?"

"It's her way of documenting things."

"No, why out in the snow?"

"I don't know, Sophia. I'm not an artist. Maybe she wants to show what the day was like when she came across the objects, or maybe she wants them to look frozen in time. I'm sure she doesn't have the same thoughts about snow as I do. Most people don't. She may find it lonely or maybe it represents death and decay, killing the nature that it covers each year. She'd probably love it if you asked her."

"You know, the world would be a better place if everyone was as sincere and self-reflective as the two of you."

He smiles at my comment, the morning sun glistening in his eyes.

"What time is the expo tonight?" I ask.

"It starts at four and will end at midnight. I thought eight would be a good time to go, after dinner and some drinks."

"Twelve hours?"

"Yeah, we have twelve hours."

Seven

COVE AND I shower together, and although we're both aroused, we keep our hands to ourselves.

He allows me to pick out his clothes, happy when I choose a grey button-down shirt. I roll the sleeves to expose a light brown trim under the cuffs. With the shirt untucked and the top two buttons left open, he looks fucking hot. Too hot to leave the room. I wish I could rip the shirt back off. I calm myself and hand him his black jeans. He rolls the bottom cuffs and slips into his oxfords, smiling, clean-shaven, and his wavy dark hair tumbled into place. I hate it that he always looks fantastic when I have to work to look half as good. As for myself, I pull on one of my short black dresses and a jean jacket with a pair of high riding boots. He adds his black baseball cap on our way out, and although I love to run my fingers through his hair, I understand that we both need protection from the sun. We leave with sunglasses in hand, ready to explore the city.

It's seventy-five degrees and sunny in Vegas, the perfect weather to walk the strip. We get a coffee and watch a crowd of tourists gather in front of Treasure Island. Cove tells stories about what they're doing in Vegas, causing me to laugh at his playful side.

"That woman over there, her name's Belle and she runs a twenty-four hour nude taxi service, but you can only ride in one of her fleet of cars if you own a turtle."

"A turtle?" I question. "Does the turtle have to have a specific name, since we're being so specific?"

"How about 'Guy'?" Cove laughs.

"Okay, so this woman runs a nude taxi service for turtle owners, but only for people who have a turtle named Guy?"

"Yep."

"And those two, over there to the right?"

"They're here on a search for a backward spoon."

"A what?"

"They have the largest collection of backward spoons in the country. They're only missing two and they heard they might find one here in Vegas."

"Can't you just flip the spoon over and it would be a regular spoon?"

"Shh, don't tell them that." He smiles.

I look at my watch and see that it's almost eleven. "Why don't we head over to the Erotic Heritage Museum? It should be open by the time we get there."

"Perfect," he says, taking my hand. "It's just a block or two off the strip so it won't take long to walk."

We stroll hand in hand through the large crowds, weaving in and out of family photos taken in front of the casinos and elaborate hotels. Every block has a line of men who snap business cards and flyers, trying to get us to take one from them. Cove places a hand up and stops them before they get too close. One person places a card in Cove's front pocket then quickly walks away. He takes it out and throws it on the ground.

"What are those?"

"Ads and coupons for strip clubs, exotic dancers, massage parlors, other places like that."

"There are so many of them."

"This is where they pick up business, especially on the weekends. They can reach more people out here on the main strip of the city than anywhere else."

"I didn't see them last time I was here."

"If Paul was with you and they recognized him, they would've stayed away, or maybe you were too drunk to remember. You did say you were wasted."

"True. Mera and I were drunk that entire weekend."

"Well, there you go," he says, putting his hand up to another guy who approaches. "Do you need anything from the mall since we're about to walk right past it?"

"No, I'm not a mall-ite."

"You don't like to shop?"

"Love to shop, just not at the mall. I like unique stores where I can find one-of-a-kind items. Mera, too, she only shops online."

"Really? That's odd."

"Why, do you like to shop?"

"Yeah, sometimes. I like to go into stores and feel the fabric. I touch everything, in search of material that's soft and comfortable."

"Well, doesn't everyone?"

"No, some people buy crap because they like the way it

looks, but if it doesn't feel good, why would you wear it? I couldn't order things online because of that. I won't wear anything that's stiff."

"Are you stiff right now?" I whisper.

"Soph." He grins. "I've been stiff since I pulled out of you last night. Your voice, body, and heart keep me aroused all the time. Your touch, your breath, your warmth... all keeps me erect 24/7. God, you saw how much I wanted you when we were in the shower together."

"Awesome."

"Awesome?"

"Yeah, that's great," I say with a smile, swinging his arm as we walk.

"You're pretty damn cute, you know that?" He grins.

"Yep."

"We're here." Cove stops, taking out his wallet.

"Whoa, this place is huge. Much bigger than I thought it would be." We step inside and find ourselves in the gift shop where there's a fifteen-dollar fee to get in. Cove pays my way and I thank him. Since we've met, he's paid for everything, which seems damn rude of me.

"Can I get lunch today?" I ask.

"That's not necessary. I want to treat you."

"Well, this relationship needs to be equal, so I'll buy lunch."

"Okay, but dinner's on me."

I agree and we begin our tour of the museum. I'm surprised by how *real* it is. I thought it would be some kind of a joke but it's actually informative. We come across a collection of artifacts, carvings, and sculptures from around the world. Many are hundreds of years old. There are stone penises and figural works of bodies entwined. It's Cove's favorite part of the museum. I fall in love with the giant penis made out of pennies and the retro electronic stimulators. I'd never put one of those things in me, no way, no how. I'd be afraid of being electrocuted, or that it would catch fire inside my vagina. Cove takes my photo in front of the penis of pennies and we ask one of the workers to take a photo of the two of us next to the Ron Jeremy fortune-teller machine. It's a blast. I'm glad Cove suggested it as one of our stops for the day.

"That was great, where to next, Babe?" I ask as we exit the gift shop still holding hands.

"I'd like—"

"Hello, Star." A low voice stops us. I feel Cove tremble as he clutches my hand. He pulls me next to him and whispers in my ear, "Don't call me by my real name." I nod, looking at the man who stands in front of us.

He twists a toothpick that hangs out of the corner of his mouth and reaches his hand out to greet Cove. I can feel the tension and hesitation before Cove takes the man's hand. I'm uneasy in this moment. I can't see the guy's eyes through his sunglasses. You can tell a lot about a person through their eyes. His hair is dark and cut short. He uses way too much gel and the ends clump and stick off the top of his head. I notice his broad shoulders and muscular build are awkward in relation to his tiny head. His jawline is covered in stubble and he rubs his chin, waiting for Cove to respond.

"There's no need to call me that. NOVA ended years ago."

"Did it?" the man asks.

"You know it did, now what do you want?"

"Sophia," he says. "Sophia, the princess. I have a message from your father."

Cove uses his arm to guide me behind his back, creating a barrier between the stranger and me. "Don't talk to her, whatever you have to say you can say it to me."

"Oh no, Paul was very specific with his instructions. He wants me to look into her eyes," he says, peering around Cove. He stares at me as Cove places a hand on his chest, halting him from any further movement. "And he wanted me to tell you that you need to wise up, Kiddo. If you think he brought you out here to get your friend back, think again. He's only got one thing on his mind, and it's not you. His entire life revolves around getting his father out of prison. Now walk away, before he abuses you just like he abused Natalie."

Cove lunges at the man but he slips away and heads for the strip. I grab a hold of Cove's arm, stopping him from a chase. "Let him go, it's not the guy's fault he had to do that, you know he probably didn't have a choice. My dad's an ass."

"And a liar," Cove says in a raised voice. "I'd never hurt you, Sophia. Don't believe him."

"Yeah, well who's this Natalie? And what did you do to her?" My voice is pissy.

"Sophia, don't. Don't let him brainwash you."

"My dad's an ass, but I've seen you be one too. Like in your mom's painting studio when you wanted to hit me. And now this guy comes up to us and tells me that you've abused someone. Did you hit her?"

"No," he repeats. "It's not what you think."

"Then tell me. Tell me about this woman named Natalie."

"I... I can't."

"What the fuck?" I yell, placing my hand on my waist. "Why would this guy say that to me?"

A crowd begins to gather and Cove looks uncomfortable. I can tell he's worried about losing me, but there's something else. I need to know more about this woman.

"Let's take a walk, back to the strip, we can get a bite to eat for lunch and discuss this."

I want to know now, but there're too many eyes on us. "No dodging this question, Cove. I need to have more details once we find a place to sit down."

"I've never lied to you, Sophia, I just keep things from you so you don't have to deal with the same shit that I deal with every day. Your dad's the bad one, not me. I just want to protect you."

I stop as he continues to walk ahead. He turns to ask what the problem is and I shake my head.

"You two sound alike sometimes," I say in a quiet voice. "What you just said is exactly what my dad would say."

"Well, I'm not him. I actually mean what I say. The words that leave his mouth are entirely for his own gain, and he doesn't care who he hurts or whose life he ruins along the way. What you just witnessed a moment ago is a perfect example." He takes hold of my hand and we walk in silence, searching for a quiet place to eat.

"Here, is this okay?" he asks.

I look up and see Neiman Marcus. We're at the mall and I'm in no mood to shop for clothes. "I thought we were getting lunch so we could sit and talk?"

"Yeah, there's a café on the second floor. We can sit and eat outside on the terrace. It won't be as busy as the places directly on the strip."

"Okay." I follow him into the store. We take the escalator to the second floor café and are seated outside. The warm sun feels magnificent on my skin. I take off my jean jacket and warm my shoulders, admiring the view of the city. "This is amazing, thank you. I'm calmer now. Who's Natalie?"

"She's part of your father's company, or was, years back."

"And what's her connection to you?" I ask as I sip my lemon water and look through the menu, keeping my cool.

Cove opens his menu and follows my lead. "She was my first."

"First what?" I look up.

"First woman I was with... forced to be with, first at almost everything. We both did what Paul told us to do, before she disappeared from the industry, when she said she was too old to be a part of it anymore. I was with other people as well, and in later years, I did a lot of stuff on my own for the camera, but I already told you about that. But she came back after NOVA was over, when Paul wanted us to be together again. By that time, I had loyal followers, and they wanted her back with me too. I guess they enjoyed the connection we had. And to be completely honest with you, I was comfortable with her. I didn't like her, for a few reasons, but it was a hell of a lot better than a circle jerk with Doron, or any of the NOVA stars."

"Oh jeez, Doron?"

He nods. "But then Natalie got pregnant, and I didn't know about it."

"Wait... I thought..."

He shakes his head. "Of course it wasn't mine, Sophia. I really did give you my virginity."

"Okay. Go on."

"Paul's a fucker. Remember this was after NOVA ended, so I was legal. He took me a step up into a new realm once I hit eighteen, then it got worse when I turned twenty. He wanted some hardcore bondage scenes from me, something I'm completely against and find sickening, but hey, that's Paul's industry for you. It's not a romantic company." He hangs his hat on the back of his chair and runs his fingers through his hair. He's nervous. Our salads arrive as he takes a sip of his water and clears his throat. "I hogtied her hands and feet behind her back a few separate times and duct taped her mouth. It was terrifying to see someone so vulnerable and helpless."

"You mean like you? Even though you weren't tied up, you were still in the same position with my dad."

"No, I should've just stopped and let Paul do with me what he wanted, but losing my father was still so fresh in my mind that I did exactly what he asked."

"And then what?"

"I'd put things inside her, and I was rough about it. Paul said no holds barred. She acted like she enjoyed it, but it was hard to tell since it was all scripted to the clients' fantasies. I pulled her hair, clamped her nipples, and made her hang from a bar by her arms." He closes his eyes. "Another time I placed a clamp around her neck that was attached to the wall. She kneeled on concrete blocks, her hands were tied behind her back, defenseless and helpless, she looked at me in a pleading way. I wanted to get out of there so I came as fast as I could. I was rough. It was similar to what happened that first time with you in my bedroom. What happened then, why I wanted to hurt your father, is related to that time with Natalie. I was lost in an orgasm and unaware that I kneed her a few times in her abdomen. I think everything we had done over a three-week span was too much for her body to handle and this was the last of it. The stress, the weight of her body when I strung her up, pushing objects inside her, then the pressure on her stomach..."

"God," I whisper.

"When we were finished I saw that she reached down and her hand had a small amount of blood on it. I thought I hurt her. When she saw the blood, she started crying. She collapsed and wept. The sound of her cries and the sight of the blood made me so fucking sick. I threw up, which I did a lot when I worked for Paul. It took me a few minutes to realize she had a miscarriage, and it was because of me. My abuse did that to her. She lost a child because of me."

"No. My dad did that, not you."

"I think it was his plan. He told me he knew she was pregnant after it all happened, and I think he wanted it to end that way. That's why he made me do the hardcore bondage scenes."

"Fuck." I groan.

"Is it possible for a person to be *that* evil? I know he's sick, but doing something like that would mean he's worse than the devil, or, he *is* the devil."

"Cove..."

"I was sick for weeks. I wouldn't work for him, I refused, and he got pissed and came out to St. Louis to talk to me. It was one of the few times I spoke my mind to him. I was angry that he didn't let her go. I couldn't comprehend why he did that, and I still don't. All of his other workers who got pregnant were fired. It's a breach of contract, and if a guy from the company is the father then he's gone too. But he didn't do that with her."

"What did he say?" I ask quietly, taking his hand to comfort him, as he's visibly upset.

"He said he knew, but that she wanted to continue to work. I thought that was bullshit. When other people wanted to continue he wouldn't allow them, so why her?"

"Tell me what else happened, with her, and my dad."

"He said I was done in another year. He had a plan to give my devoted followers a gift on my twenty-first birthday. It was a way for him to make a bundle in one shot... he said I could then take over Doron's job in St. Louis, since Doron and his wife were headed for Vegas. I no longer had to be online. Instead, I could film, edit, and be in charge of the sites in our region.

"But not 'til you were twenty-one?"

He nods. "I was glad I would soon be done, but after Natalie, nothing was ever the same. I couldn't perform like he wanted me to. I wasn't into it, not like I ever was before that time, but I couldn't even fake it. It became so routine, machine-like, automatic, and in the end, I never gave him what he wanted. I let him beat me up instead, both Dayne and Paul. That was my choice, and a choice I had all nine years, only I was never man enough to back out until that time. Dayne had me on the ground and kicked my chest, giving me two broken ribs, and Paul broke my arm. It was like a gang initiation, only I was on my way out, not in. Since I was no longer online, Paul didn't need to keep my face clean anymore, so he gave me a black eye and a swollen lip. It made his day to finally be able to leave marks on my flesh. My mother was hysterical, as you can imagine, and my father tried to sic the dogs on Paul from prison, what few he had left in his pack, but I stopped him. I made both of them let it all go... and it was over. I wasn't in another scene again until I took you into my bedroom the other day."

"Cove, I... I don't know how to respond," I say in a small voice. "I guess I can tell you that it's not your fault, but I've already said that so many times. I wish there was something I could do. Some way I could comfort you."

"Just believe me, not him. Realize that I'm not the dick Paul makes me out to be."

"I believe you," I say, finally relaxed enough to eat my lunch. "Do you know what happened to Natalie? Did you ever see her again?"

"She was the woman you saw me with in the park. That day you were on the steps."

"No way, really? You said you didn't like her, for a few reasons, what reasons? Now I'm curious."

"Paul showed me a video of her with my father. It hurt me so fucking much to see it. She knew he was married."

"Your dad knew he was married too."

"Yeah, but it was Doron's bachelor party, he was drunk. He looked like he couldn't even stand. He was completely wasted."

"That's no excuse."

"I disagree, but only because I've been in his position. I know how much Paul and the Rosens drink. They used to give me shots, lots of shots before I had to be in a scene. They said it would relax me and make me last longer. I was often given four to six drinks before Doron would film, or did it myself, before I turned on the camera. I can only imagine my father had plenty more that night, if you consider the company he was with," Cove says, taking large bites, like he hasn't eaten in days. I think a weight has been lifted off his shoulders now that more of his past has been exposed.

"So Natalie. Is she okay now?"

"She's married and has a son. Her husband's a chef and she's a stay-at-home mom. I meet her in the park once or twice a year to catch up on her life. At first, we would meet to apologize to one another. She was always saddened about what she was involved in when I was a teen. But I still can't get that miscarriage out of my head. I guess we may be friends, but I don't believe we speak often enough to be considered friends. I'll be excited to tell her about you next time we talk, though. Hopefully you can come with me to meet her. I'd love to introduce you."

"Um, that's kind. I'll think about it. I'm not sure after what you just told me if I could handle to hear anything about the two of you. That situation might be a bit awkward for me to crash in on. Did you ever ask her about my dad? How he was involved?"

"Yep, she said he gave her a choice as to whether or not she wanted to leave. He doubled her pay to stay, and she couldn't turn down the offer, not with a kid on the way. She planned to stop part way into her second trimester."

"Yeah, she would start to show after that. Her breasts must have been so sore with those clamps if she was pregnant. When I was—" I stop, quickly realizing I haven't disclosed that part of my life to him.

He puts his fork down and leans back, folding his hands. "Go on," he says in a concerned voice.

"I pass."

"What do you mean you pass?" He smiles.

"I pass on this conversation. Thank you for being so open with me, I know that must've been hard."

"No way, this relationship isn't going to work like that. After everything I just said to you, you can't even tell me you were pregnant?"

"I never said I was pregnant."

"Yeah, I'm not dumb," he says, finishing his water. "How old were you?"

"It was a long time ago," I say, thinking back to college when I had second-guessed myself about the situation, but now I know I made the right decision. I was nineteen and not in love. Wait, I was nineteen? Cove was twenty?

"I want to know more about you, the good and the bad. So how—"

"You said your were twenty when that happened with Natalie?"

"Yeah, it was during the spring, around Easter. Why?"

"I was nineteen when I had an abortion, it was March, just before Easter. I think my dad took his anger about my situation out on Natalie. He punished her for what I did."

"What?"

"I never told him, but now that I know he's had his eyes on me for years, he was aware of what happened. He knew I had an abortion. I bet Natalie told him around that same time. If he was upset by what I was doing, he could've easily taken it out on her, transferring my situation to her."

"Well, let's not get into conspiracy theories just yet. It's hard to know what really happened, but yeah, for once it actually makes a little sense. That's why he didn't fire her.

He either thought he could help her, since he wasn't able to help you, or he wanted to punish you and that was the only way he could figure out how to do so. The latter is probably true, knowing Paul. That prick."

"Fuck. I had no idea any of these things happened with my dad. I still don't know what to say."

"Focus on why we're here and don't think about the past, especially my past. And if your father tells you directly that I abused a woman and caused her to have a miscarriage, that yes, unfortunately that's true. But it needs to be placed in the right context, and he won't tell you the whole story."

"I understand."

"Let's just continue to enjoy the day, hopefully we can get back on track after that exchange."

"Who was that guy outside the museum anyway?"

"Just one of your dad's employees. He goes by Carl Caverns."

I laugh with a mouth full of food. "Really? That's hilarious."

"He's a middle of the road porn star. Not in the top tier, but known by a few. He does odd jobs for Paul, which includes being his messenger. Hopefully we won't have to deal with him again."

"Or anyone."

"Yes, beautiful. Or anyone." He smiles, shaking his head. "Jesus."

"What?" I ask, my eyes gazing into the exposed area around his neck. I lean forward and release another button, needing to see more of his skin.

"You. You're gorgeous. I'm one lucky bastard. I don't even think I can walk right now. I wish I could take you to bed and kiss every inch of your body, ending down between your legs. I want you, Sophia. I need you."

I moisten my lips and rest my palm against his cheek. Those dark eyes and chiseled jawline send my mind into a passionate daydream of him fucking me on the table. "If only you could feel how wet I am for you," I whisper. "I wanna go back to the hotel and fuck." I lean back and take a sip of water, trying to cool down. Cove swallows hard and places a finger up to his mouth, rubbing his upper lip.

"Tonight, Baby. When the day is over. I'm gonna enjoy it when my dick is in that wet pussy. You'll beg for more. I can't wait to feel you tighten around my dick when you cum."

My hand touches his jeans and travels up to feel his stiff cock. My God, how can he even breathe? "I'm glad your shirt's untucked so you can hide that giant thing. If we were alone, I'd kneel before you and suck you off."

"Fuck." He exhales, his hand stopping mine from any further contact. "We haven't done that yet."

"No, we haven't, but we will. You can count on that," I say, placing my napkin on the table as I put my jacket back on. I stand and bring my mouth down to his ear and whisper. "And Babe, I'm really good at it too. You'll be the one who begs for more."

He stands and adjusts his shirt, trying to hide his erection. He takes his hat and heads for the front to pay the bill. I follow, holding his hand, completely in lust and in love with this man. If I hadn't said no to sex for the day, we'd already be back in the hotel having a quickie. No. We wouldn't make it. We'd stop somewhere on the strip, maybe in a dressing room here at the mall. Yeah, I've never done it in one of those spaces. But I guess I'm glad we're not. It's important that we have these conversations and not just fuck. I feel more connected to him with each hour that passes and that's the reason we need to hold out for the day.

When we reach the register, I take the check, reminding him that lunch was on me. We pay and leave the café.

"Okay, Sophia. My balls ache and my head is mush, but I think I can continue on."

"Maybe you need to jerk off. We just passed a restroom."

He laughs. "You think I'd be able to relax enough to masturbate in a mall restroom? And what if I got caught and arrested? How would I explain that to my mother?"

I laugh along with him, knowing that Leondra would probably try to ground him, even though he's twenty-four. "Hey, that reminds me, when's your birthday?"

"Masturbation in a mall restroom reminded you to ask me about my birthday?"

"Yeah, you know how my mind works."

"I know. Well, I'm a Capricorn."

"No way, me too. What's the date?"

"January fifth."

"Are you fucking with me?" I ask, stopping dead in my tracks. Cove frowns, not sure what he did wrong.

"Seriously, this is a joke, right?"

"No, why?"

"Mine's the fifth. That's so fucked up!" I scream. "You *have* to be playing a joke on me."

"Baby, calm down. You're causing another scene," he says as we walk onto the main strip, once again surrounded by tourists. "I'm serious. It's the fifth."

"Isn't that exciting! We share the same birthday. How crazy is that?"

"Totally cray," he responds.

"Cray? You use that word too?"

"Yes, totally awesome to the max, since we're speaking all slang and shit."

"Come on," I plead, slapping his arm. "Humor me. This is exciting. It means we were meant to be together."

He turns and smiles. "Well if you put it that way, then yeah, it's great. I'm not much for birthday celebrations. I usually spend mine alone, but maybe that will change now that I can center the day around you."

"Hey, you were born in—"

"Don't worry, I know what you're thinking. And no, I'm not your twin brother. I'll be twenty-five soon, a year older than you."

"Thank God, could you imagine our lives being any more fucked up than they already are?"

"Actually, yes," Cove says, lifting his head to gaze at a giant billboard. "I think I can."

Eight

"FUCK PAUL JAMESON. I can't believe him. Your fucking father."

I look up to see what's got him so upset. It's a billboard for Jameson Industries XXX Adult Expo. There's a bikini-clad brunette with a perfect body down on all fours sticking her ass in the air. Her full lips are caked in dark red lipstick and her mouth is slightly open. Behind her are three men, photographed from the chest up, shirtless with flexed muscles. Their abs are clenched and covered in oil. With heads tilted down and eyes on her like they're hunting a wild animal, all three predators have staked their claim. The sign reads: *Porn stars, captured, trained, and always obedient. Come tame your own beast this weekend at the Jameson Convention Center, inside the Fox Palace.*

"You okay?" I ask, knowing that my dad's presence, even through something as simple as a billboard, is enough to piss Cove off.

"Take another look."

I study the billboard, but don't see anything out of the

ordinary, besides the fact that it's in poor taste, even for Vegas. Then I see *his* eyes, Cove's eyes, on one of the bodies in the background. His tattoo and scar are gone, they must've been edited out from the shot, but it's him. It's definitely him, a few years younger with shorter hair. "Shit," I mumble. "When was that taken?"

"Years ago. It's from his wild beast series. I don't know why the fuck he still uses my body for billboards. That asshole."

"Let's walk away so you can try to get it out of your head. There's nothing we can do about it."

"This must've been made before everything happened this past week, he didn't just put it up today, which means your dad and I were still on good terms. It makes me feel like he expects me to do shit online for him again. I don't like it that he's got me on display. That's supposed to be over."

"Come on, let's do something fun." I pull him in the opposite direction of the billboard. He looks back at the sign and grumbles under his breath. "You were about to tell me about our next destination before we were interrupted outside the museum earlier. So where to?"

"The Venetian. The Erotic Heritage Museum was interesting, but not as romantic as I thought it would be."

"Well, duh."

"Hush, Baby. I'm trying my best to make you all starry-eyed over me. My next plan may just do the trick."

"You don't have to try. I'm already starry-eyed. So what's the plan?" He holds the door open with a smile and the two of us step into the Venetian. My mouth drops open and I gawk at the beautiful space that envelops me. I'm in Italy, literally, it's like I just stepped off a plane and I'm overseas. "My God, this is breathtaking."

"So, you approve?"

"Wow."

"I'll take that as a yes." He laughs, taking my hand in his. We walk and I admire the classy architecture and brilliant faux-painted blue skies with puffy white clouds overhead. It's bright and feels like the sun still shines down upon us even though we're indoors. We walk past stores with unique gifts before we stop on a pier. I gasp at the sparkling water and long boat in front of us.

"Does a private gondola ride interest you?" he asks.

I nod, grinning from ear to ear. Cove pays an outrageous amount then holds out his hand and helps me onto the boat. I take a seat in the back and he sits next to me, placing his arm over my shoulder. A man above us rows, and we begin to glide through the water, observing the tourists shopping, and the incredible blue skies above.

"I can't believe this. I've never done anything like this before."

"Me either. It's not the type of thing you can do by yourself or with your parents." He smiles, kissing the side of my head. I turn toward him and capture his mouth, pushing my tongue wildly inside. He groans and his tongue takes chase. I place my head against his chest, grazing his nipple. He laughs and pushes my hand away.

"Okay, you did it. I'm hard again," he whispers. "Will you ever stop the torture today, or is this how it's gonna be?"

"I just got wet for you, so yeah, as long as I'm aroused, I'll make sure you're right there with me," I reply, inhaling the spicy vanilla scent that's on his shirt. "You smell wonderful again, Babe."

"I try."

We float past people who dine along the water. It's lovely. The buildings and atmosphere are dream-like. Finally, this is a perfect moment in our day.

"I love you, Sophia," he whispers, pressing his body against mine. I give him a soft kiss in appreciation.

We return to the pier and we exit the gondola. "That was amazing. I can't believe you did that for me."

"For *us*. But the romance is over for now, let's have some fun," he says. We walk past rows of shops and down a corridor, stopping in front of a group of celebrity wax figures. The sign in front of us reads Madame Tussauds, and I give him another kiss in approval.

"What a cool idea, but this time it's my treat," I insist. Cove hesitates but allows me to pay the admission. I make him take my photo with almost every figure, requesting three separate angles when I sit with Will Smith, and two of me lying next to Hugh Hefner. He only requests one photo of himself, with George Clooney, telling me that Clooney reminds him of his dad. I give him a warm smile as I shoot the photo.

"This is terrific, Cove. It's so nice to be out with you."

"I've never been this happy. Hopefully we can do it again soon." He beams. "You interested in going to an art gallery?"

"You bet. I'll do anything."

"Follow me," he says. I hold his arm tight as we stroll down the strip. We sightsee, shoot photos of the casinos, and admire fountains along the way to our next stop. I'm like a child on Christmas morning, eager to see what's next. He's just as energized, and at one point, he buys me a white rose from a street vendor. He snaps the stem and places the flower over my ear and through my hair, planting a soft kiss on my mouth. His lips and tongue are as warm as his heart, and I wish I could be half as loving.

"I adore you, Babe."

He blushes then nods to our right, stopping next to the Bellagio fountain.

"Now that's impressive," I say.

"I know. I love it. It's a spectacular hotel. And nothing's as grand in Vegas as this fountain." We take a seat on a bench and watch the show. Soft music plays as water shoots toward the sky. Lights glow and disappear under the water. "Have you ever seen it at night?" he asks.

I shake my head, completely mesmerized, sitting quietly through two songs. The water moves freely and flows with the music.

"It's beautiful at night. Meditative," he says, standing back up. "You ready?"

"Yes, but I'd like to come back here again. It's so pretty."

"You got it."

We walk inside the Bellagio. It's obvious that I'm a tourist. I stare wide-eyed at every square inch of the elegant interior.

"Jesus, marble floors and massive columns? Whoa, look at that fountain... and that glass on the ceiling. Cripes! Where am I?"

"That's the Fiori di Como chandelier, it's a Chihuly," he says, trying to snap me out of whatever world I just fell into. "Can you hear me?"

"Yeah. You have to remember I grew up poor, so—"

"You did?"

"Well, yeah. I told you my dad left when I was little. And later he was upset by the way we had been living. I had nothing as a kid."

"But didn't you see all of this when you were here last time?"

"Mera and I partied. Isn't that what Vegas is all about? Gambling... getting shitfaced?"

"No, this city has a lot of culture. And yes, tons of people come here to party, but there's so much more to it than that. Look at this place," he says, holding out his hand at the massive space that surrounds us. "Look at the opulence. It's magnificent. I could spend an entire week just studying the architecture. People miss out on this stunning city when they spend all of their time in the casinos. There's a whole other world outside of those dark gambling rooms."

"I see that now. Look, there's the gallery," I say, pointing ahead. "Have you ever been here before?"

"I come here every chance I get."

"Really?"

"Yeah, my mother has placed a love for art in my bones, especially photography. It's hard to grow up with an artist and not have some appreciation for it."

"Now that I've spent time with you, I completely understand. Your love for certain things is rubbing off on me."

We enter the gallery and spend an hour admiring the current exhibition. Cove knows a lot about the artist. I listen to him discuss the work, captivated by his knowledge. I can tell he's intelligent and would've done well in college. I wonder if he would want to attend now. He asks me what my favorite piece in the show is, and I take him over to an acrylic silkscreen of a pile of colored shoes. Cove smiles and nods; commenting on the composition, unity, and movement in the piece. I ask about his favorite work and he points at a series of Polaroids.

"I love the facial expressions and the feelings that radiate from the eyes of each person. He really captured their personalities," he says, as he walks me through the set. I feel like I have a personal guide for the exhibition and just like the other events of the day, I'm a bit sad when we're finished.

"You hungry?" he asks when we're leaving the gallery.

"Yes, what time is it?"

"Five. I think we should get a bite then head back to the room to change before we talk to Paul."

"Oh," I say with sadness. "It's that late?"

"Hey," he says, wrapping his arms around me. "Let's have a nice dinner together. Then, I promise you, I'll be back in that hotel room with you after I speak to Paul."

"Promise?"

"Yes, you can count on it. I want to sleep next to you, naked. My hands need to be all over you tonight. I'll suck and lick that clit of yours, make you moan and beg for my dick," he whispers, kissing my cheek. "You wet for me, Baby?"

"Hmm-mmm." I whimper.

"You gonna suck me tonight?"

"Yes." I exhale.

"I can't wait to make love to you. We'll be in that room together, just you and me. Promise."

"Okay," I say in a wavering voice. "Let's have dinner. Every moment with you means the world to me." He sweeps in and presses his mouth passionately against mine, giving me a deep kiss. He cups my back, guiding me down the hallway and out the front of the hotel. I see the beautiful fountain and wish we could just stay here forever.

"You see that?" He leans in, pointing across the street to a replica of the Eiffel Tower.

"Yes. I saw it earlier when we walked down this way. It looks just like the real thing."

"But look up there." He points to windows partway up the building. "I made a reservation for us at a restaurant up there for five-fifteen. You'll have your own private view of this fountain while we dine."

"Are you serious? When did you make the reservation?"

"Yesterday, when you were in the shower in the hotel room." He smiles.

"Thank you, thank you, thank you," I say, planting soft kisses on his cheek. "This whole day has been perfect."

We walk to the Eiffel Towel, take a glass elevator to the eleventh floor, and are seated at a table overlooking the strip. As the sun sets, the city lights sparkle across the quickly approaching night.

Cove orders two glasses of pinot noir and the slow roasted salmon filet for each of us. I smile in approval, enjoying the Bellagio fountain from a different perspective.

"Don't tell anyone your name when we're out tonight," he says. "When I sent Paul a text, I mentioned we'd both be at the expo, but I still haven't heard back from him. I guarantee he's not happy that I'm taking you there, but at least he's prepared and knows we're coming. But he'd be furious if people found out that you were his daughter, so don't say your name."

"I don't think he cares anymore, Cove, but I won't. I

don't want anyone to know that I'm a Jameson."

"No, he cares. He cares about having to deal with problems. He's at his best when the company runs smoothly. Let's keep who you are private."

"I'll go by Sara. No last name."

"Okay, Sara. Be prepared for everyone to call me Star. That name stuck even after NOVA ended. My online name was White Dwarf Star, then it turned into Shooting Star when I got older."

"Oh God," I say, rolling my eyes.

"Hey, it's better than Carl Caverns."

We laugh as our food arrives. It tastes delicious, and I'm surprised I can eat with all the anxiety I feel about the expo.

"So that's what NOVA stood for? White Dwarf Star? Mera and I saw that definition online."

"I was Paul's NOVA Star. That explosion was me."

"Ugh."

He hesitates and takes a bite of his salmon, closes his eyes and swallows. He swirls his wine before taking a sip, then continues... "NOVA as a whole stood for Night of Virgin Adolescents." I scrunch my nose in disgust. "The scenes were all shot in the late afternoon or at night. We were promoted as pure and young, or made to look young. And I don't think any of us had a clue as to what we were doing, but that was the draw for Paul's clients. People love innocence. It's rare and hard to come across in the porn industry."

"Cove?"

"Yeah?"

"Can I ask you about your dad?"

He looks at me then at his wine. I wait for an answer as he takes another drink. He gulps it down and pours himself a second glass. "I suppose," he finally says.

"What happened?"

"You mean in the end?"

"Yes. When he was arrested. How did that happen?"

"Dayne picked me up, like he did a lot when I did something wrong. He said it was my biggest and last mistake."

"You mentioned to me before that you went to the police. That was the mistake?"

"Yes, I tried to. Twice. The first time I was fifteen. It was when the Rosens still lived in St. Louis. Dayne, Doron, and a few others who were involved would pick me up on my walk home from school. They'd take me to a brownstone that Paul purchased from the Rosens' father. Originally Paul had a few rentals, but later he bought two properties, the brownstone being one of them."

"So you were fifteen?"

"The first time, yeah. Dayne grabbed me as I was about to walk into the station. I have no idea how he knew I was there, besides the fact that I wasn't on my usual path home. Your dad was in town for something too. I was surprised to see him in the kitchen of that place when Dayne brought me in. It was like he had read my mind. I got what I deserved that day, dunked in a tub of water, and was scared enough that I didn't think to try it again for years."

"I hate it when you say things like that. You always make it sound like it's your fault."

He refills my glass and sends a half-smile my way. I take a drink, prepared to hear more.

"The second time was years later, when I was eighteen. Paul had warned me of what would happen if I ever talked, but I thought I could beat him. Someone else also wanted out and was supposed to come out with me. I thought it was the right time. But he turned on me, and the only reason he didn't go down with my father was because of Dayne. Brotherly love."

"Doron?"

He nods. "He loves the money like the rest of them, and he doesn't mind the other sites, but was never thrilled about NOVA. He ended up ratting me out to Paul. Dayne waited for me on the street by the station. I didn't run, or fight back, or try to deny anything. It was over. I walked in silence with him to his car and he drove me to the brownstone where Paul was waiting. He told me my father had already been taken in. I was a wreck. He wanted me to testify against him, and if I didn't, my mother would *run into some problems* as well."

"Did you?"

"No. I couldn't do that to my father. I told on Paul. But of course, no one would believe me that it was Paul and not my father behind it all. And no one could pin anything on your dad. He had someone tip off the police about the child porn, sending people to our home and my father's office. Paul had planted some videos of me in both places." He stops to drink, his voice breaking apart from the memory. "The videos found in the office were my fault."

"How?"

"Doron gave them to me a day before my father was arrested. He asked me to leave them there. I didn't know what they were, and I never questioned it. I had delivered things before so it didn't seem unusual. Then, and I still don't know how this happened, Paul was able to place some files on my father's home computer." He finishes his second glass of wine and pours a third, his hand shaking as he puts the bottle down.

"You can stop. I get the picture."

"No. Let me finish. I think you need to know this."

I cross my legs and lean in, allowing him to lower his voice so people can't hear the conversation. He holds my hand and brushes his thumb over my fingers.

"He paid off two incarcerated men to testify against my father. They said they distributed the porn for him. Then the police 'magically' came across a few phone conversations with my father talking about NOVA. The person on the other end was never identified."

"Of course," I say, pissed off. "I think I'm going to scream right now."

"That's how I felt. I couldn't get anyone to listen to me. The police thought I was blaming Paul to protect my father. Then my mother's job came under scrutiny. Her years as a nude photographer didn't play well in the courtroom. My parents were portrayed as the wicked ones. The jurors were appalled that they had involved their underage son. There was absolutely no evidence linking my father to the Rosens or Paul. I even took the police to the brownstone, but it was wiped clean. No furniture, freshly painted, and newly carpeted. There was a 'for rent' sign out front and a woman confirmed that she had rented the place from Paul for years, and that nothing unusual ever happened there. I looked like a fool, just like your father had planned."

"That's fucked up."

"I went mad, and so did my mother. She was furious

that both my father and I never told her what went on for all those years. The bank account that my father set up also didn't help his case. Paul always gave me cash, and that's what my father deposited. It was a lot, and he couldn't explain where it came from. We were all in a hole, unable to climb out."

"Couldn't anyone find the other people in the videos?"

"Yes, they did. Natalie was one. She testified against him. That was another reason why I said I didn't like her, but I also understood where she was coming from. If Paul did some of the things to her that he did to me, then I get why she testified. I can't blame her. The other two were the brothers from LA, but they died in a car accident."

"And that wasn't suspicious?"

"No proof, Soph. They were drunk. Well above the limit. Paul had it planned out so well that if anything ever went wrong during those years, well... he knew what to do. It was always set to end this way from day one."

"So all of that because you were outside the police station? Dayne couldn't have just taken you back to the brownstone and, I hate to say it, punish you?"

"It was time to end NOVA. We all knew it. Age had become an issue, and Paul wasn't going to bring in any random teens that he didn't have a connection to. It was too dangerous to start over. Doron exposed my plan and that was enough for Paul to let it all go. He could still make money from me, but as an adult."

"So why not just end it? Why go through all of that and ruin people's lives? Why not just move and let it all go?"

"Good question, and I'm not Paul so I can't answer it. Lack of trust perhaps. He could've felt that something could still go wrong in the future, even though it was over. Or maybe just because he's a dick."

"How can your mom stand to even look at my dad now?"

"It took some time, but eventually she realized she needed him, as sick as that may be. My father gets beat up in prison. Paul steps in and pays off some of the inmates and guards to protect him. He's kept him safe, unless I fuck up, then it always seems like my father pays for my mistakes. My mother says it's a coincidence, but no way, I know Paul, it's never a coincidence."

"Dickhead."

Cove clinks my glass. "You bet he is," he says. "My mother's keeping her enemies close, as the saying goes. Plus, she still makes a shitload as the head photographer for his magazine, and she knows I'm still working for him, too, or I was. I think, like me, she's waiting for the right moment. Waiting for Paul to slip up, or for something to happen, something to open, like a magic box with a key that sets my father free. That's how she can stand to look at him."

I hear a high-pitched ding and turn to see a man tapping his fork against his wine glass. He stands and looks around the room, smiles, then takes the hand of the woman at his table.

"Excuse me everyone. I'd like to have your attention for just a moment. Please look at this beautiful woman who I've been blessed to have in my life for two wonderful years."

He kneels, pulls a small black velvet box out of his pocket, and continues his proposal. The room is quiet. The woman raises her free hand to her mouth, a tear running down her cheek.

"Karen, you've captured my heart. My love for you continues to grow with each passing day. It will never end."

"Sounds like he memorized that one," Cove whispers.

"Shh," I hush him.

"Will you do me the honor of—"

"Yes!" she screams before he can finish his sentence. A few women in the room wipe tears from their eyes and others say *ahh*. There's a refined round of applause as the two hug and kiss.

"So what do you think they'll do after dinner?" Cove whispers, smiling.

"The same thing as us," I respond.

He turns toward me, not sure if he really heard what I just said. "What? Not after the expo? You mean right after dinner?"

"We've spent the day together, just like I wanted. We've been good. I think we both deserve a sweet, hot, sticky dessert. Don't you?"

"Oh." He grins. "Do you like vanilla?"

"How about you try that chocolate roll again?" I smile, remembering my quick introduction to anal sex yesterday. He laughs at my request.

"You're so dirty," he says, shaking his head. "I love it."

I clutch his knee with my hand. He stares at me, his eyes heavy with passion.

"The first thing I'm going to do when we get back to the room is go down on you. I know that you're hard for me, Babe. I can see the tension on your face. Don't you wish I could reach under the table and unzip you?"

He nods, wetting his lips with his tongue.

"Can't you imagine me sliding my fingers in your

jeans, grabbing hold of that stiff dick?"

"God." He closes his eyes.

"My tongue can't wait to lick your shaft, up, up, up to your sensitive tip," I whisper.

"Sophia—"

"Shh," I hush him, running my hand up his leg. "Picture me below you, my eyes looking into yours, as I have your giant cock in my mouth."

"Baby." He pants.

"I'll let you shoot that warm cum into my mouth, allowing each burst to slide down the back of my throat."

"Can I get the two of you anything else this evening? Another bottle of wine, or perhaps some dessert?" the waitress asks.

I smile at her, but Cove keeps his eyes on me, without any acknowledgment of her presence.

"No, thank you," I respond. "Just the check."

Nine

COVE LOCKS THE DOOR to the hotel room in a rush. He charges to my side, grabs my waist, and pulls my dress over my head. He devours my mouth with a deep kiss and doesn't hesitate to slide two fingers inside me. I unbutton his shirt as he kicks off his shoes.

"Fuck. Fuck. I think I might burst any second," he says, escaping his jeans and boxers. He presses his body against mine and I feel his cock pulsating, moments away from an explosion. I push him onto the bed, sliding my tongue up and down his shaft. He takes my hair and wraps it behind my head.

"That's it, Baby." He tenses and throws his head back. "Oh fuck."

I flick my tongue around his crown before taking him entirely into my mouth.

"Fuck," he cries out. "That mouth of yours is so warm and wet, just like your pussy."

I suck fast and hard, driving him crazy, pushing him close to the edge the second I grab his balls.

"Sophia, I'm gonna cum," he says. "I'm gonna cum all over you. Release me... don't touch..."

I keep him inside my mouth, bobbing up and down, sucking and twirling my tongue as fast as I can. I pull on his nipple, opening wide for his cock to reach deep into the back of my throat.

"It's coming Baby... Fuck..." He erupts in my mouth. I swallow, trying to keep up with his gushing release.

"Jesus." He gasps. "Sophia. I can't believe you just did that."

I sit up and wipe my mouth. "What Babe? Make you cum in like, thirty seconds?"

"No." He pants. "Well, yes. But you swallowed. You didn't pull your mouth away and jerk me off."

"Why would I?"

He sits up and takes my head in his hands. "I love you," he says. "I love how different you are. I love that you're real. I love that we can be together and be ourselves."

I straddle him, parting his lips with my tongue. His hands travels down my legs and comes to rest on my knees.

"And I love it that you still have on these riding boots," he says, looking down with a grin. He lies back, placing his hands above his head, gazing at the ceiling. "You're perfect."

"Should we get ready to go?"

"No. What about you?" He looks back up. "I want to pleasure you before we go."

"When we get back, not now. You're on my mind, but so is Mera. I haven't thought about her all day and I feel bad about it."

"I think that's because of her text."

"Yeah, she sounded happy."

"She probably is, for now. Most of Paul's girls are for a few months, then they try to leave the house or want to go home and things get ugly. He's such a control freak. So is Dayne. The two of them in that house together are a disaster waiting to happen. I'm surprised they haven't killed each other yet."

"Really? I thought they were best friends."

"They are, but there's a lot of competition between the two of them. You should see them when they're drunk. It always ends in a fight."

"A fistfight?"

"Sometimes, but mostly just verbal attacks. Then Dayne becomes all apologetic before he passes out. I see it happen every time I'm there."

"Well, I think we should go. Sorry, but I need to think about my friend."

"Soph, if you want to go, then let's get dressed and go."

I smile, giving him a long kiss, twisting his nipple as I release my lips. He clutches his chest and laughs, slapping my ass as I head for the bathroom to freshen up. I need to look my best if I'm going to be surrounded by porn stars.

• • •

"You're gorgeous, Sophia," Cove says as we travel down the elevator to the basement level of the Fox Palace. "Don't be nervous. Stay next to me, and remember, no names. The Expo Hall is giant and we'll have to walk past a lot of shit before we can get to the back area where Paul usually sits. He has a stage from where he observes the floor."

I nod, starting to sweat, feeling slightly panicky. I

decided to go with a sophisticated look for the evening—a short, scoop neck sweater dress with a white tank underneath. Cove suggested my two-inch heels, adding a gold ankle bracelet and gold hoop earrings. I left my hair to fall naturally, the ends curled and resting over my breasts. My makeup for the evening is heavy, with dark eyeliner and a deep shade of lipstick. I feel as if I'm headed to an elegant dinner party, but know that's far from the truth.

Cove looks uncomfortable, but it's not because of his expensive sport jacket and black tie. He's just as nervous as I am, and his palm is sweaty when he takes my hand. He holds it against his heart, staring straight ahead. Giving his hand a squeeze, he snaps out of his daydream, looking at me with a smile. I hear music as the elevator reaches our floor.

"I know that song," I say.

"You'll have it memorized by the time we leave. Paul plays it at every expo, sometimes he has it set on repeat for hours."

"It's Marky Mark and the Funky Bunch, isn't it?"

He nods as the elevator door opens. We walk down a short hallway to a set of double doors. The music is louder, putting a bit of a swing in my hips.

"I remember my dad used to play this song all the time when I was a toddler. That's how I know it."

"It's called 'Good Vibrations.' Totally old school. It annoys the hell out of me. It's about to start again, just wait."

I listen for a moment. Sure enough, the song repeats. Cove touches my back, leading me to the door.

"Doron and Dayne kind of look like Mark Wahlberg."

"Holy shit, they do!" I exclaim, as I think back to the

one time I met Doron in Vegas. He reminded me of a professional football player when I saw him, with his massive chest, arms, and legs. My dad's big, but he looked tiny next to Doron. "God, from what I recall, he was a stud."

"Thanks, Soph. Now get him out of your head. You ready for this?" he asks.

"Bring it," I say, walking with my shoulders back and my chest forward to the entrance of the XXX Expo.

He opens the door and I step inside, my eyes wide, my brain trying to process what's before me.

"Jesus." I grip Cove's arm.

He pays our entry fee and we walk into an enormous heavily ornate room. The gold chandeliers are the largest I've ever seen. The lights sparkle and reflect off the gold walls, and the ceiling's painted with cupids and plump nudes. I feel as though I've entered the St. Nicholas cathedral in Prague.

"Jesus."

"You just said that."

"Look at this place," I say, taking in the room, gawking at the *real* decorations roaming around us—the ones with their shirts off, sporting nipple pasties as a top and thongs for pants. The women. Big-breasted women. Giant. Humongous. Tits.

"Whoa. We're surrounded by an army of triple E's."

"I'd say some of those are much bigger than that."

"Holy shit, Cove." I tug on his arm like a child. He sees the woman I'm gaping at and nods.

"Yep," he says. "She's a big one."

"She has to rest them on a counter. Look at how big

those things are. How does she stand?"

"I've seen her before and she always has someone with her to help carry them around."

"No way. Is this for real?"

He laughs, rubbing the back of my neck. "No. It's not. Consider it a freak show, that's how I've always been able to get through it in the past. It's a circus. And if you're not drop dead gorgeous, you have to be an oddity to survive and make money."

"So you were one of the gorgeous ones?"

"I was one of the lucky ones. I never had to do drastic things to my body. But I also worked for your father; his employees had a list of do's and don'ts. No implants over a certain size." He looks around the room. "A lot of the people in here are randoms from the industry. He'll bring in extras to fill the space. You'll be able to tell who's who after a while. It's just like any other trade fair, except the product is a body, not a boat. They're high-end products and products for mass consumption."

"And the bizarre."

"Yes, and the bizarre. Think of it in terms of cheese. You've got a small basket of Caciocavallo Podolico, a table of Brie, and the rest of the room is full of cheddar."

"Okay," I reply, giving him a crazy look. "Whatever you say."

"Um." He pauses, and tries to come up with a better example.

"No, it's okay, I get it," I say, still staring at the massive titty woman. "Cove, seriously, how can she even breathe?"

"It's just for money, Soph. She'll probably have the implants removed once the thrill is gone and her followers have moved on. Then she'll have to find something else to enlarge."

"Oh, maybe it will be her ass."

He laughs and pulls me forward, away from the spectacle and on to the next.

"Are those what I think they are?"

He shakes his head in disgust. "Unfortunately, yes."

I release his arm and walk over to the display, a desire to touch and play with each one. He follows close behind, not letting me out of his sight.

"My God, it's a wall of fake vaginas."

"You can try em' out if you'd like." He smirks.

I place my finger inside one and Cove quickly grabs my hand. "Soph, that was a joke. You don't know where those things have been."

"What? They're up too high for a guy to stick his dick inside."

"That's what you think, just don't touch them. I've seen people test these things out. Make sure you wash your finger the first chance you get, and don't touch your mouth anytime soon."

"Oh, yuck. Are you serious?"

His face is grave and I look down at my finger, checking to see if anything's on it. He cracks a small smile then begins to laugh. I slap his chest, smiling at the absurdity that for a brief moment I thought my finger was about to fall off.

"You fucker."

"Hey, Paul probably has eyes on us right now. I'm sure he's not happy his little girl poked her finger inside one of these things."

"Well good thing no one else here knows who I am, I wouldn't want to embarrass him," I say, prodding my index finger back inside.

"So what does it feel like?"

"Lubricated latex."

"And cold, right?"

"Yeah, but look, they have different ones." There's a name above each vagina for who it's modeled after, and a drawing beside them that shows the inner space. Some are ribbed and others are smooth. And there're wide, deep interiors, and short, tight models.

"You can buy some that are heated, or you can get warming lube," he says.

"Yeah, kind of like my dildo," I say, removing my finger from the display.

"Oh, really?"

"Hey, doesn't everyone have a rubber rod?"

"Well, no. I don't."

"Women, Cove. Women have dildos."

"News to me."

"Oh, come on. I bet your mom has one."

"Sophia. Not cool. I don't want my mother to have one, so don't place that picture in my head." He shakes his head.

"Okay, well women have them."

"What do you do with it?"

"Excuse me?" I say in a long drawn out voice. "What do you think I do with it?"

"Well, you probably won't need it anymore, right?"

"Feeling insecure?"

"Yeah." He grins. "How big is it?"

I turn away and continue down the aisle, leaving him to wonder.

I can't believe the number of women who sign autographs and allow close-up photos of their breasts. One woman has her legs spread open on a table, and a group of men are photographing her crotch. She wears a thong, but still, it's rather small and doesn't leave much to the imagination.

"Holy fuck."

Cove covers my eyes and pulls me past a woman going down on a guy. His dick is massive, the woman looking like a tiny mouse next to him, able to be squashed at any moment.

"Let's get to Paul. I think you've seen enough."

"Is that even legal? Can they do that in public?"

"I'm not sure if you would consider this to be public, and I also don't think anyone in here really gives a shit."

If I didn't already look like a tourist in the Bellagio with my mouth hanging open, I sure do now. I scan all the posters that hang above the booths, flip though the magazines, touch the life-size cutouts, and photograph the silicone dildos. Then, a hand grabs mine. I turn to see a large man standing next to me. I recognize him immediately as one of the Rosens. He has pearly white teeth and a formal hair cut that's trimmed short around the back and sides. The dark hair is slightly longer on top and swept back. He's dressed in a dark grey pinstripe suit, with a black dress shirt open at the neck. Cove takes his hand and pries it off mine, then pushes him away.

"Well, well. Little Sophia Jameson."

"Don't call her by that name in here, Doron."

"Well then, don't call me by mine either, you prick. Does Paul know you're here?"

"That's none of your business."

"Oh, Star," he says, shaking his head. "You know it is. Why don't the two of you walk with me? I'll take you to him."

"Thanks, but we don't need an escort. We can get there on our own," Cove says.

"I'm not giving you a choice. Start walking."

Cove whispers in my ear, "Stay close to me. Don't talk to anyone. Let me speak to Paul then we'll get the hell out of this place."

I nod, not sure if I can be silent around my dad, but decide to follow along with Cove. It does seem as if he knows him better than I do. Plus, I just want to see Mera. The two of them can say whatever they need to say to one another, and I'll keep my eye out for her.

We follow Doron down two more aisles of merchandise and nudes, then stop at a booth where Doron whispers in a woman's ear. She looks at Cove and smiles. I tighten my grip around his hand and he squeezes me back, not fazed by the naked woman who stands before us.

"Hi Star, long time no cum."

Cove nods, placing his arm over my shoulder.

"Is this one of Paul's newbies?" she asks.

"No, Aundrea, she's a friend of mine. Her name's Sara."

I place my hand out, trying my best not to reach out toward her giant boobs. I don't want to seem like I'm about to feel her up. "Andrea, it's nice to meet you," I say.

"Aundrea," she replies. She takes my hand and places it

against one of her breasts. "I know you want to touch them schoolgirl, go ahead, they're real."

I pull my hand away and step back, slightly humiliated. I've only felt Mera's chest in the past. She's been the only woman I've been comfortable with, and she doesn't have massive behemoth tits like this woman.

"This your first time, Miss Sara?"

"No. I've been with a woman before."

"No, girlie." She laughs. "I meant your first time to one of Paul Jameson's expos?"

"Yes, it is." Cove steps in, as I feel more and more uncomfortable. "Now, if you'd excuse us, we have—"

"Oh, Star. You're always in a rush. When you gonna slow down and really enjoy some of us hotties?"

"I have an appointment."

"No you don't, you shit. Show some respect to her," Doron says. "If I remember correctly, she's been more than kind to you in the past." Cove's trying not to look at either one of them. Instead, he scans the room, in search of our goal for the night. Doron fidgets, pulling on the cuffs of his suit coat, just like Cove had mentioned. He moves constantly, unable to relax. I can tell that neither one of them wants to be here, but Aundrea, she's a whole other story.

She waddles over to Cove, sliding her finger across his chest and around to his back. At about five feet tall and plump, she reminds me of a Heirloom tomato. Her hair is bright red, with braids of silver streamers flickering like fireworks when she moves.

Doron made it sound like Cove's been with her, and I can't imagine she's from my dad's company. She's not the

Caciocavallo Podolico type, more like cheddar, as Cove would say.

Cove completely ignores her, his eyes cold as he stares straight ahead. I look up and see my dad in the distance, seated on a stage in the corner of the room. He's at a round table with a man next to him and two other people across. No question it's Dayne by his side, both he and my dad staring directly at Cove. He takes my hand and steps hurriedly past Aundrea, pushes Doron to the side, and heads toward my dad.

"Let me know when you're ready to party again, Star," Aundrea yells. I look back and she blows me a kiss.

"Don't look at her," he says. "Try to forget that just happened."

"I thought my dad had high-end products?"

"She was high-end six years ago. Paul dropped her after she gained a lot of weight. I don't know who she works for now."

"What the fuck?" Doron says, catching up to us. "Paul's in the middle of dinner with clients, you can't just walk up there."

There're other people seated at tables around my dad, and the area is roped off to the public.

"He can leave his private dinner party to talk to me," Cove says.

"Do you want your face bashed in again?" Doron pants, barely keeping up with us. "I'll give him a message, but you can't go up there."

Cove stops, looking Doron in the eye. "You need to stop smoking. Listen to you wheeze and pant. You know I could run to that table and sit down next to Paul before you even moved two feet. You're not a good watchman, Doron."

"Bodyguard, and I may not be able to outrun you, but I can still beat the shit out of you, so you won't... you won't run."

Cove turns to me. "I have precious cargo with me, so no, I won't run."

The three of us look at the table. My dad leans back, smacks Dayne's shoulder, and whispers in his ear. He never takes his eyes off us. Dayne stands, buttons his dark pinstripe sport jacket, adjusts his tie, and excuses himself from the table. I immediately see and feel the difference in the two Rosen brothers. Doron shuffles his feet, looks at the floor and back up at my dad. He's insecure, where the man walking toward us has his eyes on Cove's face, and only his face. He walks with a purpose, shoulders back, fists clenched. His hair is slightly shorter than his brother's, but they both have the same perfect teeth and the dark beady eyes of a rodent. He's threatening, and not someone I'd ever want to cross.

Doron walks toward him, and when they pass, Dayne slaps his brother on the shoulder. Doron nearly trips, but catches himself and takes Dayne's place on the stage next to Paul. They're like a comedy team, but only one of them is remotely amusing.

"What do you want?" Dayne asks harshly.

"You know why I'm here," Cove responds.

Dayne's cell beeps and he looks at the screen down at our hands.

Cove gets the drift and releases my hand. "Please forgive me," he whispers.

"You're not welcome here, I don't know what you

think—"

"Dayne."

"You douchebag." He grabs Cove by his collar. "Don't fucking interrupt me."

Cove relaxes and surrenders himself to him.

"That's better. Now I don't know why you're here, fuckwad, but we have a dinner party that you've interrupted." He releases Cove's shirt and straightens his tie. Cove doesn't move, allowing Dayne to fix his clothing.

"I want to talk to Mera," I say, unable to keep quiet like Cove had requested. "Where is she?"

Dayne shakes his head, aggravated by my outburst. "You haven't trained her, have you?" he asks, placing two fingers under my chin and lifting my head. His cell beeps again. He looks down and quickly removes his hand from my body.

"Tell me what you want. Paul wants to know, then he wants you the fuck out of here."

"Tell him I'm here to please him," Cove responds, standing straight, his hands clasped behind his back.

"One last time. I won't do this back and forth shit. Exact words, what do you want? Say it now or I'll take you to that back corridor and bash your head into the wall."

"Tell him I came for an exchange. I'll give him Blackjack for Mera."

"Who the hell is Blackjack?" I ask, completely confused.

Dayne laughs and cracks his knuckles. "If you think I'll let that new house whore go that easily—"

"Tell him," Cove says.

Dayne looks back at my dad who still has his eyes on

Cove. He hasn't looked at me, and if Dayne wasn't next to us, I'd walk right onto that stage and give him a piece of my mind.

Dayne sends a text. My dad finally turns away to look at his phone. He leans back in his chair and looks at Cove, his eyes narrowing, his fingers tapping the table. He whispers to Doron who takes my dad's cell and sends a text back.

Dayne frowns at his cell. "Tomorrow. Be at the office. Nine in the morning." He places his cell in his pocket and starts to turn and walk away, then hesitates and places a hand on Cove's shoulder.

"This isn't just up to Paul. Not this time."

"I can get you another whore."

"No. There's more to it than that. You're in my game now," he replies, standing with his feet apart and his hands clasped in front of his groin.

Cove nods toward my dad and places his hand on my back, leading me away. I turn around, but my dad's already in a conversation with the men at his table. He glances my way for only a split second, then back to his clients.

"We didn't even get to talk to him," I say.

"Yes, we did. It was a good meeting. We'll be able to speak to him in person in the morning."

"Well, I don't think it went well at all. Where's Mera? When do I get to see her? And who the fuck is Blackjack? You've kept secrets from me again."

"Soph." He stops, taking both my hands and pulling me close to him. "Look at me. I want you to chill out for a sec. Mera's safe. She's at the house."

"How do you know that? And who's there with her?"

"They'd never bring their house... they wouldn't bring her here. She's home, I guarantee you she's probably watching a movie or reading in her room."

"Mera doesn't read. And that's *not* her home. Don't say she's home," I say heatedly. "I thought we were coming here to get her back. Something's wrong. Where is she?"

Cove exhales, speaking softly to calm me down. "Maybe she's in the pool having a late night swim. She's okay. You'll see her tomorrow."

"Don't make shit up. I don't appreciate that you've lied to me," I say, in spite of his kind words. "Who's Blackjack, Cove? You said you didn't really have a plan, but who's Blackjack? Is that another woman?"

He ignores me and searches for the exit. "This way," he says, pulling my hand to follow. I escape his grasp, pissed that he won't answer my question.

"Screw this!" I shout, walking away. "I'll find Mera myself."

"Wait," he demands. "Hold on a second." He grabs my arm and spins me around, an apology flashed across his face. "Blackjack is off limits."

"Then so am I," I say, trying to escape. His hand is tight and I'm not allowed my freedom.

"Trouble in paradise?" A familiar voice cuts in.

"Dad," I whisper.

"Hey, Kiddo. Come here. Star, take your fucking hands off this young woman, do it quickly."

A crowd starts to form and the Expo Hall is suddenly quiet. All the flashes of cameras, the autographs, and the excitement have come to a sudden stop. Dayne appears next to Cove, ready to attack at my dad's request.

"Give Star a moment to make his decision, Dayne, I think it will be the right one if he considers all the fans we have here this evening."

Cove releases me and kneels in front of my dad, his head down, eyes closed. I'm disturbed at the sight, feeling nauseous and empty. Cove surrendering, being submissive to my dad in front of all these people cuts deep into my heart. I can't watch this.

"Miss?" my dad calls out, keeping my identity a secret. "Do you see how powerless he is? Do you see him here on his knees, surrendering himself to me?"

Cove's motionless. A grown man conditioned to bow to my dad at a moment's notice. I want to drag him out of here, but deep down I know he needs to do it on his own. He needs to tell my dad to fuck off. Then he needs to stand and get on with his life. *Stand up, Cove. Stand up.* I want to say it, but then I'll become my dad. I don't want to control him. I want him to be his own person, separate from Jameson Industries, and apart from NOVA... *Stand up.*

My dad wears an evil grin. My body is tense as I look into his eyes, those reddish brown eyes that the two of us share. That's the only thing we have in common.

I can sense that he's angry that we're here... that *I'm* here. I decide to turn and leave. I don't need to be a part of this. I know where he lives. I can go and get Mera right now, on my own.

"The house is locked and she's in safe hands for the night. Don't even think about going there," my dad says.

I stop, my back still turned to them. How the fuck does he know what I'm thinking?

"Besides, Kiddo. She's happy."

I clench my fists, wanting to turn around and lunge at

him, screaming, arms swinging, knocking him to the ground. Instead, I continue to leave, whispering my hatred for him. "Fuck you, Dad."

"Did you hear that?" someone in the crowd says.

"Is that his daughter? Is she a Jameson? I didn't know Paul had a daughter," people whisper, as cameras flash around me. "She came in with Star. Is she in the business?"

I disappear around a corner and squeeze my way through skin and breasts, walking quickly by Aundrea, past the blowjob still in progress, past the display of vaginas, past big titty woman, and out the door. I race to the elevator. The door begins to close, but I reach it just in time, pushing the first floor button repeatedly until I'm out of the underground level.

I shouldn't be so hard on Cove. I understand that he's stuck in the middle of trying to keep our relationship intact, helping me with Mera, dealing with my dad, and trying to shield his family from further harm. I just wish he wasn't so secretive about what his plans are. Who is Blackjack? And how will that exchange get Mera back? I should turn around and demand answers, but I shouldn't *have* to ask. Goddammit! My mind races a mile a minute. I need to go for a walk and clear my head. Then I'll go back and discuss this with him.

The elevator dings and the door opens. I eagerly leave my dad's casino, stepping onto the strip. I head south, not sure of my final destination. I have no desire to go back to our room, and I know I can't get to Mera. If I had the keys to our rental, I'd probably head back to Wayne and Lydia's. I need someone to talk to and I know they'd comfort me. But that's a fantasy world. Fuck, I should just call Mera.

I take out my cell and touch her smiling face, placing

the call as I walk. It goes to her voicemail.

"Mera, I miss you. I hope you're okay. I'm worried about you. Call me. I *need* to talk to you."

I hang up, not feeling any better. Without Mera in my life, I'm limited to whom I can call for support. I flip through my contacts: Mom, my brother Mark, Cove, Dad, Leondra. *Leondra?* I didn't put her number in my phone. I wonder if Cove did, or if she did it on her own.

Frustrated, I put my cell away and decide to stick with my original thought of being alone. Cove and I have spent the entire day chatting back and forth, leaving little time for me to reflect.

I walk across an overpass of Las Vegas Boulevard, ending up in front of Caesars Palace. The streets are busy this time of the night, and the strip is alive with drunken fools. People on their way to get married, people in newly wedded bliss, groups of friends out for a good time, and a few loners, likely out gambling.

I see the water of the Bellagio fountain straight ahead. My feet can't move fast enough to get back to that beautiful spot that took my breath away earlier. Cove's right, even from this distance I can see how extraordinary it is at night compared to the day. The lights of the city and the lights in the fountain are radiant, glowing, moving, and changing colors. I find a bench to sit on, tilting my head back to see the water stretch high into the dark sky.

Wow. Pretty.

The water glows gold as Christmas music plays. Holiday music always radiates a warm feeling deep inside my heart, and although it isn't even Thanksgiving, I'm still immediately consumed by the thought of spending that time with the people that I love, spending more time with

Cove.

My phone rings and displays an unknown number. I wonder if that's Mera?

"Hello?"

"Sophia," Devery says. "Where are you?"

"Devery... why are you calling me?"

"I'm worried about you. I'm sorry that I hung up yesterday. Something came up. Are you okay?"

"Yes."

"Yes?"

"I'm fine. But confused as to why you keep calling me."

"Where are you?"

"None of your business," I grumble.

There's a pause and I hear papers rustling in the background. "I'd like to help you, Sophia. Please tell me where you are."

"What makes you think I'm out somewhere?" I say, pissed off that she knows something that she isn't telling me. Just like the rest of them. She asked me that same question when I spoke to her yesterday in the hotel room.

"I received a text from someone who's worried about you. He said you left your father's casino... alone. Vegas isn't the place for a twenty-three-year-old woman to walk around by herself at night." She sighs and more papers move around. "Wait. Cove is twenty-four, right? And you're twenty-three?"

"What does it matter?"

"Is he there with you?"

"God, Devery. What gives," I say, frustrated by her lack of direction. "What do you want? And who sent you a text? I'm so tired of everyone's shit. Tell me what you want and why you called."

"My brother Doron called me. He saw you leave without Cove and he said you looked upset."

"Well duh, my dad had Cove submit to him on his knees, and like I already told you, he has Mera. So if you want to help me, wise-up. The Evertons aren't the *bad guys*. My dad's not a Saint."

She's quiet. I watch the fountain, but no longer hear any music, tourists, or sounds from the busy street. My ears only hone in on the call, waiting for Devery's voice to return. The water ballet falls and disappears. Couples who were captivated with the sight return to their business, leaving me alone with my shrink.

"I'm torn, Sophia. I hear different things from different people and I don't know whom to believe. My family has a long history with your father. My parents love him, and treat him like a son, but I sense that something's not quite right with the current situation."

"*Now* you sense something's wrong? Just the current situation? Geez you're slow. Past situation. You know about Cove's father."

"No, I don't know much about that."

"Then why won't you speak to Leondra?"

"We've had our differences."

"Devery, I don't trust you."

"It seems to me that you don't trust anyone."

"Fuck you," I say, wanting to scream into my phone. "You know, for a therapist, you sure do have a knack for making one of your patients feel like shit about herself all the time. What do you know anyway?"

"Sophia."

"Tell me what you want."

"Are you okay?"

"Yes, right now, I'm fine. I left the casino to clear my head. The sights at my dad's expo were too much, and the control he has over Cove ripped my heart out. It was awful, and there's so much going on behind the scenes that I'm confused. All I want is to go to my dad's house, grab Mera, find Cove, and have the three of us head back to St. Louis."

"So you and Cove didn't go to Vegas for the expo? You went for Mera?"

"What? Are you serious? No, we're not here for a fucking porn expo," I say as my nostrils flare in anger. "Who told you that?"

"I just... I knew you were going there, to Vegas. Your father told me after Cove purchased two tickets. He said you might need extra therapy after you attended the event with him. He made it sound like Cove brought you into a dark world, against your will."

"My *dad* needs to stop tracking people. How does he know what Cove spends his money on? Never mind, don't answer that. I'm not surprised to hear that he knew about the flight as soon as Cove bought the tickets. My dad isn't honest with you, Devery. I didn't come here against my will, and Cove didn't bring me into a dark world. It's just the opposite. He wants to protect me from my dad's way of life."

"So you weren't forced on a plane?"

"Of course not. I think you're just as brainwashed by my dad as everyone else. I'm not going to do anything I don't want to do." I sigh, wanting to hang up. This conversation isn't going anywhere.

"Sophia... I need to know if you truly believe everything that Cove Everton has told you. Deep down in your heart, what do you believe to be true?"

"I've never doubted him, Devery. I don't know what you know, and I can only imagine you've heard horrible things from both my dad and your brothers. But I feel that I've made the right choice and I believe what he tells me."

"So let me ask you again. Where are you?"

"I'm outside the Bellagio, watching the fountain water soar."

"By yourself?"

"Yes."

"So you're on the right path and you truly believe the words of Cove Everton, but you're outside on the Vegas strip... alone? Without him?"

Devery Rosen wins again.

Ten

"I TOLD YOU I need some time to clear my head." I groan to Devery, trying to explain why I'm not with Cove right now.

"I understand, but my brother knows Vegas well and he wouldn't have texted me that he's worried unless you were in danger."

"Why would he care about me? Besides, he's part of the problem. Both of them are."

She sighs. "Sophia, head back to the casino so you're not out in that strange city all alone."

"Tell you what. Even though I'm confused and upset, I'll head back, but only if you do something for me."

"What is it?"

"Call Leondra."

"I'm not sure you understand... I can't... my family wouldn't..." She pauses, shuffling papers around. "...I'll try."

"It would mean a lot to her. She's lonely. And with Cove gone and her husband's recent beating, I can only imagine she has nothing to do but worry about the two of them."

"What happened to her husband?"

"Ask her. Call her up and ask."

"Sophia, go back to the casino."

"Bye, Devery." I end the call. God, I need a drink. I always need a drink after I talk to her. But she's right, again. I shouldn't be out here. Not because I'm in danger, but because I shouldn't have overreacted back at the expo. I wonder if Cove will even speak to me if I go back, taking off the way that I did, leaving him with my dad.

"Cove," I whisper.

His head hanging low, shoulders slumped, he sits next to me. Sadness radiates off his body. I place my hand on his thigh and he winces.

"Cove, I'm sorry. I didn't mean to walk away from you."

He rubs his eyes. "I should've gone by myself."

"No."

"I didn't want you to see me like that, down on my knees, your father in complete control. I made a mistake."

"No," I say softly. "No, you didn't. You asked me to trust you no matter what was said, no matter what happened between you and my dad, and I didn't. I left. I made the mistake." He leans back, takes my hand in his. "How did you know where to find me?" I ask.

"Gut feeling. I knew you wouldn't go back to the room alone, and you loved the beauty of this fountain earlier. I couldn't picture you anywhere else. By the way... that was nice... what you said to Devery was great."

"What?"

"About my mother. I heard the last part of your

conversation. You're a good person. I only wish I didn't have to put you through all this."

He finally looks at me, all the joy in his face from earlier is gone, replaced with regret. "He's upset that you called him *Dad* in front of all those people."

"Good for him. I don't care."

"And he said you can speak to Mera tomorrow, but only after you come with me to his office for a meeting." My eyes light up. "I didn't want to take you there. I knew you wouldn't like what you saw at the expo, and it will only be worse tomorrow, but he insists you come along. And I know why." He sighs. "Let's go back to the room, Sophia. I want to spend the rest of the night with you, just us, without any interruptions or arguments."

"Why does he want me at his office?"

He leans in and kisses my earlobe, gently tugging and nibbling, his fingers raking through my hair. "I'm tired of sharing you with this city. The past two hours really sucked, and I want to make it up to you. Let's head back."

"Cove," I say firmly, in need of answers. "Why does he want me there?"

He stands and pulls me up with him. "Because he likes to see me suffer, because he wants you to watch me submit to him, and because he's an ass."

"I get it. Okay, but I'm still not happy that you have a secret called Blackjack."

"I'm not either."

"Huh?"

"I'm not." He looks at me, his face serious and sincere. "Don't you think I would tell you if I could? I've kept it to myself because I need to figure out how to separate you and me from Paul's business, even though that seems impossible. I'll give him a choice tomorrow. Something's that very personal to me, but to him it will be all about the money. It just needs to be enough."

"What are you going to do, offer to buy me from him or something?"

He laughs. "I wish it were that easy."

"Hmm. But it's nothing involving underage porn or anything illegal?" I ask. He pauses and I immediately worry. "Cove?"

"I don't think it's illegal, no."

"Well, that doesn't sound promising. You don't think?"

"Tomorrow, Soph," he says, squeezing my hand. "Nine in the morning. You'll be there too."

"And Blackjack will be there?"

"Yes."

"Okay, then I'll let it go for tonight," I say, beginning to feel a need to have his lips on my ear again.

"Yeah?" he questions.

"Yes, I'm tired of sharing you with this city too. I just want the two of us to be alone."

He smiles. Our steps are hurried as we work through the crowds and traffic back to the hotel. I'm anxious, my stomach full of butterflies, a feeling that I heard happens with puppy love.

He takes out his cell and orders a bottle of wine and the Romance Special for our room. I laugh, not knowing what that special is, but take off my heels and start running in order to find out.

We make it to our modest, yet romantic off-the-strip

hotel, out of breath, taking the stairs fervently up a few floors to our suite.

"Where's the card?" I ask.

Cove frantically pulls out his wallet, finds the card and slips it into the reader. He turns the handle without waiting for the green light. We're still locked out.

"Do it again. Hurry!" I demand, laughing.

The elevator dings and we see room service with our cart. Cove places the card on the reader, slowly swiping it through the device. He waits for the green light, opens the door, and I rush in under his arm.

"No wine, sex," I say. "Now."

He wheels the cart through the doorway and locks us inside. "Now?" He eyes me from head to toe when I slide out of my dress.

"Yes, now."

"You wanna see the Romance Special first?"

"Actually yeah," I say, walking over in only my black lace lingerie. I place my hand on his back and rest my head on his chest, looking into the basket. "Oh good, condoms."

"I expected three and not an entire box. That's a bit intimidating."

"Don't worry, Babe. We can save some for a rainy day."

He laughs and pulls out a bottle of oil, peeling the plastic off the cap to sniff the contents. "Hmm, perfect, it's vanilla."

"Yeah that *is* perfect. What else do we have?"

"Chocolate truffles, a rose... yikes."

"What?"

Cove takes out a wooden spoon. "Wow, that's not one

bit romantic. I wonder if the kitchen staff threw it in as a joke?"

"I think it's intentional, look, there's a box of Firecracker candies as well. Oh yay! And two candles with matches." I beam, lighting them as Cove dims the lights in the room. "Now that's sexy."

"No, you're sexy. Look at you, standing there practically naked in the soft candlelight, arousing me with your gorgeous body. I feel like I've won the lottery."

"Yeah?" I reply in my sexiest voice, hot and in need of his cock. I tilt my hip and run my finger down the front of my chest, licking my lips. I leisurely slide my lace underwear down my legs, stepping out when it drops to the floor. "You know, it's been an entire day since you fucked me," I tease.

"That was your choice." He grins, taking off his sport coat and tossing it over the chair next to the desk. "But I promise you, it will be worth the wait. Lie across the bed for me and spread your legs. I want to stick my tongue in that wet pussy of yours before my dick takes over."

I rush to the bed and throw myself onto the mattress, smiling in anticipation. He unbuttons his shirt and slides out of his black oxfords. His movements have deliberately slowed since our sprint to the hotel. He swaggers to the edge of the bed, takes my legs in his hands and slowly raises them toward my body until my knees are bent. His hands glide over my skin, down my thighs, to my knees. He spreads them apart and explores my wet lower lips with his eyes.

"Beautiful," he remarks. "You wet for me, Baby? You want me?"

I nod, biting my lower lip. He kneels and places soft kisses across my belly. His tongue's warm, traveling down to my clit.

"Cove," I whisper, needing him more than ever. "I love you."

"I love you too," he says in his softest voice, his body descending off the bed, leaving just his head between my legs. I tilt my head back, my chest high, eager for him to pleasure me. Shadows from the candles flicker on the ceiling, reminding me of the glowing desert stars from last night. His tongue slides between my inner lips, freeing a longing moan from deep within me.

"You're so beautiful," he says, circling my clit, his hands caressing my legs. He grips my hips so there's no escape from his tongue lunging deep inside my pussy.

"Cove."

I feel him smile.

He tightens his hands as I try to close my legs, his lips surrounding my clit. Warm air rushes out of his nose and swarms into my most sensitive areas. Goose bumps rise over my skin. I can feel my release building quickly. It's impossible to last more than a few minutes when he's down on me. He knows exactly what to do, producing a fast explosion without any direction. My legs tense as his tongue massages my clit. But he stops before I cum, standing over me.

"Take off my pants," he orders.

I rock my hips, in need of his mouth to return, but comply with his demands. I unbutton and unzip, yanking his pants and boxers down to the floor. He waits with his hands on his hips, hair mussed, eyes full of passion and want. His cock fully erect with pre-cum on the tip.

Grabbing hold of him, I lick the stickiness off. He exhales and grips the back of my head when I fill my mouth with his entire length, deep to the back of my throat.

"Hold it there, Baby. Just for a second, then I'm going to fuck you."

I look up, his mouth open in ecstasy. He holds my hair behind my head, slowly gliding his cock out, then walks over to the romance basket to get a condom.

"Put it on me," he says.

I take it and grin. Tearing the wrapper, I immediately smell cherries, something we both find funny. I place it on his tip, leaving a small amount of room at the top for his release, rolling the rest down his length.

He nods in approval. Then in one quick swoop, I'm off the bed and on the desk. I run my hand over his chest, take a heavy breath, and wait to feel him inside me.

"Now, Cove. Fuck me, now," I say.

"Demanding this evening, aren't we?" He places my legs around his waist, his tip touching my outer lips. He moves slowly in, parting my wet flesh.

"Fuck," he whispers.

"Babe, I want you to lose control tonight. Don't just make love to me, fuck me."

His cock twitches. His mouth races to mine. He moans, shoving deeper and harder inside. The furniture rocks and the lamp next to us rattles against the wall. He pushes it off the desk and it crashes to the floor. He lays me down, placing one leg to my side and keeping his other planted on the ground. He drives his entire body over mine, looking down with narrow eyes, his hips rocking steadily, his muscles tight.

"Jesus, I can't believe how wet you are, even with the condom between us I can tell. Cum for me. I won't last much longer. Cum."

He pounds faster. Sweat forms on his chest. He leans forward, putting more pressure on my clit, only wanting to please me, not asking for anything else but my release. I close my eyes and lift my hips, sliding along with his cock.

"That's it. Cum for me."

He changes his movements to slow and steady thrusts.

My body trembles as my pussy explodes around his shaft.

"Yes."

"Cove!" I scream, unable to take his slow pace. He laughs and powers faster inside, just as I requested: a firm, strong, hard fuck. My head hits the table and a notepad digs into my back. We breathe like beasts, our bodies dripping with sweat, his rigid mass widening, stretching my insides. My orgasm lasts forever, waiting for his to begin. Muscle spasms flutter throughout my body, and every thrust causes a rush of warm waves to encase his cock.

"Oh fuck, Sophia. I wanna cum all over you." He pulls out and I grab his cock, quickly tugging the condom off. "I'm cumming, Baby."

His stomach tenses. He grabs hold of his dick, his mouth slightly parted as he shoots onto my stomach and chest.

"Oh fuck!" he yells, placing his hand against the wall for stability. His release makes it all the way up to my face. He collapses over my body, spreading his semen between us.

He pants. I shake.

He sighs. I exhale.

We lie on the desk for a good five minutes, smiling, kissing, until I can't handle the hard wood and office supplies poking into my body any longer.

"Cove, Babe. I need to get up. I love you to death but this is really uncomfortable."

He helps me off the desk. A pen that was stuck to my back falls to the floor, along with the notepad. Cove spins me around and rubs my body to ease the pain.

"Sorry. I didn't realize all that shit was under you."

"No worries. I didn't either until it was too late."

"Did I hurt you?" he asks.

"Nope, that was amazing."

He wraps his arms around me, lifting me off the ground into a big hug. "Wine?"

"Yeah, definitely. And one of those chocolates too."

"You got it."

He hands me a glass and fills one for himself. "To us," he says, clinking my glass. We both take a small sip then in unison, gulp it down.

"Great minds think alike," I say.

He tosses me a chocolate truffle and pours two more glasses of wine, handing me one and placing the other on the table next to the bed. He turns down the comforter and sheets, props the pillows, and leaves a cozy spot for us to snuggle. I place my wine on the other table, my mouth full of chocolate, resting my back against the headboard.

"This is great," I say, loving the fact that we're alone.

"Yeah, I wanted to have a relaxing night after that busy day," he says, as a text comes through his cell. He looks at me and I roll my eyes, knowing that we spoke too soon. "Well, fuck-a-duck," he says, taking his cell out of his sport jacket.

"Who is it?" I ask.

"My mother. She wants to know if we're okay. I forgot to call her after the expo like I told her I would. Do you mind if I make a call?"

"Of course not, tell her I said hello and that she should give Lewis a hug from me."

Leaning over the bed, he places a kiss on my forehead. "You're the best."

"I know." I smirk, taking a sip of wine. "Throw me that other chocolate."

"Yes, dear." He laughs, tossing the chocolate on the bed. I must look like a spoiled brat, sprawled out naked in bed, sipping wine, eating chocolate truffles... and I love every minute of it.

He pulls on his boxers and shirt before sitting in the recliner to place the call.

"You don't have to get dressed."

"Yes. I do. I can't talk to her when I'm naked."

"She can't see you, Cove."

"It's just weird... hello, Mother? Yeah, something came up." He listens and starts to pick at the leather armrest, just like he did earlier to the steering wheel in the car. It must be a nervous habit. "No, everything's fine. We went to the Bellagio fountain after the expo and lost track of time. Sorry."

There's silence and I start to sense tension in the room.

"I know," he says. "I didn't mean for that to happen. I didn't know she was going to leave the—" It's quiet again as Leondra cuts him off. He sighs and pulls the lever on the side of the chair, releasing the footrest to tilt back. "Uh-huh, I see. So you've talked to Paul?"

I sit up, not happy to hear those words.

"No, tomorrow..." He hesitates. "About a hundred grand."

I gulp at the information. How much did he say? A hundred grand? For what?

"I said *about*, I don't know for sure. And no, she doesn't..." He sighs again, frustrated by the questions. "No, she doesn't. I couldn't. What do you want me to do?" he raises his voice, upset. "Tomorrow morning. I'll try to call you after it's over, but I can't promise anything."

"Tell her what I said."

"Sophia says hello and she wants you to give Lewis a hug from her. Okay?" He looks at me and nods. "She said she hugs him every hour."

"Ahh, that's so sweet. What a lucky cat," I say.

"I love you too. And Mother?" He pauses. "I'm sorry." He hangs up the phone and places his index finger to his mouth, sliding it over his lips. He stares off into space and I decide to give him a few minutes to think before I start asking questions. What's all that money for?

I sip my wine in silence, waiting patiently for his return. *Cove? Hello? You in there?* Finally, he uses one foot to move the chair, turning it in my direction. I look at him and flash a concerned, yet sensitive smile. He moves his finger from his mouth and smiles back, raising his arm for me to join him.

"You okay?" I ask, snuggling alongside his body with my arm across his chest. He rests a hand on my waist and kisses my head, rocking us back and forth with his free foot.

"Yeah, I'm okay. My mother's worried."

"Why did my dad call her?"

"I think he probably knew she'd call me, and that

would throw me off. He doesn't want me on top of my game tomorrow. He'll do anything to keep me on edge... at all times. That's why I think he called her. Don't worry about it too much."

"Well, you know I have to ask about—"

"Don't. I told you it's a business deal with him. That's it. Just don't. Okay?"

I rest my head against his chest and listen to his racing heart. It's obvious that the conversation upset him more than I thought. I let it go. Completely out of character for me, but something I'm finding myself doing more and more lately. I'll allow Cove to take control of the situation.

"Sorry, I'm not trying to be an ass," he says, rubbing my thigh. I place my hand on his nipple and squeeze, making him laugh and squirm. "You know, we should really wipe this sticky stuff off our bodies."

I nod and walk over to the bathroom, grabbing a towel for the two of us to use. "It's already crusty," I say, trying to clean my chest.

"Sorry."

"You can't apologize for that, Cove. It's not your fault it dries so fast. There, that's better," I say, tossing him the towel and returning to my cozy spot next to him.

"God, Sophia. I've never met anyone like you."

"And you never will again." I smirk.

"Yeah, that's what I'm afraid of." He stirs in the recliner, unable to get comfortable. "Do you mind if we go back to the bed? I thought this was a good idea, but now I realize there's barely enough room for the two of us."

"Sure thing," I say, crawling onto the mattress. "I want to get back to my wine anyway. That's more important than being close to you and touching your body."

"Oh really?" he asks, sitting next to me with his wine.

"Yeah, women can't live on cocks alone. We need wine and chocolate too." He laughs. I clink his glass, drinking to my tipsy words. "Cove?"

"Yes, Sweetness."

"That was one hell of an orgasm."

"Mine or yours?"

"Mine. And yours, too, I hope."

He gives my hand a soft kiss. "Yeah?"

"Yeah. One of the best."

"One? Not *the* best?"

"Maybe the best. I've never kept track. It could've been the best. Definitely in the top three."

"Take another drink, Soph. I love the shit that spews out of your mouth when you're drunk."

"Okay, *the* best," I say with a grin.

"No, no. That's okay. You don't have to say that just so you don't hurt my feelings," he teases. "I'll have another chance to pleasure you, and when I do, there won't be any doubt in your mind as to whether or not it's *the* best. Just wait."

He places his wine down and blows out the candles, then sets the alarm on his phone for seven. We meet under the comforter, arms wrapped tightly around one another's bodies. He makes sure my skin is covered with the sheets and gives me a soft goodnight kiss on the cheek.

"Sophia?"

"Yeah, Babe?"

"Just so you know, that *was* the best orgasm I've ever had."

Eleven

"WHY DO THEY *fight every time Paul throws a party?*" *Natalie asks.*

"*They're both alpha males and want to be head of the pack in this house. Only they're the only two in the pack. I think it's fucking ridiculous that Dayne even moved in here, but Paul doesn't trust anyone else. If he wants protection while at home, Dayne's his guy,*" *Cove says. He takes Natalie's hand and they walk into the backyard.*

"*The pool's empty tonight. I'm surprised no one's swimming. Do you want to go in?*" *she asks.*

"*I don't like to swim, Natalie. I haven't liked it in years, not since I met Paul and the Rosens.*"

"*They're inside, and it looks like Dayne's about to fuck that new blonde,*" *she says.* "*Besides, I'm already in my bikini. I should use the thing for something other than showing my body to Paul's clients.*"

She tests the water with her foot and dives in, coming up with her long, brown hair slicked back.

"*Star, come on. We never get a chance to enjoy ourselves*

when we're here. Take a break for a couple minutes and get in the water. You'll feel better."

"I fucking doubt it," he grumbles. "I really fear the water, Nat."

"Then face it for once. You're afraid of every fucking thing," she says. "Take off your shirt and pants and get in. You're not going to get over being a pussy, as Paul calls you all the time, unless you do something about it. Maybe you'll get some courage for once if you fucking get in here."

He stares her down, clenching his fists. At sixteen, he's had enough. Enough shit and name calling from everyone. He wants to dive in and drag her underwater until she's about to pass out, until she understands the terror of teetering on the edge of death. He'd like to do the same to Paul and Dayne.

"You gonna come in, you pussy?"

He looks toward the house and sees Paul with his hand on one of the NOVA brothers from LA. They just arrived and Paul's ready to sell them off for the night. The room is full of his regular employees, mostly women in skimpy bikinis, drinking, laughing, and touching the clients. He looks back at Natalie who has her bikini top in her hand, tossing it to the edge of the pool.

"Don't. I don't want to make a scene out here and have Paul drag us back in."

"Like I said, you're being a wuss. Come on, little chicken shit, get in. This is my last night of doing this crap."

Cove looks into her eyes and sees a happiness and joy that he hadn't noticed earlier. Last night? Where's she going?

"Don't look so worried, Star. I can't be in NOVA forever. I'm starting to show my age with fuller hips and a bigger ass. I don't look like a teenager anymore. Paul said it's time for me to move on."

"So that's it?"

"Yeah, for now at least."

He looks back at the sliding glass doors to see where Paul is and quickly takes off his pants and shirt, slides out of his dress shoes, and takes a seat on the edge of the pool. He places his feet and legs in the water, enjoying the warmth on his skin.

"Why does Paul make you guys dress up for these things and the rest of us are practically naked?" she asks.

"He wants us to look pure and innocent. I guess it's like a catholic school boy outfit."

"Ah, makes sense, I guess. So where'd your father take off to?"

"Doron took him to dinner. He doesn't like being at these things. He gets upset when I disappear with one of Paul's clients."

"And your mother? I've never met her."

"I've never seen your parents at anything for the company either."

She laughs and floats around the water. "No, I suppose you wouldn't. I can travel by myself without the help of mommy and daddy."

"Hey. My mother doesn't know anything and I plan to keep it that way. My father and I are on vacation right now, supposedly, and she's at a surprise dinner for her sister here in Vegas. Usually, it's just my father and I who come out. He tells her he's teaching me the business, and when he travels, he takes me along."

"What business? Porn?" She laughs.

"No, he does some kind of security for websites," Cove responds, aggravated that she thinks it's a joke.

"And you're not sure exactly what that is? I guess he's not

doing a very good job training you."

"Fuck off."

"Are you gonna sit on the edge and talk all night or are you getting in? We don't have much time before we're considered MIA."

Cove slides into the water and walks across the pool to Natalie. He takes her feet, pulling her through the water on her back. She laughs and flutters her hands to stay afloat, enjoying the ride.

"You try it, Star. Get on your back and close your eyes. Don't think about where we are or what we need to do later, just feel the water lift you to the surface. Relax and enjoy yourself."

"I don't know how to do that."

"Well, it's time you learned. Now float."

Cove lies on his back with his legs stretched. He moves his hands under his body, trying to steady himself in the water. He tilts and places his feet on the pool floor, then tries again.

"Free your mind. It's the only way to last in this world."

He lifts his legs and leans back, his hands flapping in the water like a bird learning to fly. His actions slow, and his hands gradually change to circular movements in the water. He closes his eyes and floats. She places her arm under his back and guides him through the pool. With a sigh, he relaxes, finally able to breathe.

"Nice, isn't it?"

"Yeah, Nat. I need one of these."

"A pool?"

"Yes, a pool. And a guide—someone to kick my ass sometimes so I leave my comfort zone."

"Ha. You don't have a comfort zone. That's one of your

biggest problems."

"Well, maybe I just found one. If my parents had one of these, and Paul and Dayne weren't around, I'd probably never leave it."

"God, you're so freakin' weird. It's not THAT good. I just want to teach you how to let go of your stress and all those bad thoughts racing through your head."

"No," he says, placing his feet back on the floor of the pool. "It IS that good. For a few minutes I didn't see Paul's God awful face when I closed my eyes."

"Star!" Paul's voice pierces his ears.

Paul leans alongside the sliding glass doors, hands in his pockets, looking down at the scene. "Both of you, get your asses in here, now. Star, dry off and look presentable, and make it quick. It's time." He slides the doors shut and walks away, leaving only the sounds of the cicadas singing in the trees.

Cove shakes. He feels anxious. Knots form and twist in his stomach.

"You need a drink."

"Yeah, I do. I'll get one before I head back into one of those rooms. He's probably pissed that my skin smells like chlorine."

"We both smell of chlorine," she says, walking up the ladder and out of the water with Cove.

"Why did you make me get in the pool again?" Cove teases, trying to make light of the situation.

"Pussy."

"Don't call me that, you bitch... Hey, I wonder who'll take your place."

"Don't know. Someone hot, I'm sure. Maybe it's that new blonde that Dayne's with, or maybe you'll just continue on

with those single live-cams you just started."

"*How'd you know about those things?*"

"*I've watched you.*"

"*Why? Don't you get enough of me already?*" he teases, buttoning his shirt and fixing his hair.

"*Well, actually Paul had me watch one so that I could do the same. He said you're good. I guess he wanted to show you off.*"

"*Ugh. Don't tell me anything else. He's such a pervert.*"

"*He's a pedophile, not a pervert.*"

"*He's never touched me.*"

"*But he likes to watch.*"

"*No, he's never watched me either, at least, not that I'm aware of. The only thing he watches is his bank account,*" Cove says, zipping his pants.

"*Star and Natalie, get the fuck inside. Now!*" Paul yells, standing at the door again. "*I feel like I'm fucking babysitting.*"

Cove picks up his shoes and walks quickly over to Paul. Natalie follows, still topless.

"*What the fuck. Enough of this shit. Get inside and head over to the dining room. The two of you are dessert. Put on a nice show for the clients gathered in there, and make it good.*"

"*What, like a strip tease?*" Cove asks. "*They're in Vegas, they can go to a club and watch a strip show any hour of the day. This is one of your lamest parties ever.*"

Natalie scurries inside, but Paul places a hand on Cove's chest and stops him from entering the room. "*Natalie, get started. There're two others in there already. Star will join the three of you in a sec.*"

She walks through the main room and down a hall toward the dining area. There's a loud cheer when she reaches *the room. Paul smiles, then turns back to Cove, his expression changing to anger and hatred.*

He takes Cove's arm and bends it behind his back, using his body to force him against the stone exterior wall of the house. Paul's arm is pressed across Cove's shoulders so he can't move. "God, I'd love to bash your fucking face into this stone. What's with the fucking attitude tonight? When I let go of you, you'll keep your mouth shut and walk into that dining room. Be nice to these people, you understand?"

"If you despise me so much, why don't you just let me go, like Natalie?"

"If you didn't have such a hold on my company, I would. Your face and body bring in a quarter of my yearly profits. But don't worry… you'll get your wish someday. You can't be young and full of cum forever, right?" Paul seethes.

Cove drops his shoes and tries to back away, only to have his arm pulled higher against his back. His eyes wince in pain, but he doesn't give Paul the satisfaction of hearing him cry out. Cove knows he would never leave a mark where anyone could see it, not if he wants to make money. He relaxes and places his forehead against the cool wall, surrendering to the industry.

"Good boy," Paul whispers. "We're both too old for this shit. I know you're sixteen and trying to sound like a tough guy, so I'll go a little easy on you. I remember that age. But someday you'll stop being such a dumbfuck. Right?"

"Yes sir," Cove replies in a soft voice.

"I love you like a son, Cove. And you need to respect me like a father. You know what I want to hear."

"I'm sorry, Paul," he whispers. "You own me."

He releases him and brushes off the back of his shirt, smoothing out the wrinkles. "Leave your shoes out here."

Paul steers him into the house toward the dining room. Cove can hear the laughter coming from the party. It sounds like a drunken rodeo.

Paul hesitates for a moment, then walks to a table, opening a large drawer full of sex toys, condoms, and hoods.

"I need you to put this on," he says, tossing Cove a leather wolf hood.

"Well, this is new. Since when do we dress up?"

"Star, look at me," Paul says in a serious tone. "This dinner party came in through the kitchen. They're confined to that end of the house, away from my clients upstairs and in the massage rooms. I need you to wear this, but don't take it off... don't let anyone else take it off either. Your 'prey' is already in there. Three of them. Catch them, devour and consume them, then leave. There's a large opening for your mouth, but the rest of the hood is a solid piece. It might be a little hard to see, but do your best. Stick to the task at hand. The Rosens paid a lot for this party, and Dayne and Doron both insisted you would be the best for it."

"Wait a second," Cove interrupts. "What sort of party is this?"

"Here, take a drink," Paul says, pouring him a shot of whiskey. Cove throws it back and holds the glass out, wanting a second. "Alright then, have two." Paul grins. He downs the drink and puts on the hood, buckling the two straps around the neck. "It's a bachelorette party, for Lydia Rosen."

"Fuck no, Paul," Cove whines, trying to unbuckle the hood, getting his hand gripped before he can take it off. "My mother's here?"

"She won't recognize you. The room is full of Lydia's former sorority sisters. You won't know anyone else except for your mother, Lydia, and Devery."

"Get serious. What mother wouldn't recognize her own son?"

"Shut up. They're all plastered. If I can't see your face, they can't either. Just do your thing and come back. Fifteen minutes, tops. Do what you're told, and do it now." Paul *unbuttons Cove's shirt, slides it off, and throws it over a chair in the room. "You'll only need your black pants on for this. You're the dark wolf."*

"God, and I'm supposed to be the kid, right?" he says, walking away from Paul, wishing he could flip him off without any punishment. "I guess this would be considered the opposite of dressing 'a wolf in sheep's clothing,' right?" he says under his breath.

He walks down the dimly lit hall of Paul's mansion. A mirror hangs at the end of the hall with the door to the dining room to the left. He watches his reflection in the mirror as he approaches the room, dawdling in the darkness, deliberately running his fingers over the walls as he walks. He stops just a few feet before the doorway, listening to the drunken screams of joy.

He flexes his muscles. Paul makes him lift weights; he's starting to have the body of a man. Soon, he'll be too old for NOVA, too, then what? More evenings like this one? Or nothing at all?

He grunts and growls, starting to breathe like an animal for the show. He can be a wolf. He can do this.

He unbuttons his pants to flaunt his pubic hair. He's ready. He takes a deep breath, his nostrils flaring under the hood.

Paul can hear the women scream and applaud when Cove enters the room. He steps outside, lights a cigar, and takes out his cell to call Doron.

"*Doron, about a half hour. Bring Everton in through the garage to pick up his son. His wife's still on the other end with Dev.*" *He hangs up and puffs on the cigar, rolling his dress pants above his knees to sit next to the pool. His eyes follow the smoke trails into the darkness, focusing on the stars that appear behind the dispersing swirls.*

"*Hmm. I haven't looked up in years. Not since...*" *he whispers, thinking back to nights in the backyard of the house he bought for his wife and kids. Mark and Sophia loved to gaze at the clouds during the day and watch the stars twinkle at night.*

He remembers the last time he saw the two of them. In the morning, he walked Mark to the end of the road and made sure he was safely on the school bus, then after lunch, he placed Sophia down for a nap. He left right after, never saying good bye to either one. It was easier that way.

He takes his cell out and looks for a number, pauses, then puts it back in his pocket. "*Fucking ex-wife. She ruined everything, lost the money I'd saved for years. Fucking bitch.*"

He shakes his head and places his cigar on the edge of the pool, pulling his cell hastily back out. He dials the number and waits; stretching his legs out in the water.

"*Elizabeth.*"

"*Don't freaking call this house, Paul. I've told you that time and time again.*"

"*Wait, I want to know how the kids are.*"

"*You... you want to know how MY kids are? The kids I've raised on my own? Your daughter is fifteen and has a mouth on her that will take her straight to hell, and your son...*"

Paul hears a voice in the background. It's Mark. He asks who's on the phone. Elizabeth immediately hangs up, leaving Paul to sit outdoors and admire his million-dollar house, smoke his expensive cigar, and splash in his glamorous pool. Alone.

He wonders if he even loves them. Would he give up everything around him for his kids? He's worked too hard. His money gives him freedom to do whatever the fuck he wants. He can have a woman any time of the day, eat at the finest restaurants, and take off at a moment's notice to anywhere in the world. This idea of having a family, like Doron and his wife, sometimes burdens him with a feeling of guilt, but only for a brief moment.

Why would he want to share his wealth with another person? The possibility that something could go wrong is far too great. This is his life, and he made it to this point with hard work. A fucking wife and kids, who needs them? But those brief moments of guilt...

Glass shattering in the main room knocks Paul out of his daydream. Cove is next to the open liquor cabinet, wearing the hood and his boxer briefs, pouring a shot. He shrugs at Paul, takes off the hood, then swallows the shot and slams the empty glass on the counter. Paul notices Cove's hands are shaking. He runs his hand through his hair, holding the hood in the other.

"Did you give them what they wanted?"

"Yeah," Cove mumbles. "I hope you fucking pay me a shitload for that one. It's not easy to do that crap with my mother in the room. You're lucky she's about to pass out and won't remember most of the night."

"So you want a lot of money?"

"Fuck yeah. At this point, who wouldn't? I want to buy a car as soon as I'm old enough, and now I'm thinking a house with a pool would be great at some point."

Paul takes out his wallet, putting a few five-hundred-dollar bills in Cove's briefs. "That enough?"

"What the hell is going on?" Devery says. Her mouth

hangs open, her eyes on the hood in Cove's hand. Doron and Cove's father enter from the hall to the right, having come in from the garage. Cove places the hood back in the drawer and takes his shirt from the chair. He dresses with his back to everyone. "Paul, how could you make Leondra's son do such a thing? Does she know about this? Is this a joke on Lydia and her?"

"Dev, calm down," *Doron butts in, walking over to her and Paul.* "It's not a joke, so don't even mention it to them. Cove works for Paul."

"What?" *she fumes.* "You're talking about the Cove standing next to you, Leondra's husband, right? Not their son. Not this young boy."

"Doron, shut the fuck up," *Paul snaps.* "The kid just wants a little extra money to buy a car, isn't that right, Cove?"

Cove nods. "It was just one time. Paul gave me a bunch of cash to do it."

"What you just did in there was illegal," *Devery scolds. She places a hand on her waist and points the other at Paul.* "And you know it. You could go to prison."

"No one's going to prison," *Doron says, lighting a cigarette.*

"Don't fucking smoke in my house. Head out back and take Star with you. Devery, let's go to my office and talk this out in private." *He cups her back to lead her away.* "The kid's fine and no one was hurt. You'll see there's nothing to worry about."

"This child in front of me has a tattoo, Paul. I'm not ignorant."

Doron follows Paul's orders, taking Cove out the back door. Cove looks over his shoulder, checking if his dad's following.

"Take him home." Paul nods to Cove's father. He obeys and leaves in silence. He closes the sliding glass doors, watching Paul take Devery up to his office suite.

"I wouldn't want to be Paul right now, Dev's gonna give him so much shit," Doron says, exhaling his cigarette.

"I wouldn't want to be Devery," Cove says, bending down to pick up his shoes. "Paul's gonna try to fuck her."

Doron throws a punch at Cove, only to have his fist caught mid-swing.

"Try that again and your head will be on a platter. Don't lay a hand on my son."

Doron lets out a laugh and holds his stomach as he falls forward. "Are you serious?" he says. "Ha, that son of yours has had more hands on him than all of us combined."

"Knock it off, dickhead," his father says, slamming Doron to the ground and kneeling on his back.

"Dad, stop. Paul can't see this. Get up," Cove pleads, frantic to put an end to the fight. "Let's go. Doron, I'm sorry. Let's go, please," he begs, running his hand through his hair. "Please, Dad. Please! You can't do this. Not with Paul so close. Let him go, Dad," he says, panicking. "Dad... Dad, please... Dad..."

• • •

My eyes flutter open in search of light. The blinds and curtains are closed and I'm in total darkness. I feel Cove's warm breath on my back. He's breathing fast, possibly lost in a dream. Hopefully it's a pleasant one this time.

I slide away, my bladder about to burst from too much wine. Way, way, too much wine last night. *Phew.* We had some at dinner too. Cove drinks a lot, even more than Mera and me. It's hard to keep up with him. Not that I have to, but sometimes I forget how much I've had while I'm in the moment.

I wash the smeared mascara off my face, brush my teeth and fix my hair, ready to curl up next to *my* handsome man. He always smells so wonderful, like vanilla, spice, and cedar all rolled into one. I take his Clive Christianson C off the bathroom counter, open the bottle and sniff the contents. Yep, that's it. Lovely. I close the bottle and turn off the light, then sneak back into bed.

"Hey, Baby," he mumbles, half-asleep. "Come here." He lifts his arm and I lie next to him. "Mmm, my gorgeous naked woman." He parts my mouth with his warm tongue. "I'm the luckiest bastard alive." He grabs my shoulders and rolls on top of me, his dick prodding between my legs. "I wish I could see more than just your silhouette," he says. "I love watching you when you cum." He gets up and turns on the bathroom light. "That's better. Not too bright, but enough light so that I can see your face when we fuck." He crawls back over me.

"Wait," I slither out from under him.

"Huh?"

"Get on your stomach," I say, searching through the romance basket for the massage oil.

"You're not looking for that spoon, are you? Am I getting spanked?"

"No." I laugh. "The oil."

"Yeah, but you stopped me. Did I fuck up?"

"With what?"

"I just want to make sure I'm giving you what you

need. Did you just stop me because—"

"Shh." I straddle his hips, pouring oil onto his back.

"Fuck, that's cold."

"It will warm up in a second," I say, rubbing it into his skin. I reach up to his shoulders, grab and massage his neck, then drag my hands down to his lower back. He moans, his body finally relaxing. "I enjoy being with you, no matter what we do. It's about the way you make me feel at *all* times, not just when we make love, or have a hard, fast fuck. This is nice too. You've done nothing wrong." I push my fingertips deep into his shoulder blades and press firmly along his spine. "Don't be insecure about it. Neither of us will be able to enjoy ourselves if we think we're doing something wrong in bed. I don't want that pressure when we're intimate."

"You're amazing," he says into the pillow, enjoying the massage.

"I know I am." I smirk, tossing the bottle of oil on the floor and rolling him over. "Look at me. Look at this awesome body in front of you."

"Self-centered, narcissistic, and egotistical too." He grins.

"Those words all mean the same thing."

"You would know." He laughs.

I grab his nipples and twist. His eyes clamp shut and his teeth clench, trying to hold in the pain.

"Yeaaaw, ah, Sophia! God that hurts."

"Serves you right to say I'm egotistical."

"And narcissistic and self-centered."

I twist again.

"Ouch! Okay. Enough." He gasps. "Stop." He rubs his

red nipples and frowns at my attack. I place a finger over his lips, trying to soothe his wounded expression. He bites my finger, hard, and I cry out.

"Ouch!"

"Oh, sorry, Baby." He grins.

"No you're not."

"Well, neither are you."

We laugh and I fall on the bed next to him, throwing my arm over his body. We kiss and roll, Cove ending up on top, still erect and wanting to fuck. I slide his tip between my legs, granting him permission.

"Are you ready for me?" he whispers.

I close my eyes in anticipation. He embraces the side of my head and slowly pushes inside. We lock in a warm kiss, our tongues sliding around and out, our hands traveling across one another's flesh.

He looks into my eyes, brushing my hair from my face. "Sophia, you're everything to me," he whispers.

"Cove." I press my lips to his. His cock slides out of me, and I feel empty. "No," I whisper. He stands and walks over to get a condom.

"Don't move," he commands, tearing the wrapper open with his teeth. He turns and looks at me, then down at my pussy. He holds his cock and slides the condom on, never taking his eyes off me. "I could cum right now, just from seeing that gorgeous body of yours open for me." He kneels on the bed and slinks over me. I've never seen so much passion in one person's eyes before. He truly loves me.

"I need you," I whisper.

I run my hand through his hair, then grip the back of

his neck, pulling him down for a kiss. A raspy moan comes from his throat as he reaches down and parts my lips with his cock, swiftly filling my body with his. Starting slow then gradually building speed, he's steady, calm. With each thrust, he watches my face as it warms and glows with desire. His cock begins to thrust harder as his body rubs against my swelling clit. I feel a rhythm through my inner lips as his shaft pushes along my insides.

"I'm gonna cum, Babe."

He slows. Something I'm now used to—a tease that makes for a longer, more intense orgasm. I push against him and take control of the movement. His body stops and he lifts his hips to allow me to slide at my own pace.

"God." I moan, closing my eyes and throwing my head back. I grab his hips and try to make him fuck me faster. I need him. "I'm cumming," I whisper. He stops to feel me, waiting for my tremors to end.

"You always do that to me," I say, brushing his hair off his face. "You slow down, and this time you stopped. No one's ever done that before."

"You like it?"

"Yeah. It's amazing. My orgasms last twice as long. And they're stronger. I lose control and want more when they end."

"Good." He smiles, giving me a kiss. "Then you get more."

The alarm on his phone sounds.

"Damn it." He turns it off, tossing it across the room.

"No. No... do we have to get up?" I ask.

"Unfortunately," he replies sadly.

"Will you finish first?"

He slides out, takes the condom off, and throws it in the trash. "No. We can't be late. Not for one of Paul's office appointments. He'll have a full schedule today, it's a Monday, and we should probably arrive a few minutes early." He helps me out of bed and into his arms. I'm given a hug and a kiss, his erection throbbing between us. I can't believe he's not going to finish.

"Let's shower," he says, walking to the bathroom. The water turns on and he starts to hum. Something I haven't heard him do before. "You coming?" he asks.

"On my way."

I walk into the room and lean against the counter, watching the steam rise around his body. He places his head under the water and his dark hair falls forward over his face.

"You coming in or you just gonna stare at me?"

"Stare."

He looks down at his erection.

I smile, shaking my head. "You know, you can't walk around like that today."

"It will go down."

"When?"

"Get in the shower, Sophia."

I step in and take his place under the showerhead, washing my hair. A soft washcloth sweeps across my breasts as Cove gently cleans my chest and stomach. He smiles and winks, our lips inches apart, water running between our faces.

I take the washcloth and place it over his cock, hanging it on him like it's a towel bar. He takes it off, finally showing slight embarrassment about his erection.

His hands press against the wall behind my head,

blocking me from any escape. "You've made your point," he whispers. "Don't think that because I'm going to do this fast that it's meaningless."

"Never," I respond, lowering to my knees.

"Will you lick my balls?" he asks, lathering his hand in soap. He begins to stroke and I watch for a few seconds before my tongue licks his most delicate area. I run it around his taut sacs, lick, nip, and suck while his hand races above my eyes.

"Baby, keep going."

I smile as he jerks off, his leg muscles tightening, his balls swelling. My tongue lowers to his perineum, and he moans when I flick it with my tongue.

"Fuck, what are you doing to me?"

His words send my tongue into a flutter over the area, back and forth, as I caress his balls with my hand. His legs part for steadiness, giving me better access.

"Keep going, do it faster."

He moans, jerking his cock madly. I release his balls and place my pinky finger in my mouth, lubricating it before nudging my way inside his ass. He clenches around it, not allowing it to move. I hear a wild moan and stand to kiss him as he cums. His hand slows as semen hits the wall, lands on my belly, then dribbles down his hand.

"Sophia," he whispers, his eyes glazed over in delight. "What you just did... the way you pleasure me... how you always know..." He shakes his head and places his hand under my chin. "You have me, forever."

Twelve

COVE PACES in the waiting area of my dad's office at the Fox Palace. He barely spoke on the ride over, humming from the time he got out of the shower until we walked into this room. He's nervous, and even though this place is ice cold, I notice a small amount of perspiration on his forehead. He's sweating, and I'm covered in goose bumps. I shouldn't have worn this sleeveless dress.

"Cove, sit down," I say.

"I can't."

I understand his anxiety. I feel the same, lost as to what's about to take place. I think he'll give my dad a large sum for Mera. I'm afraid to push for more details and haven't brought it up since last night. I have to trust that he knows how to handle the situation.

I look over to the administrative assistant. A pretty woman with blonde hair pulled into a bun. Her face is thin and defined, but hidden by a pair of large, red-rimmed glasses.

"He knows we're here, right?" Cove says to her

impatiently.

"Yes. He said to have a seat and he'll be with you shortly," she responds.

"Hey, Babe. Why don't you come and sit down next to me. You're making me nervous," I say.

He sighs and walks over, taking a seat on the sofa. "Something's wrong. What time do you have?"

"One minute past nine."

"Yeah, he's never late. If anything, he's always early. We've been here for ten minutes. What the fuck?"

"It's *one* minute past nine," I repeat, placing my hand on his bouncing leg. "Take a deep breath. We'll be in and out and on our way in no time."

"Sophia."

I swear he's stopped breathing.

"What?"

"I don't know if I can leave with you. I've told you that already."

"Isn't this an exchange?"

"It is. But I may be part of it, and..." He hesitates, looking around the room.

"And what?"

He holds my hand in his. "Remember what I've told you. No matter what you hear, what I say or do, it's business. Remember that I love you. I'm not trying to hurt you, Sophia, but I've kept something from you." I take my hand away. "I didn't know Paul would want both of us here today, so I didn't think you'd ever find out."

"Tell me now," I demand.

He wipes the sweat off his forehead and loosens his tie. I place my hand on his black dress pants to stop his bouncing leg. He turns away and stares at a flat screen in the corner. There's no sound, just images of the morning news.

I'm getting pissed. Besides the fact that I'm confused and scared, now the one person who's comforted me over the past two days has yet *another* secret. Something other then Blackjack?

"Hey. You gonna answer me or are you gonna prove Devery right? She said I was falling for the wrong person. What does she know that I don't?"

"This is for you and Mera."

"What about you, Cove? What about us?" I raise my voice.

"Baby." He sighs. "You have to promise me that you understand it's all for you. So you and your friend are happy and safe."

"We can have it both ways. The three of us can be happy. You're not the only one who has a say today. I won't be quiet this time, not like I was at the expo."

"Soph—"

"Hello, kids," my dad interrupts. "Why is it that the two of you are always arguing?"

I turn to see him in the doorway, his hands in his pant pockets, an eerie grin on his face. Cove closes his eyes. I don't say hello, or smile, or even nod his way. I just stare and wait for him to speak. His black suit looks a bit too formal to be Monday morning office-attire, and I can tell it's been tailored to fit his body, expensive, like the gold rings on his fingers. The room immediately fills with the smell of Amouage Dia cologne, overpowering Cove's vanilla woodsy scent. A man older than my dad makes his way out his office door with a briefcase in hand.

"Cove," my dad's voice thunders, "you have an appointment and yet you sit on that sofa like a frigid pussy. Don't waste my time."

"Get in here, douchebag," a Rosen says from inside the office.

Cove stands and reaches for my hand. I give him the benefit of the doubt and allow him to help me up, keeping his words clear in my head. I'm focused. What he has to do is okay. It doesn't matter what it is, just remember that he loves me.

"Lauren, take a twenty-minute break. Lock the main door on your way out," my dad says to his assistant, closing the door behind him.

Doron pats both of us down and takes our cells. I'm humiliated. My dad is having me frisked. What the fuck?

A large glass table is centered in the room with enough black leather swivel chairs to seat eight. The rest of the furniture is rather bland, dark wood, typical for an office, and somewhat of a disappointment. I pictured a room with a bar and a fireplace, full of paintings, elaborate furniture, and rugs from foreign lands. This space is clean and barren. It looks like an FBI office—modern and minimal—perhaps used as a front for something else.

"Do I have to be here?" I ask, overwhelmed and queasy.

"Doron, turn the fluorescent lights off and tilt the blinds slightly to let a little light in."

My dad sits down at the table and Cove takes a seat across from him. Neither one of them looks at me, but Cove at least acknowledges my existence by pulling out a chair.

"Dad, I want to see Mera. I'm taking her with me...

back to St. Louis."

He ignores me, staring at Cove. Doron sits next to him, rocking back and forth in his chair. He looks out of place, wearing jeans and a button-down shirt, rolled at the sleeves, far more casual than the rest of us.

"Cove, I heard what you said at your mother's. You've agreed to help bring NOVA back. That's why I've decided to meet with you, and it's the only reason. I need someone for this project. Doron is the only other person who has the time to work on it. But you know the ins and outs better than him. You've lived it. Now you need to take charge of it."

"Dad. Why the hell did you place a bug in Leondra's home? She doesn't deserve to be treated that way." He ignores me again. I don't exist in this place and his world.

"I knew you were listening," Cove says, placing a hand on my leg. My dad looks down and sees the contact through the glass table. Cove withdraws, focusing on the discussion. "I knew you were listening, Paul. That's why I mentioned NOVA to my parents. It was one way to keep you off my back until I made it here. It's how I got in this office."

"Doron, stop fucking swiveling in that goddamn chair," my dad yells, his face turning red with deep twisted lines across his forehead. He glares at Doron then looks back at Cove. "Don't say you fucking played me you little prick, you know Doron carries. I'll take it out of his belt and shoot you between the eyes before you have a chance to blink."

"Dad! Stop it!"

Cove raises his hand, signaling me to calm down. I sit back in the chair and fold my arms in defense.

"What are you doing here, Star?" he asks.

I roll my eyes, unable to hear that porn name one more time. My dad's fingers are interlaced on the table. He leans forward, his body language prodding for an answer.

"Answer him," Doron says, preparing to stand.

"An exchange. I'll give you what you wanted from me three years ago."

"Ha, I don't believe it," Doron says. "Dayne told me last night that you had Blackjack, but I thought he was fucking with me. I even bet him a grand that you didn't."

"Doron, shut the fuck up," my dad says.

"Did you kidnap someone? Did you find a new employee for my dad?" I ask.

"Shh," Cove hushes me, stretching his arm toward Doron. "Give me my cell."

Doron looks to my dad and gets a nod to go ahead. He slides the cell across the table. Cove picks it up, quickly typing his password.

"I need an agreement, Paul."

"You don't fucking make the deals in my company. Show me what you've got, then *I'll* tell you what happens next."

"No. I want Mera to go home with Sophia. I want them out of here and away from this. Don't you want that for your daughter?"

"You tell me, shithead. You're the one who brought her here."

"I was going to come no matter what," I say. "You took my best friend, Dad. Did you think I would just sit home and say, oh well, that sucks, I guess there's nothing I can do."

He finally looks at me, his face tense. "You left my

protection, Kiddo. You made your choice. Besides, Mera wanted to come. She works for me now. She's happy. You'll see that for yourself soon enough, now shut your mouth."

"You callous, insensitive—"

"Sophia," Cove interrupts, turning toward me to whisper in my ear. "Stay strong, let everything you hear go. This is business."

"No, both of you, this is *not* business. This is my life, and Cove's life, and Mera's life. What the fuck?"

"Do you want me to take her out?" Doron asks.

"What does that mean, are you going to shoot me?"

He laughs, swiveling his chair again. "No, it means physically take you out to the waiting area so we don't have to listen to you bitch."

"Let her be," my dad says, smiling at me. "You done?"

I stop talking and wait.

"Show me," my dad demands.

Cove types into his phone then trembles and falls back into his chair. "How about a drink first?"

"Goddammit, I'm tired of this shit. Last time, and if you're lying, your father won't make it out of that infirmary."

"Jesus, you're such an ass," I murmur.

His fist slaps the table, nearly breaking the glass. Cove quickly types and pushes his cell across to the two of them.

My dad picks it up and looks at the screen, while Doron slides in close to see what he has.

"Oh, sssshit," Doron hisses.

My dad's chair hits the back wall as he stands and grabs Cove by the collar. He pulls him forward and drags him across the table. I gasp and my eyes widen, frozen in my chair by the scene. "YOU DUMB FUCK!" He yanks him off the table and throws his body against the wall, slamming his face into the hard surface. He knees him then positions his kneecap under his balls. Cove's like a ragdoll, allowing my dad to toss him around. "You better not have fucking posted that anywhere. If I find out that's online, you'll never be seen or heard from again."

"Dad, stop!" I shout. "What is it?"

"Sophia, sit your ass down."

"No. Let him go!"

"Paul." Cove groans. "I didn't post it. It's not to get back at you. It's to make you money. I'll give it to you."

"Give it to me?" he says. "You hear that Doron, he'll give it to me." He turns him around and plants a hard fist across his jaw, sending him to the ground.

"You still have my followers. They're still your loyal customers," Cove blurts out, his voice strained. "Market it, hype it up, and charge a few bucks for people to download it. I know when NOVA ended we had thirty-five thousand wanting that as the finale. Give it to them now, they'll still watch it, I guarantee it. That's an easy hundred grand for you in one shot."

"Shit, he's fucking right, Paul," Doron says.

My dad paces then swiftly kicks Cove in the gut. He curls into a ball on the floor.

"Dad, no!" I start to run over to Cove, but Doron grabs hold of my arm. "Dad, please!" Cove starts to sit up, but my dad places a foot on his side, keeping him down.

"You know I can't fucking post that, you fuck. Does she know?" he asks, his fists clenched and body tense. Cove's silent. "Does she know?!" he shouts, commanding an answer.

"No sir, she doesn't know," Cove says. "Just take it and let Mera and Sophia go home. You can do with me what you want."

"I can't fucking post it. You know that."

"Tell me what's going on. I want to see that phone."

He takes his foot away and allows Cove to sit up. He walks over to me, picks up Cove's cell, and looks at the screen.

"It's gone."

"I have the screen and video locked. You can't view either one without my password."

"Bring it up. Show Sophia."

Cove wavers to his feet, gripping the table for stability. He takes the cell and unlocks the screen and video, allowing it to play again. He lays it on the table. I try to walk over, only to be restrained by Doron.

"No, Cove. Fucking pick it up and show her."

He closes his eyes and exhales, picking up the phone on his way over to me.

"I'm sorry," he says, holding it up. "It's the two of us in the airplane bathroom, my first time with a woman. Paul wanted my virginity when I was twenty-one, but I wouldn't do it. I wouldn't give it to his clients. But he can show them now."

"You fucking used me? That wasn't real?"

"No, it was. Sophia, Baby, it was. I wanted to be with the right person my first time, something Paul doesn't understand." I watch the video, horrified that he did this. "People were willing to pay a bundle to see me lose it. His clients were with me for years, watching my every move.

They never saw me with a woman, not like this, but many of them dreamed about it. I was in their lives for years. They tuned in every week, every day, like I was their favorite television show. And the final episode is usually the most watched... the moneymaker. I was the company's virgin."

"This wasn't real? *We* weren't real?"

"Don't say that. It *was* real. It *is* real. I love you. Remember to ignore this. Its business. It's an exchange for your friend. I didn't do this to hurt you. You weren't even supposed to kn—"

I put all my strength into a swing and slap his face. "Fuck you, Cove." I try to release my arm from Doron's hold. "Let me go, asshole," I yell, pushing on his chest to get free.

"Doron, sit her down. Cove, sit down. Both of you, now!"

"You used me! I hate you! I hate all of you! Let me out of this room, now!" I scream, punching Doron's chest. He pushes me onto a chair then holds my shoulders so I can't escape. Cove takes a seat and leans forward, placing his hands over his face. "Turn me around. I can't look at either one of them," I say. My dad nods and Doron turns my chair so I'm facing the wall. I let out a high-pitched scream in frustration. "You should've told me your plan. You lied to me and set me up!" I kick the wall. "I want Mera, now!" I kick the wall again.

"Knock it off!" my dad shouts.

"Where was the camera, Cove?" I ask in a heartbroken voice.

"I had it in my hat, the one I took off and placed on the shelf next to us. The camera's tiny... you wouldn't have seen it... I turned it on when I went into the restroom before we boarded the plane."

"And how'd it get on your cell?"

"I set all that up the first morning in the hotel room, when I was using my laptop."

"You had this entire fucking thing planned out, and I fell for it! I loved you. I can't believe I fucking loved you and thought that you actually loved *me*."

"Soph... I do. Remember, everything was real. Everything *is* real."

"Shut the fuck up! I can't think with the two of you whiny ass kids bitching back and forth," my dad says.

"Paul... you've got fifteen minutes until our next meeting," Doron says.

"Yeah, well our little Star just fucked me over again. I'd like to just leave him in the desert or take him out to Lake Mead and have some fun with him in the water."

"I gave you what you wanted. It's an easy hundred grand, just take it and let Mera and Sophia go."

My dad and Doron both laugh. I need to get out of this room. My chest is tight and I'm starting to hyperventilate.

"I wanted the new NOVA, shithead. Not Blackjack. Twenty-one should've happened years ago."

"It still can. You know it. They're still out there, waiting."

"Hey, fuckhead," Doron says. "Don't you get it, it's Paul's daughter. He's not going to use it. We just went through this shit with you last week. I say we just kill him and be done with this chapter of our lives. Or use the video and kill him anyway."

"If I kill him, then I'll have to take care of Leondra, and possibly Wayne and Lydia. There're too many people involved."

"And me... you'll have to kill me too," I say. "As soon as I'm out of this chair I'm going to the cops, so just go ahead and dump me in the lake with the rest of them."

"You can block Sophia out of the shot," Cove says.

"People don't want to watch a woman's face blurred out," my dad says. "That's not going to turn them on. They want to see tension, the eyes, the mouth, that's all part of how they get off."

"Why do you care if she's online? You don't even love her, so what does it matter? Just use what I have."

"Don't fucking tell me how I feel and don't feel."

"Hundred grand. Money or family? What's more important to you?" Cove mumbles.

"What's more important to you, Cove? Money or love?" I snap. "Just post the fucking thing. I don't care. Make your money. The two of you mean nothing to me."

"Bring the video back up," my dad says. "Let me see it again."

I'm suffocating. I can't breathe. I think I'm going to pass out. The room quiets, and all I can think about is my dad watching me fuck. I won't say *make love*, since that's no longer the case. He's watching that scene right now. My dress was off and I only had on a garter and thigh-highs. Don't look at me... don't fucking look at me. Don't.

"How is it Paul?" Doron asks.

"Not bad. Nice angle. The lighting's good too. It seems real, unplanned, which always gets our highest ratings. His face is a mess, and people might turn away from that. He's not pretty, that's for sure. Then again, women like that wounded man shit, and some men like the tough guy look. Is there sound?"

"No," Cove says. "You don't need to hear what we said to each other. And I have *you* to thank for my face."

My dad chuckles and Doron's body moves in quiet laughter. "I suppose we can easily place our own sounds in... wait, hold on a second... you dumbass. There's no cum shot," he says, slamming the phone on the table. "How can you work in this industry for so many years and not pull out for the cum shot?"

"Ohh." Doron groans. "Rookie mistake, Cove. What happened, you get too excited that you finally got some pussy?"

"Fucking edit one in," Cove says. "That's easy enough. I can do it for you and make it look real."

"Why don't you just reshoot it? No one will know you've already done it," Doron suggests.

"He's not touching me ever again. You'll have to find someone else." I gasp, still fighting to breathe.

"I'm not doing this with anyone else. It was meaningful to me. That's why I waited so long. Don't you see the passion in what you just watched? It's real. You can't recreate that."

"It *was* real, but only for a brief moment. It's not anymore," I fume.

"Think about what you have, Paul."

There's silence again. I hear my dad pace as I stare at the cold grey wall. He walks across the room and I hear him pick up his office phone.

"Dayne, he has it, but there's an issue. Sophia's in the

shot."

"Put him on speaker," Doron says.

There's a click and I hear Dayne's voice in the room.

"Hey douchebag, remember what happened last time you fucked with us?" Dayne says. "I thought you finally agreed to do this project and get it over with, and now you show up today with this shit. *And* you had the nerve to show it to Paul? You made him watch you fuck his daughter? I bet that was pleasant. What do you say you and I go for a ride this afternoon, outside the city?"

"There's no cum shot, Dayne. He came inside of her." Doron laughs.

"For fuck's sake. And no condom I bet."

"Nope." Doron laughs harder.

"I hope she's on some form of birth control, otherwise we'll have to bring back the in-house doc to take care of things."

"What?" I gasp.

"Enough already. Don't take me to that place right now, any of you!" my dad shouts. "Dayne, if we kill him, we'll have Leondra to deal with. If Cove's gone, she'll have nothing left and she won't think twice about going to the cops. And if we take care of her, we have Wayne and Lydia, plus my daughter is in the middle of all of this. What do we do with her?"

"What do you mean, what do we do with her?" I ask. "What... you want to kill me? Then you have Mera to deal with. So kill her, too, right? Then Devery will wonder where I am, so you'll kill her too."

"No one's touching my sister," Doron says.

"Just post the damn thing and be done with the three

of us, or at least Sophia and Mera," Cove says.

"Stop it, all of you. Dayne... come up with a different plan. We're not going that route, but we need to discuss some things today. Think about how attached you are to Mera, and how we can fix the situation. We'll meet tonight at the house. Make sure Trey's there."

Dayne laughs before he hangs up the phone.

"Turn her around."

Doron turns my chair and I'm face to face with the two men who I despise most in this world. Cove cleans the tears off his cheeks, staring at the floor through the glass table.

"I'm not sure I'll make enough for this exchange to take place, plus it's too high a risk to send my daughter and her friend out into the world after everything they've seen."

"Making a hundred grand isn't enough?" I snap, my panic turning to rage, now able to breathe, but furious that I can't move.

"It's not worth the security that's involved to keep the two of you silent."

"I'd say I'm not going to talk, but whether or not that's true, you wouldn't take the chance, right?"

"No. Not after the past week."

"You can triple your profit," Cove says, sitting up in his chair and raising his head to look into my dad's eyes. "If you don't think it's enough then don't just market the loss of my virginity, but market your daughter. That targets your entire company and not just the NOVA followers. People would flock to see Paul Jameson's daughter on an online site."

"Really, Cove? Now you're selling me off? You're specifically marketing ME?" I try to stand, but Doron holds me down. My dad leaves his chair and comes around to Cove's side of the table, grabbing his arm and pulling him out of his chair.

"Paul, you could triple your sales. That's a good deal," he says.

My dad hits him square in the eye. He slams his back against a window then holds him by his collar. Cove turns away, closing his eyes.

"Doron, take her to the house and keep her there until I get home. I'll take care of him and the rest of our appointments for the day."

"Thank fucking God," I say, finally able to stand and get out of the room. "I hope the two of you kill one another."

Doron laughs, leading me out of the office.

"Sophia, wait!" Cove yells.

I hear another smack as fist meets face in the room behind me.

Punch him back, Cove. Stand up for yourself!

A small part of me, a very small part of me, still wants Cove to win this game.

Thirteen

DORON PULLS HIS LEXUS through the black iron gate of my dad's home. He parks in front of the four-car garage. We haven't said a word to one another since we left the office, leaving Cove and my dad to fight it out, or I should say, my dad to beat the crap out of him. I'm pissed. All I want is to find Mera and go home.

He leads me to the front door and types a code into the keypad on the sidewall of the entryway. After a click, we're allowed access to the inside.

Doron calls out for his brother. The house is quiet, the smell of vanilla prominent. The memory of waking up in Cove's loft to the same scent enters my mind.

"Mera!" I yell, listening for a response.

Nothing.

"It's a big house," Doron says. "You need to stay here until your father finishes his work at the Fox."

"Where am I gonna go? And anyway, I'm not leaving this city without my friend... and Cove's balls in a bag."

"That can actually be arranged. Be careful what you

wish for." He looks up. "Mera and Dayne must be busy. Feel free to explore, except for the third floor and your father's office. Both of those areas should be locked. All the exterior doors can only be opened with a keypad, so don't bother trying to escape. I need to call my wife and take care of some business. I'll be in the backyard by the pool if you need anything. Just knock on the glass doors and I'll hear you," he explains, walking through a massive two-story great room. "Oh, and there's no land line, so no need to search for a phone."

He reaches the back, presses the keypad on the wall, and lets himself out. The door closes and I'm alone in my dad's mansion.

"Mera," I call out. "You here?" I listen. Nothing.

The great room is a cross between a medieval castle and a ski lodge. A staircase leads to a balcony that extends along the back of the room, running to the left and right into separate areas of the home. There's a colossal stone fireplace with a long sword that hangs above the mantel. A beautiful photograph of a woman shot in black and white is above the sword. She's nude, her chest pushed forward with her arms behind her body. She has her head tilted back and only her chin and neck are exposed in the shot. It reminds me of the photograph above Cove's fireplace that his mom took of herself, and I wonder if this was also shot by her.

The walls are stucco and a large iron chandelier hangs in the center of the room. A canopy attached to the ceiling is in the shape of a star, and each arm ends in a cluster of votive-shaped glass. Wide pine floors are stained dark, matching the color of the overhead beams that run across the space.

Doron puffs on a cigarette as he talks on his cell. The

backyard looks intimate compared to this enormous room. There's a pool surrounded by short palms and a high, bamboo style fence. A lounger is next to the edge of the pool and I imagine Mera's recently been out there.

Brown leather sofas and chairs are placed throughout the great room and arranged in groups of four, with a coffee table in the middle of each set. A fully stocked bar is to my left with stools facing a flat screen. The rest of the space is rather bare, except for a few indoor palms by the back door.

There's a hallway to my left and one to my right. I walk left and open the first door, stepping into a pitch-black room. Not finding a light switch, I wait for my eyes to adjust. I can make out the outline of a large U-shaped couch and a few recliners. The room slopes downward into the darkness and I remember Cove mentioned a theater room in the house. This must be it.

I close the door and open another. Red walls, a black massage table, minimal objects placed here and there; a shelf stacked with towels and white candles, and a chair and coat rack in the corner. The next room is identical, only reversed, with a red massage table and black walls. The final door leads to a four-car garage. There's a speedboat in the farthest space and a custom motorcycle for Jameson Industries in the next. I had no idea he had either one. The next spot is empty. But a grey Aston Martin is in the space closest to me. Every object in front of me could be from the money he made selling Cove's body in NOVA. Fuck, this is crazy.

I close the garage door and walk quickly back to the great room. "Mera!" I shout. "Mera, I'm here."

There's no response.

I know she's here. Cove said the house whores... God I

hate that term... he said the house whores rarely leave.

I walk through the great room and head down the other hall. There're no doors on the right, only a dark shelf at waist level stretching a good twenty feet down the wall. The shelf has a line of evenly spaced white candles, with melted wax fallen down their sides. When lit, I can imagine this hall resembles a church... or a séance. I pass a suit of armor, something totally cliché for a wealthy man to own, and open the first door on my left. It's a small room containing a stack of towels, a shelf full of white candles, like the one in the hall, and a shower. One large glass-enclosed shower, placed directly in the middle of the room. There's no sink, or toilet, just a shower. This whole house disgusts me. I shut the door and quickly open the next—a bedroom, or rather, a bed in a room. Two black robes hang on hooks next to the door, and again, there's a shelf with white candles on the left wall. Cove's guest bedroom had a dresser full of white candles. I thought it was romantic, but now I can see that it's all just part of the company. Like the tattoos on Mera and Cove's bodies, the white candles are a signature of my dad and his products.

An ornately framed mirror greets me as I reach the back of the hall. My reflection reveals a troubled and sad young woman. My insides are broken. Shattered. To think, just three hours ago I was madly in love with *him*.

I turn away and step into the final doorway of the hall, entering a massive dining room. The table that runs through the middle of the room is the same dark color as the floors. It's a good forty feet in length. The thing must weigh a ton. The oak high-back chairs emit the same sense of power as the table they surround. I feel like I've stepped into a king's castle and this is where the barbaric and bawdy men gather shamelessly in the evening for meat, wine, and women.

Where the fuck am I?

I flip a switch and an enormous fireplace comes to life, with gas logs in the hearth and small white twinkling lights placed along the mantel. It casts a warm glow on my skin and flickers across the walls.

"Mera!"

Nothing. I thought both she and Dayne were here, and yet the house seems so empty and cold. I have no sense that there's been any human presence in these rooms for weeks, months, possibly years.

The final doorway off the dining area leads to a large kitchen. The counters are empty except for a bowl of fruit placed in the middle of an island. How surreal. There's not a crumb or a dish in sight.

My dad's home is not at all how I pictured it. I thought the interior would be warm and alive like Leondra's, yet stylish and opulent like Cove's. A mix of the two. But there's no sense that anyone actually lives in this house. People just come here to work. It's not a home, it's a massage parlor, slash sex hotel, slash meeting hall. Fuckin' A.

I stomp back to the great room and over to the glass doors, giving them a hard kick. They're unbreakable, of course, and Doron quickly responds to the noise. I give him the finger when he turns around. He walks over, waving his hand for me to step back. I kick the door again and he opens it, pushing me in then sliding it shut.

"What the fuck are you doing?"

"Where's Mera? She's supposed to be here, but this house is nothing but cold air and dead rooms. It's nothing but a fuck palace. No one lives here. Is this a front for the business? For filming? Cove said this was my dad's house, but there're no personal items anywhere. So tell me what I'm doing here and where she is!"

"Chill the fuck out! Just because you're a Jameson doesn't mean I can't smack you around to shut you up."

"You ass!" I take a swing at him. He catches my hand. My arm is quickly twisted behind my back and he pushes me onto one of the sofas. My face hits the hard surface and I howl from the pressure of his mammoth body on top of mine. "Ow, get off! You're going to break my arm!"

"Shut up and listen to me," Doron shouts. "Calm down."

I struggle for a few seconds, certain that my arm will snap at any moment, and disgusted by the cigarette smoke that leaves his mouth and enters mine. I turn my head and relax, surrendering to the titanic mass on top of me.

"That's better," he says, stepping away. I turn over and place my feet on the coffee table, wiping my hair away from my face. "This *is* your father's home and he wouldn't appreciate it if he found out you tried to wreck the place. You can't break this glass. It's like everything else in the house, once you're in, you're in. There're only a few of us here, and Paul takes security seriously. That includes alarms, keypad security, windows, doors, and cameras."

"Of course he has cameras in here." I groan.

"This floor is for business. This is where we meet, party, fuck, and make money. That's what our life and our company are about."

"My dad's company."

"*Our* company. The three of us started this and we're in it together."

"Four. There were four of you, remember?"

Doron sits in a chair across from me, shaking his head. "You know too much. That boyfriend of yours put you in danger when he opened his mouth."

"He's *not* my boyfriend."

"So you just fuck random people? You should join the company if that's the case. And anyway, we'll see if he's your boyfriend or not."

"What does that mean?"

"Have you been upstairs?" he asks, looking down at my legs. I realize with my feet on the coffee table that he can see under my dress, and even worse, between my legs.

"Like what you see?" I ask, placing my feet on the ground. "No, I haven't been upstairs."

"Then you haven't seen the house. Before you try to break through the glass doors and throw a bitch fit, you should head upstairs," he says, pointing to his right. "I'm sure the house whore is up there with Dayne."

"Her name's Mera."

"Well, she's a house whore now, get used to it. I don't think Paul's gonna let the two of you leave for a while, so you'll hear that term used a lot in this house." His cell rings and he holds up a finger for me to wait.

"She's on the sofa. We're in the middle of a little chat. And yes, she's fine." He looks down at me then paces. "I could have any woman from the company over here in a second, why would I touch your daughter, Paul."

"Tell him to go to hell!" I shout. Doron covers the phone and furrows his brow, shaking his head.

"I think they're upstairs... and don't ask me to go up there. You know what a dick he is when people interrupt him." I stand, but Doron places his hand on my shoulder. "You sure about that? She's feisty."

I roll my eyes, knowing that the day's not going to end without my fist firmly planted in someone's face.

"I'll be right there," he says, ending the call. "Paul seems to think you'll be fine on your own. I need to take care of some things at the office."

"Cove?"

"*Things*. We'll be back this evening," he says, walking toward the front door. "Go upstairs. You'll find your friend. She's around here somewhere."

As quick as he's out the door, I'm up the stairs. I head left and enter a family room. Large windows run along the back wall, filling the space with sun. Dark shelves line one side of the room and are full of books, photos, and small objects. The room is comfortable and bright. I explore a few of the shelves and see that the photos are of my dad with well-known actors, football and basketball players, and political figures. Most are from the Las Vegas, Los Angeles, and St. Louis areas, but I only know that by the athletes' uniforms and the city landmarks in the background of some of the shots. There's also a photo of my dad in college, with Dayne and Doron and their fraternity brothers all standing in front of their frat house. Looks like a party. My dad and the Rosens have aged well, just as muscular as they were years ago... wait... is that Cove's dad in the photo? Yes, I think it's him. It's someone who looks like Cove, anyway. I only saw his dad briefly on FaceTime that one night when I stayed at Leondra's, but... it's him... yeah, it's him.

I find no photos of me, or my brother, Mark.

"Hmph, what a selfish bastard," I grumble, leaving the room to enter a hall that leads further into the second level.

"Mera," I call out, taking a moment to listen. Still nothing.

The door to my left is locked, so I try the one across from it.

"Jesus. What the fuck is this?"

Another sex room, definitely designed for his clients, or maybe his own fetish. In the middle of the black room rests a circular mattress. There're no sheets or pillows, and it's surrounded from floor to ceiling by metal bars that form a cage, a jail, a cell, or a holding area, or... God, whatever it is, it's gross.

The metal is painted blood red and there's only one-way in and out; a small door at the bottom that a person has to crawl through in order to enter. There's also a flat screen on the wall with a full-length mirror underneath it. I walk in and reach out to touch the metal. I need to prove to myself that everything I'm seeing is real. My hands run up and down the bars. I place a firm grip on one... it's solid, securely set into the ceiling and floor.

"That's about the right size," a low voice says. I jump and turn to see Carl Caverns, my dad's employee who stopped us in front of the museum. He's leaning against the doorframe in a white t-shirt and black jeans, sporting black motorcycle boots. A toothpick still hangs out of his mouth and a pair of sunglasses rests on his head. He smirks, looking at my hand as it holds onto the bar. "I said... that's about the right size. How does it feel in your hand?"

I drop my arm and take a step back, feeling threatened and trapped by this man. "Do you ever take that thing out of your mouth?" I ask.

"Does it bother you?"

"Yeah, a little bit. It makes you look seedy."

"Well maybe I am... *seedy*," he says in a slow drawl.

"Maybe, I'd like to see you in that cage, trapped like a bird. I can be the house cat and prey on you, devour you until your insides burst. Then I can lick the mess clean."

I roll my eyes, unable to hold in my repulsion for this man. "I'm not into that whole role-play thing."

"Star is one of our finest role-playing men, at least he used to be. I find it hard to believe that you don't enjoy it if you're with him."

"First of all, shithead," I say, walking toward him with my finger pointed at his face. "I'm not his girlfriend, and I wouldn't allow him to play any games with me if I was. I'm tired of this crap."

"Ha. A Jameson, tired of this crap. Yeah, right. I'm sure Big Daddy has your bank account full."

"Second, you dumbass. You don't have a chance with me. And third, how did you get in this house, and does my dad know that you're here?"

"Follow me," he says, reaching his hand out for mine.

"I'm not touching you."

"That's fine. Have it your way. I just want to show you to your room. You shouldn't be in these private spaces anyway. Paul has them cleaned after parties and they're off limits until the next function."

"My room?"

"Two doors down, next to Paul's office. Come on, you don't have to touch the *weird* guy in front of you, but you can at least follow along."

I give him a suspicious look as he places his hand in his pockets, rocking back and forth, twisting his toothpick around with his tongue.

"Look, my hands will never leave my pants, alright?"

"Nothing better leave those pants," I reply, taking a step to the door. He walks out and I follow him down the hall.

"That door we just passed is another bedroom, a *normal* one. And here, my little Jameson princess, is your room... can I take my hand out to open the door?"

"Go ahead," I say, entering a beautifully lavish bedroom suite.

"Bathroom's in that far right corner, desk area under the window. No, the window doesn't open. Fireplace. Sofa. Um... walk-in closet in the bathroom."

"My suitcase! How'd that get here?"

"My specialty, Madame. Professional gopher at your service." He takes a bow. "Your father says jump, and I jump. He wanted your things, and I got them," he replies, standing back up.

"And Cove?"

"Well now, I thought you weren't his girlfriend. Open relationship, yet still curious as to where he'll be?"

"No relationship, and yes, still curious."

"Not a question I have an answer to," he says, taking the toothpick out of his mouth and placing it in his front pocket. "And not one I care to know."

I throw my suitcase onto the bed, in need of more comfortable clothes. I have to get out of this dress.

"I'm heading out. Paul checks our code numbers to see when we come and go, and I'm taking far too long to drop off a bag. You good?"

"Yeah," I say, pulling out a pair of blue jeans and a tank. "Wait, no. Do you know where Mera is?"

"If she's not by the pool or in the kitchen, then she'll

be over in Dayne's suite. It's on the other side," he says, disappearing out the door.

I run and look down the hall, watching him scurry away like a rat in a New York City subway. "Hey Carl. Thanks," I yell.

"You're welcome. And you can't blame me for wanting to fuck you, Sophia Jameson," he says, waving a finger in the air.

Fourteen

I PASS THE STAIRWELL that leads down to the great room and head across the balcony to Dayne's side of the house. I feel better now that I'm wearing my comfortable jeans and favorite white tank. That is, as good as one can feel locked in a porn king's mansion.

At the end of the balcony is a large barn door that hangs on an antique metal track system. It's painted black and is close to seven feet wide, solid and heavy. With its size, I'm surprised how easily it slides open.

"What a fucking mess," I whisper, stepping into a room that's bursting with male testosterone. I won't find any romantic white candles in here.

Mera's light blue underwear is on the floor by a recliner, her bra hanging over the back of a sofa. A small bar area is full of empty beer bottles and dirty shot glasses. The room smells like a bar and my bare feet stick to the floor from the booze that's spilled everywhere. Dayne's obviously unable to leave behind his frat boy days, still looking to drink and fuck whenever he gets the chance, slightly different from Doron, who may also enjoy the same things, but has a wife and a life separate from all this.

An iPad has been left out on the sofa. Maybe I can send Leondra an email. I need someone to know what's going on out here, and she's the only person I can think to contact besides the cops. I'm not ready to take it to that extreme until I talk to Mera, then we'll decide what to do together.

Damn it, I need Dayne's passcode to use the Internet. I toss it back on the couch and walk through the room to a hall. I hear music. A strong beat. Some rap song.

I pass a set of French doors on my right. They're locked, but I have a clear view into Dayne's office: a desk, two leather chairs, and piles of porn magazines from the company. The music's louder now. Blasting, and I recognize the song. It's the Beastie Boys, "Root Down," an old-school band I often heard playing in the dorms during 'eighties night' parties. Dayne and my dad, although they look and act hip, still let their real age show. Marky Mark and the Funky Bunch? Beastie Boys?

I head to the last door at the end of the hall. A heavy bass vibrates my body as I push the door open.

"Shit." I groan. I've seen Mera fuck people in the past, but I'm not prepared to see her with Dayne.

She grips a low dresser, her chin up and head back, Dayne tugging her long hair. He pulls it with every drive into her body, his other hand on her breast as they fuck. With their backs to the door, I have a clear view of a large tribal tattoo that crosses his back.

"Say it," Dayne demands. "You love me in your ass. Say it." He yanks her hair.

"I do. I do, Dayne."

"Don't fucking shit on me, you understand? Don't shit on me."

"No, I won't," she says, breathless, her eyes closed.

"Goddamn, you're tight."

I'm afraid of what might happen if I interrupt Dayne in the middle of his fuck. He seems more violent than Doron. Not knowing him makes me take one step back. I believe this is how Leondra must have felt when she walked in on Cove and me. Nervous. Reluctant. Ashamed.

"Fuck, don't say anything. Keep that mouth shut while I get ready to cum in your ass."

"Dayne!" Mera exclaims in a voice I know well. She's about to cum, and I take another step back.

"You whore. You dirty little house whore." He pulls out and pushes her to the bed. "Don't you dare cum first."

She's face down as he kneels over her. He grabs his dick and separates her ass, about to push in when he sees me in the doorway. He smiles and my eyes widen, frightened by his sinister grin and scarred chest. The long mark across his heart looks like an old injury, possibly from a knife, and his right nipple is disfigured, like someone cut it off and sewed it back on slightly off center.

"Well, well," he says, walking toward me with his long erect cock bouncing in the air. "Baby Jameson is here... in my bedroom."

I look down at his stiff erection and see a tattoo of a swallow on his groin.

"She is?" Mera squeals, lifting her head off the bed.

"Where's that cock you like to suck? Did you bring Star with you? Maybe the two of you can join us... not that I'd want an Everton naked in my bed, but I wouldn't mind—"

"Jesus, Dayne. She's my best friend, don't play games," Mera says, rushing across the room and into my arms. "Oh Soph! I've missed you." She places soft kisses over my face, ending with a giant kiss on my mouth. Her breasts brush against my tank and I'm immediately comforted when I touch the warm skin on her back. Her body, her voice, and the soft flowery perfume that she wears—it's all so familiar and calming.

"Fuck, get back into bed, Mera. I can end in about a minute after seeing two women kiss and grab each other like that."

I ignore Dayne and take Mera by the shoulders. "Are you okay? I've been so worried sick about you over the past three days."

"She's fine," Dayne says in a lower, more direct voice. "And we're in the middle of something. When you're in this house you'll learn not to snoop around and intrude on peoples' lives."

"Dayne," she scolds, looking back at him.

He walks over and separates our embrace, picking her up and carrying her back to the bed. "Sit there and wait," he says, then looks at me while pointing at the door. "Get out. You can see her in a few minutes. I'll send her out when I'm done. Now get the fuck out until I'm finished."

I look at Mera for her reaction, but she's staring at Dayne. I can't tell if the expression on her face is lust or if she's play-acting, like she did with Trey. I turn and leave the room, walking down the hall as the music continues to blast. I wait in front of Dayne's office, listening to him groan as he pounds into her. I'm emotionally exhausted. I wonder if Mera has the code to get out, and if she does, if the two of us can leave without Dayne noticing. I need to figure something out before my dad gets home. With just Dayne here, we may have a chance.

"Fuck, you fucking whore." Dayne moans, making indescribable sounds as he fucks her. Mera's quiet, which is unusual for her.

I walk back to his room, tired of waiting. After going through three days of fights, passion, disgust, and hatred, I'm not waiting another second.

She's lying on her back with his hand over her mouth, his head in the blanket, both of them heaving for air.

"Mera, we need to talk, *now*."

Dayne rolls over with an arm across his stomach. "Get the fuck out of my bed and go talk to Paul's whiny-ass daughter," he says. "Get her out of my room before I catch my breath. You're both lucky I'm in system failure after I blow my load."

"Like all men," she says, getting out of bed. "You sound like a fucking dork sometimes, Dayne."

He slaps her ass and she laughs, pulling on one of his button-down dress shirts, the sleeves rolled, front open. It runs down to her knees and could be a nightshirt on her. Dayne's slightly bigger than his brother and twice the size of my dad, making Mera seem like a Chihuahua living with a Doberman.

I take her hand and we leave Dayne's room. I need a private place to speak to her, but I know that won't be possible in this house. We head down the stairs and I point to one of the barstools where she takes a seat in silence. I mix us both a Greyhound from behind the counter, needing liquor, yet craving juice.

"That's a good afternoon drink," she says.

I gulp mine down like it's a shot and make a second.

"Jesus, Soph."

I look down at the floor with my hands on the counter, confused about what just took place upstairs, needing an explanation. "I've been fucked by a lot of people over the past few days, trying to get to you, and I'm *not* happy right now. So before I fly off the handle on yet another person, my best friend no less, why don't you tell me what happened the night you left, and what you're doing here, and if you're interested in leaving with me. You sounded happy in your text messages. Are you happy here, Mera? I don't understand what's going on."

She comes around to my side and rubs my back. "Sorry," she says. "I don't know."

"What don't you know? Are you happy or not? What do you want to do?"

"I'm sorry I haven't been able to talk to you. Dayne was the only one who let me use my phone, but only to send you a quick text. He wanted me to tell you I was enjoying myself."

"Dayne was the one who told you to send the text?"

"Yeah, he wanted you and Cove to back off. He thought my text might make you guys might second guess trying to meet with your dad. That you might go home and just enjoy each other and not make a mess of the company."

"Why? Why would he care?"

She sighs, her hand still on my back. "He said Cove's jinxed. Every time he comes here, something goes wrong and Dayne has to work to fix it, then your dad's in a bad mood for weeks. Dayne said he's tired and doesn't want to deal with Cove anymore. He said if it were up to him, he'd just get rid of him."

"And that doesn't bother you?" I ask, voice glaring. "This guy you just fucked says he wants to get rid of someone, and that doesn't make you want to run?"

She steps back. "I don't know your boyfriend, Soph. I've never seen or met Cove Everton. I know nothing about the guy except for what you've told me, which is very little."

"And what do you know about the men in this house? If you haven't noticed, they have you locked inside and fucking them at the drop of a hat."

"I knew what I was getting into," she says, her voice growing with mine. "It's for protection that these doors are locked."

"Oh, fuck that. You're not that stupid, Mera. For your protection? You're a prisoner and now so am I."

"Paul will probably let you leave once he knows I'm not going with you. He can't keep you here forever."

"He doesn't trust me. I already said I'd go to the cops!" I shout.

"Don't yell at me. I helped you get past Trey so you could see the man of your dreams." She pauses, looking around the room. "Where is he anyway?"

"I don't care where the fuck he is. I hate both him and my dad. I want out of this house and away from all of you!"

Mera immediately wraps her arms around me, holding me so that I calm down. "Soph, I didn't mean to do any of this to you, it all happened so fast," she says. "Your dad came over that morning and was furious that you had left. He threw the dummy out of the bed and punched Trey, then told me I needed to pack. He said I'd start at his company that day. I wasn't sure what to do or say. I tore my room apart and packed everything I thought I might need, not knowing where I'd end up and for how long. Paul talked to me about things later that night in the hotel room. And he *did* give me a choice between working in St. Louis or here. But the offer to be here was too good to turn down. Just look at this place." She raises her arms. "It's beautiful, especially the pool. I can swim, watch television, or listen to music. I get beautiful clothes, and believe it or not, Dayne and Paul are nice to me. They put on some weird tough guy show in bed, but it's all for fun." I shake my head and drink. "Your dad also pays me a lot. I mean, *a lot*. It's more than I made at the Pillsman Center and I don't even have to do anything."

I laugh. "Except get fucked in the ass. You have to do that. What ever happened to that college degree you earned? You just gonna forget about it?"

"Excuse me?" she says, backing away. "This, from a nude model? What about that degree you got? Talk about the pot calling the kettle black."

I run my hand down my face and take a deep breath. "Cove and I flew out to get you. My dad left me a note that he took you and he won because he got what he wanted."

"Yep, that sounds like Paul. His business is a competitive sport."

"Cove knew how upset I was that you were gone. He came up with a plan for my dad to make a bundle of money in exchange for you."

"Really? You guys tried to cut a deal for me? But why would you do that if you didn't even know what *I* wanted?"

"Because I thought my dad kidnapped you. Cove thought it was all a setup to get him to do something." I put my hand on my hip and furrow my brow. "You know, I thought you'd be happier to see me. That we'd come and get you and the three of us would fly home together."

"And live happily ever after?"

"Well... yeah. And live happily ever after," I say.

"Where is he?"

I put my glass down and run a finger along the bar, biting my top lip to fight back tears.

"Soph?"

"I thought I really loved him, Mera. But he hurt me, just like my dad."

"What happened?"

I feel humiliated. "It's too hard to talk about right now. When I left my dad's office, the last thing I said to the two of them was that I hope they kill each other."

She laughs, forcing me to smile a little. "It's not funny," I say.

"Then why are you smiling?"

"Because you are, and I'm so angry I don't know what else to do. I'm either about to have a nervous breakdown, or I need to get wasted and laugh it off." Mera hands me my glass and I chug it down.

"We need something stronger," she says.

I pour us two shots of vodka. "Bottoms up," I say, throwing mine back. "So did you fuck my dad?" I ask, pouring another shot.

"Soph... I..."

"No, I already know the answer. No need to explain. I just needed to say it."

"He's not what I expected. There's no intimacy or foreplay with him like with the Rosens."

"I don't want to hear about him in bed."

"No, Listen. I was terrified of him and Dayne that first morning in the room."

"Dayne was there too?"

"Yeah, he was at the hotel when we arrived. I was with both of them."

"At the same time?"

"Um... kind of. Dayne watched, then Paul watched, then Dayne left and Paul and I were alone."

"That's nasty," I say, passing another shot to Mera.

"It was scary until I realized the two of them have some alpha male thing going on."

"I've heard that before."

"Yeah, they act like dicks in front of each other, but your dad was actually really nice to me after it was all over, and when Dayne and I are alone, it's nice. He's fun. He says stupid things and tries to act like a monster, but he really isn't. I think I'm starting to—"

"What the fuck are you two doing down there?" Dayne hollers, walking down the stairs. "I want you on that floor, Mera, on your knees at all times and ready to suck me off."

She rolls her eyes.

"Pour me a shot, house whore," he demands, wearing only a pair of jeans, a baseball hat, and a thin silver chain. For someone in his mid-forties, he's ripped, and I blush when he catches me admiring his body. I turn away and shift my concentration to Mera.

She gets Dayne a glass then combs through the liquor cabinet. "Whiskey?"

"Rum and coke."

"Coming right up."

I stand and take the bottle of vodka to one of the sofas.

"Soph, you want your glass?" Mera asks.

"Nope, just the body," I say, sitting back with my legs

stretched out on the coffee table.

"Body or bottle?"

"Did I say body? I meant bottle. I think the liquor's starting to hit."

She hands Dayne his glass then follows me, shirt open and breasts bouncing as she moves. She sits on the opposite sofa, placing her feet next to mine.

"So you're *really* happy here?" I ask.

"Who wouldn't be? I get whatever I want from Paul, and all I have to do is fuck him and the twins, which you know I would've done before all this happened anyway. So yeah, now that they've made me feel welcome and I understand what they're like in bed, it's great. And you know you'd do the same."

"No, I wouldn't."

"If you think back to before Cove, yeah you would've. What happened to you anyway? A few weeks ago you were a completely different person."

"I think I'm growing up, or setting higher standards for myself... or something."

"Well, don't."

I drink, watching her hands travel down her beautiful soft white legs as she leans forward and stretches her back.

"A few weeks ago, my dad was a completely different person too. Remember when he was angry about my fling at Giorgio's? Today I could see in his eyes that he's actually considering putting me on one of his sites."

Dayne hovers around us. "I don't blame Paul for wanting to make a little money off you and Star. He planned to make some money off him anyway, now he has the chance to double that."

"Triple, he can triple his profits, like Cove said."

"Whoa, I missed a lot today," Mera says, sitting back in the chair. "So your dad has to choose between you and money?"

"I don't think it's much of a choice anymore. It will be an easy decision for him."

Dayne laughs and walks behind the sofa. He takes my hair in his hand and pulls my head slowly back. I look up into his brown eyes, unable to turn away. "Paul's a great businessman. There's no choice to make. You're not of his blood if you didn't see what was coming. It was completely planned by us."

"What? So my dad really did plan on Cove and me getting together?"

He releases me. "What do you think?"

"I think that's shitty, if that's what happened. So he knew Cove would fall for me?"

"Nope," he says, shaking his head. "We knew *you'd* fall for him. There's a difference between the two."

I take another drink and try to think about what Dayne's pointing out to me. Am I just too drunk, or too stupid to get it? "What?" I ask.

"After NOVA ended, we lost a big chunk of income. But Paul had the genius idea to market Cove's first fuck when he turned twenty-one, calling it Blackjack, but Cove wouldn't do it."

"So, why didn't you just leave him alone after that?"

"We couldn't. If you could see all the emails we get about him, it would blow your mind. He's famous in this company. We made him, and yet he's destroying us. People have fallen in love with the little shit. Still, years later, they still fucking ask for him. They want to know where he is, what he's doing, how much they can pay to see him again. It was time for us to try another approach."

"Me." I sigh.

"Yeah, you. Plan B. We thought he'd be attracted to you, but more importantly, you to him. Being in a shitty experience together is a great way to jumpstart a relationship—your dad beating him in front of you, his past, you wanting to save him, your dad insisting you stay away from him, blah, blah. It was all there. You lost your heart in the guy because of your connection to him, because of Paul. That was great, since Cove wouldn't give his heart to a woman, and to him that meant his dick, unless love was involved. He didn't want to fuck a woman who didn't have feelings for him. I think his father ingrained that into him, that somehow love is more meaningful and powerful than a fuck."

"Isn't it?"

"Not to me," he says, downing his drink. "And you two falling so fucking hard for one another is what makes this better than anything we've ever done. Clients will see and feel that connection. It's different from our other work. The only thing that was planned was that penthouse you moved into. It couldn't have worked out better than it did."

"And Cove wasn't aware of any of this?"

"Nope."

"You tricked him. You tricked both of us."

"How so? How is it that you falling for that douche was a trick? He got an opportunity to get some pussy, and now we get to rake in the dough. It's a big win for all."

"What about me? What do I get out of this? Or doesn't it matter?"

"You get whatever you want. That's up to you."

"So Cove was right? My dad threw a fit in St. Louis and put on a show at the expo for business? For his clients? It's all a stupid performance?"

"Aha, now you're starting to get it. I have to say, Paul was truly pissed about you in the parking garage, and that video Cove posted from his penthouse. You both jumped the gun on us, putting yourselves out there before we had everything set. It was tense. We had to clean up a lot of shit because of your mistakes. We didn't want anyone to see either of you before it was time."

"Cove put that video from his loft online to hurt my dad."

"True. We knew that. We figured he was testing us. If Paul hadn't reacted, he would've known you were a plant, and it probably would've ended right there for him."

"I feel like I'm in a movie or some surreal world. What the fuck? You guys really screwed us both, and Mera, too. You made her send those texts? Why, if you really didn't want Cove and me to leave?"

"So you'd know she wasn't hurt or in danger, so you wouldn't come rushing over here, or go to the cops. And it made Mera happy. She wanted to contact you. As far as I'm concerned, Mera's the bonus prize in all of this."

"Aren't you worried about my dad listening to us? Should you be telling me his dark secrets?"

"He can't listen and be in a meeting at the same time," Dayne says, looking at his phone. "Besides, some of these are my dark secrets, not Paul's. We'll split the profit between the two of us."

"What about Doron?"

"My brother has his own projects. This isn't one of them. Paul has kept him away from Star since an incident occurred years ago, and I know, given your boyfriend's big mouth, you've already heard about it. But Doron's still working on that part of the company, where Cove used to be."

"The new NOVA? So that *is* a real thing?"

He nods. "Paul's serious about it. We're not, but we all have our own jobs to do that we're good at, and Doron's been in NOVA since day one. I think Paul was hoping Star was serious when he mentioned it to his parents."

"Can you please stop calling Cove by that name?"

"Is douchebag better?"

"Soph, I can't believe how calm you are right now," Mera says. "Slow and still, relaxing your legs on the table. You should be pacing and throwing things at this point."

I squint and throw back another swig of vodka. "I'm drunk, my mind is fuzzy."

"Well, if it makes you feel any better, Dayne's right. I did want to talk to you, and I *am* excited to see you," she says. "Let's go hang by the pool and chill for the day. Dayne, let us out." She looks up and bats her eyes at him.

"You've got to be fucking kidding me. You think I'm gonna let my drunken house whore and Baby Jameson lounge shitfaced around the pool? You'd both pass out and drown. Then what?"

"Then Cove will find you a new house whore," I joke, taking another sip of the vodka. Mera holds up her glass to imitate a toast before she drinks. I look up at Dayne who's still hovering. "Why don't you sit down with us, Mark?"

"Mark?" he questions.

"Yeah, Cove was right, you look like Mark Wahlberg."

"Did that come up because of that fucking music Paul was playing at the expo?"

"Of course, it's not like we were just sitting around one day discussing your looks."

Dayne's cell rings before he can respond. "Yeah, I'm here," he says. "They're together, getting piss drunk."

"If that's my dad, tell him to bring home a pizza and a gallon of ice cream so I can drown my sadness and disappointment about Cove in food."

Mera laughs. "You're doing a good job of that already with the vodka."

"What? What the hell, Paul? I'm not locking up all the liquor. She's your fucking daughter. You come deal with her. I'm not your babysitter."

"Oooooh," I tease. "Trouble with your master, Dayne?"

"Soph." She sits up, shaking her head. "Don't piss him off. Maybe you have had enough."

"I can do that," he says, staring at me with a huge grin. "I'll make sure of it." He hangs up and pours himself another glass of rum from the bar, then walks over to me and yanks the bottle out of my hand. "You need to use a glass in this house. I'm not gonna let you get plastered and spill that entire fucking thing on the floor." He walks back to the bar and pours some vodka in a glass, then slams it on the table in front of me. "I can't believe after all these years you're actually in this house, and as it turns out, you're a total fucking bitch. If you were actually sweet and respectful it'd be a lot easier to figure out what to do with you, maybe let you go. But here you are, a drunken, foul-mouthed, cunt who's fucking that douchebag."

"Fuck you!" I shout.

"Dayne," Mera says. "That was nasty."

"Fucking asshole!" I add.

"Yeah. Right back at you." He smiles, taking a seat in the chair next to Mera and across from me. I pick up the drink and swallow a large gulp, exhaling in frustration. "Well look at you. Aren't you the lucky one who has two lawyers for parents and was born with a silver spoon in his mouth? You know nothing about me, how I grew up, who I am, what I'm like."

"Oh, Sophia Jameson." He shakes his head. "I know *everything* about you."

Mera and Dayne start to blur. I try to open my eyes, but I can't focus. I'm drunk. No, something else is wrong. The room spins. Crap, how much did I drink?

"Don't fight it, just close your eyes," he says.

"W-what did you put in my drink?" I ask in a slow, trailing voice. "You d-drugged..."

"Let go."

Fifteen

THE RED NUMBERS of an alarm clock glow next to the bed. I'm unable to move. I can't figure out how long I've been fading in and out of consciousness. My head throbs, probably more from the alcohol than the drug Dayne must've slipped in my drink. Ten. The clock reads ten. Is that morning or night? I look at the window and it's light outside. Must be morning. The house is quiet.

"Why did you drug me?" I whisper.

I try to push myself up, only to place my hand in vomit on the bedspread. It's cold, probably from last night. There's more than one spot, some on the pillow, some on my tank, and a lot running down the edge of the bed. Where was Mera when I was sick? It's not like her to leave me alone.

I take off my tank and toss it on the floor. Someone already took off my jeans and placed them on the back of a chair by the window. I hope that was Mera and not Dayne.

My eyes are blurry and I can tell that the drug is still in my system. I shake my head and try to focus. That doesn't work. I stand, waver, and have to sit again. My legs shake and my head spins. "What the fuck?" I whisper. "What kind of game are you playing, Dayne?"

Fortunately, no vomit is inside my suitcase, but some has dripped from the bedspread to the hardwood floor. I'm sure a watermark will show underneath it when it's wiped clean. A white rug is about a foot away, free of vomit. It got lucky.

I look around the room. A sitting area with a sofa and a side table are positioned in front of a white stone fireplace. A miniature chandelier hangs above the space, and a second white rug completes the area. The room is quiet and calm. The only window is long and narrow, on the wall opposite the bedroom door. There's a desk and chair underneath it. A flat screen TV is on the entry side of the room and a metal roll cart with breakfast has been left just inside the door. I'm too nauseous to eat so I turn back and face the window, easing my body off the bed. I waver again, but I'm able to stand, walking slowly toward the bathroom. I enter a narrow hall that has a kitchenette with fully stocked cabinets. I wash my vomit-covered hand off in a small sink while staring at a wine rack filled with red and white wine. My legs shake as I hold onto the counter for stability. I can't believe I had all that vodka. I'm in so much pain. My head, my arms, everything hurts, especially my shoulder and neck. I must've slept wrong.

I continue past a closet and into a two-story bathroom. It's enormous. Two skylights bring in the Nevada sun and the walk-in shower has three showerheads... three... and double glass doors. Light green glass sinks sparkle in the sun. A half-wall mirror soars above the sinks, reflecting more light throughout the room, and a set of marble steps lead up to a clear glass door—a balcony. Jesus. I feel like I'm at a spa. I understand why Mera doesn't want to leave.

I relieve myself, feeling slightly better, with clearer eyes and a sounder mind. I'm starting to come out of whatever drug Dayne gave me. I still don't get it. If he had just told me I was going to sleep in this suite, I would've said fine. He didn't have to drug me to get me in here. Where else can I go? I wonder if he drugged Mera too. Maybe they didn't want me around for their evening meeting. Maybe they were afraid I'd hear something I wasn't supposed to.

I walk over to the sink and wash my hands, enjoying the warmth of the water. I need a shower. That will help. Then I need to see what's going on outside this bedroom suite.

There's a pinch in my shoulder like I've just been stung by a bee, then an odd tingling sensation travels around the area, causing me to grab my shoulder and scratch. My hand touches plastic wrap. I slide my fingers over it and feel tape along the edges. I look into the mirror. My body shudders, my eyes widen, and I let out a long high-pitched scream.

Property of Jameson Industries is clear as the light of day, tattooed across my shoulder in fancy script, giving it some false sense of beauty. I move closer to the mirror, touching it again.

"Fuck you, Dad!" I yell at the top of my lungs, almost losing my voice. "Fuck you!"

I pace until my legs finally work with my brain to run to the bedroom door. It's locked. I pound on it and kick it with my bare feet. I'm locked in.

"Mera," I cry out. "Mera, can you hear me?" I smack the door with my palms, frantically trying to escape.

"Sophia," a voice calls out. I turn around but see no

one.

"Who's there? Where are you? Come out so I can see you."

"It's Carl, look at the screen."

I take a step back and look at the wall next to the door, seeing Carl's face on the flat screen. He's in an office, still chewing on that fucking toothpick.

"Tell my dad to open this door, RIGHT, NOW!"

"Sophia, calm down. You're okay, right?"

"No! I'm locked in this room and I have a fucking tattoo. I'm not staying here. I don't know what you guys have planned, but I'm not doing shit for any of you! Open the goddamn door... now!" I scream, kicking it again.

"You need time to cool off, which is why the door is locked."

"Where are you? Are you in this house? Tell my dad he better let me out of here!"

"Like I said, you need time to chill. It's Tuesday and everyone's at work, maybe this evening you can come out and play. And the way you look, you probably need all day to freshen up. Take a shower and put on some clothes." He looks down at my breasts.

I give him the finger, putting my arms across my chest. I find a solid black t-shirt in my suitcase and throw it over my head.

"Ahh, that's too bad. I was starting to enjoy my job for once."

"Listen, Carl—"

"Sophia. Eat your breakfast, shower, and shave, or do whatever you women do to fancy up, keep that tat covered, then fucking chill and wait. It could be worse. You could be dead." The screen goes blank and he disappears. I scream and pound on the wall underneath it, wanting to kill all of them.

"I hate it when people say that!" I shout. "It could be worse, your arm could fall off." I pace in front of the bed. "It could be worse, you could go blind, or fall off a cliff, or get trampled by a horse. It could be worse, the house could be on fire. Then what? Then what, Carl?" I scream. "Would you let me out if the house were on fire?" I look at the fireplace and quickly kneel in front of it. "Why not?" I whisper. "I'll burn this house down if I have to."

And with that, the fireplace blazes in front of me, turning on in a split second.

"Sophia," Carl says.

I hold my middle finger high in the air.

"It's electric, basically an oversized space heater. You're not going to burn down the house with it."

I ignore him and watch the flames, leaning against the front side of the sofa. With a long exhale; I bow my head in defeat.

"Where's Cove?" I ask. I turn and look over my shoulder to see that the screen is black once again. "Fucker," I mumble.

My shoulder throbs and so does my head. I need something to ease the pain. I walk back to the bathroom and run the shower, taking off my shirt and sliding out of my underwear. I search through the drawers by the sink and find a bottle of ibuprofen. Thank God. I swallow three hoping they kick in soon.

I'm careful not to get the tattoo wet. I can't believe it's even there. My first one. My first tat and it's an advertisement, no, it's a contract for a porn company, AND it has my name on it. How belittling.

"This is going to be one fucking long day," I say, rinsing vomit off my body. I sit on the shower bench and let hot water pelt my face and chest. I open my mouth, swallow water, then take more in, letting it roll out of my mouth and flow down my chin.

I wonder what happened to Cove. Maybe they really did take him to Lake Mead. They have the video, what else do they need him for? Then again, why do they need me? I hate all of this. I feel like I've been blindfolded for weeks.

I turn off the shower in complete aggravation, dry off and get dressed. Putting my black t-shirt back on and the short black and grey skirt I wore to Wayne and Lydia's. Won't *they* be worried? And Leondra? Of course they will. They'll be here soon. Paul can't keep them away. They'll know something's wrong when they don't hear from us. Shit, did I say Paul? I didn't even call him 'dad.' If I'm his property, I guess he isn't really my dad anymore. That's how I'm going to process this. I'm his employee. He's my boss. What is he going to make me do? Maybe nothing. Maybe they're all just trying to scare me. Perhaps it's all a joke.

I walk back to the bedroom and try the door. Still locked. This is no joke. I give in and sit in front of the fireplace with the metal roll cart at my side—cold eggs, bacon, a spice muffin and some cantaloupe. I eat it all accept for the eggs, unable to stomach them with the vodka and vomit still fresh in my mind. There's also a menu on the cart and a pen to fill in my order. I look over the list, assuming it's for lunch or dinner, only to see names running down the front, along with a description next to each one.

"What the fuck is this?" I whisper. "Hey Carl," I say.

"Carl, you still listening?"

It's quiet. Not a sound comes from inside the house or the screen. I read the names, finding Cove part way down the sheet.

Larry Lick - *Want a happy clit? Larry's known to have the fastest tongue in the west. Drop your panties for a flicking fun night.*

Shooting Star - *Make a wish. Our Desert Shooting Star will be your submissive, willing to make your wildest dreams come true. Take control, be tender or brutal, the night is yours to explore.*

Rough Rider - *Like it long and hard? RR's our hardcore expert. If you're not afraid of ropes, he's the rancher with the rod. Get ready to be mounted, branded, and prod.*

"My God, really? You guys want me to pick a guy off a menu? How pathetic is that?" I toss it back on the cart and laugh, shaking my head at the ridiculousness of all of this. I wonder what would happen if I circle Cove's porn name. Would he really show up here? Would he submit to me? Or is this just another form of entertainment to them? They know I'm not going to select some random stud.

I pick up the menu and circle Shooting Star then slide it under the door.

Fuckers.

I want to know what they did to him... I kind of hope

he shows up. Yeah, he can be my submissive. He deserves that, I want him to suffer and have his heart broken, just like mine. That's cruel, I know. But it's not fair that everyone around here gets to walk around and act like love doesn't matter. This is my first broken heart, and like the movies, I'm supposed to run sobbing to my mom for love and support, to my dad for comfort and security, and to my friends for a shoulder to cry on. Instead, I'm stuck with these sick thoughts racing through my head. This isn't healthy, being alone in a room with no one to talk to after everything that's happened. Fuck, I'd even talk to Devery right now... I wonder if she ever called Leondra?

"Hey Carl," I say, needing human contact.

"Yes," his face reappears, surprising me that he's still around.

"I can't just walk around in circles with thoughts from the past few days stuck in my head. I'm going insane. I need to talk to someone."

"Talk away."

"Can you hear and see everything that I do?"

"Not exactly, and not by choice, no. Paul wants to make sure you didn't get sick from the drug and that you're not trying to kill yourself or break out."

"I *did* get sick from the drug, I'm *not* the suicidal type, and I *can't* get out."

"You got sick from the alcohol."

"Fine." I sigh. "Why do you have your sunglasses on inside?"

"Sorry." He raises them to his head. "I just got back from lunch," he replies, with his trademark toothpick hanging out of the corner of his mouth.

"I selected a man from the menu."

"I'm sorry?" he questions with a look of confusion.

"The menu you guys gave me to select a fuck buddy for the night, I made my choice."

"Oh. I don't know much about what goes on in the house at night. I've only been to a few parties. I'm more of a day runner, watchman, and serviceman."

"I see," I say on the edge of the bed, watching him poke at his teeth.

"So did you select the right one?" he asks.

"I don't know if there is a right one. I picked the familiar one."

"That's probably the right one then."

"Do you have a girlfriend?" I ask, watching something that looks like a squashed pinto bean getting picked away from his gum.

"Nope, don't need one."

"Don't need or can't get?"

"Maybe I should get back to work and you can go back to being alone."

"I only meant that you might get some women if you didn't pick your teeth in front of people."

"Men. And it's none of your business."

"Oh, I thought... well you came on to me, and—"

"I prefer men, but you're Paul's daughter, I mean, I'd be famous if I fucked you, just like Star."

"*He's* famous without me."

"True."

"So do you have a boyfriend then?"

"Perhaps."

"Too personal?"

"Yeah, is there something else I can help you with, Chatty Kathy?"

"I'm bored and I have cabin fever. What am I supposed to do?"

"There's an iPad over in the desk drawer. You can go online, but we'll monitor everything, so no emails. You'll get cut off immediately. Shop, read, or play solitaire."

"Sounds dreadful."

"What, you don't like to read? It will take your mind off your present *situation*."

"I read. It's just that this doesn't seem like the time to start a new novel, that's all."

"Suit yourself, I need to get back to work before Paul kicks my ass."

I open the desk drawer and find the iPad, unplug it from the power source, and pull the blanket full of vomit off the bed. I lie chest down with my feet swaying in the air.

The homepage when I open Safari is set to the Jameson Industries Website. The advertisement for the expo that just ended takes up half the page. There's a photo of the woman with the breasts the size of Montana, and the wall display of vaginas. I enter the expo page and see that you can register for a private dinner with my dad, which must have been what we interrupted that evening. It costs five hundred dollars to dine with him, five hundred fucking dollars.

I go back to the company homepage and click on the products tab. There are eighty-four pages of items for purchase. "Jesus," I whisper. "I can only imagine how much this brings in. They must have a constant flow into their bank accounts." Magazines, books, posters, videos, toys, clothing, even coffee mugs and shot glasses with the company name. There's a top ten products tab that I click, finding that the *Butterfly Kiss* by California Exotics, and a 3-speed waterproof clit stimulator, are top sellers. Thank God you can't buy any used products on their site.

I scroll through the cock rings, anal beads, bullets, and magic wands, ending with the *soft and sensual realistic feel* dildos. I see my new friend Carl has a nine-incher for sale. Yes, I can buy a Carl Caverns dildo and have it delivered in a discreet package by tomorrow. I close the page in case he's watching. I wouldn't want to send out the wrong message, but like he said, whether he's on that screen talking to me or not, they can monitor my usage. He probably already knows I'm viewing his dick.

I shift my position on the bed and lean against the headboard with my knees up and the iPad on my upper thighs. I've never researched my dad. I never had a reason to. I mean, I've seen his Fox Palace Hotel and Casino, but it's just like all the other online hotels in Vegas. You click on the site, view a few photos, check out the schedules for upcoming events, and make a reservation for a room. Nothing I needed to look at more than once. Now I'm curious as to what's on his company's website.

I come across a photo book of female nudes by Leondra, and the magazine that she's the head photographer for. I can watch numerous three-to ten-minute videos, but find nothing about Cove. I don't see one product, photo, or video... nothing with his name. How can someone so famous in the company not exist on their site? I read the ABOUT page to see how much information my dad will divulge.

Jameson Industries offers adult products and services for

private, business, and home usage. Our main office is located in Las Vegas, Nevada, with smaller branches in Los Angeles, Denver, and St. Louis.

Below the short paragraph are three mugshot style photos of my dad and the Rosen twins. I click on each one and read a description of their titles in the company, education, and interests. I had no idea my dad enjoys golf and fly-fishing. Where can you go fly-fishing in Nevada? What a load of crap.

I click the Facebook tab and a new window opens, taking me directly to their site. The cover photo shows an aerial view of the crowded expo floor from this past weekend. I'm horrified to see the second photo down the page is of Cove kneeling in front of my dad. It's a photo set with the title *A Star's reappearance in the desert.* The set is from that moment. There's a photo of me with my back to Cove, a close-up of Cove with his head lowered, another of my dad turned toward me, and one of me as I leave. There's a description next to the last photo that reads: *Is this the future of Jameson Industries?* Hundreds of comments follow. People, clients, fans, whatever you call them, want to know if I'm really Paul's daughter. Some say they'd like to fuck me, others write that I'm hot, then there're a few who write long paragraphs analyzing what I could do for the company and where I should be placed for the best exposure. What the fuck? I type my own comment, signed in as a Jameson Industry guest on the iPad.

Get a life, people!

I see the comment and smile, then watch as it disappears. "What the?" I type it again. Gone. What, I can't even type a simple message? Fine. I close their page and go to Google's home page. Now what? Can life be any more boring? I'm not the sort of person who can sit around and wait for things to take place. It's not in my nature. "Errrrgh." I wrap my arms around my legs and rock on the bed.

"NOVA," I whisper. The last thing Mera and I did together before I left her place was to search online for NOVA. She texted that she had opened the search and that I needed to call her. What did she see?

I type it in and scroll past the obvious pages we already researched, ending with two Wikipedia sites. One for NOVA stars, and one for NOVA court case. That must be it.

I read about Cove's dad, that he was found guilty of the possession, production, and distribution of child pornography, endangerment of a child, and tax evasion. He was sentenced to twenty years in the Plains City Correctional Center. There's no mention of Cove, Leondra, or Jameson Industries, only a link to child pornography laws in the United States.

The screen on the iPad goes blank and Carl reappears next to me.

"Can't you just fucking be like other women and shop online or look at recipes?"

"That's quite stereotypical of you. Is it the '50s?"

"Find something else to do," he says, disappearing, and my Internet access blocked.

I toss the iPad back in the drawer and spend the rest of the afternoon in a state of unrest. I nibble on cheese and crackers from the kitchenette, explore the closet that's packed with clothes, all different sizes, try to get the flat screen to show an actual channel besides Carl, do some sit-ups, and gaze at the tattoo. I walk up the stairs in the bathroom a few times and stand outside on the balcony in the warm sun. The door wasn't locked, but at three stories up, I'd never be able to jump or escape without breaking a leg... or my neck. I have a clear view of the pool that's been empty all day. If I find out Mera's aware of all of this and she's done nothing to help me...

I go back inside and pace and sigh for hours. Loud music plays in the evening. I start to wonder if they forgot about me. Did they get my menu choice? Will they pick up the breakfast cart? Will I get dinner? Are they going to leave me in here to starve to death? Is that how they'll get rid of me, a slow painful death through the deprivation of food and human contact?

It's ten at night. An entire day has passed and my only contact with the outside world has been with a porn star through a flat screen.

"Carl? You there?"

Sixteen

HE'S NOT. No one's around. Not Carl, my dad, the Rosens, Mera... Cove.

"What the hell?"

I pound on the bedroom door, letting out a burst of frustration. It accomplishes nothing. My hands throb. My head and shoulder still hurt. But surprisingly, I haven't had a panic attack since I've been here.

My eyes scan the room looking for a camera. I don't believe Carl views me through the television. There must be something around, some way he's watching me. I check the chandelier, alarm clock, chairs, pillows, and fireplace. All the obvious places are clear. My eyes examine all the smaller items placed throughout the room. A vase of fake flowers on the desk, pen and notepad, lamp, small ceramic bird statue, and a photo of the Fox Palace... all free of electronic devices. I lie on the bed and watch the ceiling fan above my head spin.

The ceiling fan... has to be. I race over to the bedroom door and flick the switch on the wall. It comes to a stop. I stand on the bed and instantly see a small camera with a tiny cord that runs into the ceiling—perfect placement, right above the bed. I wonder how many clients they've recorded in here, or if it's solely for their employees' "protection." I believe the latter is what they'd say.

I write my dad, or Carl, or whoever, a quick note...

1) I want OUT.
2) What did you do to Cove?
3) You *won't* get away with this!

I place it on one of the blades of the fan, about a foot below the camera, and hope they can read it at such a close proximity to the lens. It's worth a try. I don't bother to cover the camera or rip it out just yet. I feel better about the situation just knowing where it is.

Laughter comes from somewhere in the house, then loud music plays for hours. It's a heavy beat, never slowing to something that lulls me to sleep. I lie in bed and listen, identifying most of the songs as Drake, Eminem, and Jay-Z. At least they've moved into the twenty-first century with their musical tastes. I'll assume that's Dayne. He's probably having anal sex again with Mera.

"Oh God." I moan and roll onto my stomach with a pillow placed over my head. "Make it stop," I mumble into the mattress.

After an hour of swearing about loud music, imprisonment, and boredom, the house finally quiets. I can think. I can think about Cove and how much I miss him. I truly miss him. It's been almost two days since I've seen him. I want to run my hands along his body, kiss his lips, smell his cologne, inhale his warm breath, and fall asleep in his arms. I want to talk to him and spend time with him. Only I'm drained and angry over his offer to my dad, the exchange, that entire morning. And yet, all I can do is think about him.

· · ·

"Sit."

"Mmm?" I moan. What was that? I listen between sleep and consciousness. The room's silent. Must've been a dream.

I hear a squeak and sit up. The roll cart vanishes from the room and the door closes. "Wait!" I throw the sheets off and race to the door. "Come back!" I yell, as my fists pound the hard wood. Whoever it was, they're gone. I'm left alone in the dark.

"Fuck!" I kick the door with my foot and yell. "Fuck, fuck, fuck... Dad?" I exhale and crawl back into bed as tears start to roll down my cheeks. I place my arm across my eyes and sob. My nose runs and my pillow's soggy. I throw it on the floor and lie flat on the bed, wondering how long it will take to fall back asleep. I wipe my eyes and sniffle, trying to clear my nose so I can breathe.

The alarm clock reads two. I sniff again. My chest rises and falls in quick jerks as my body tries to settle itself. The room feels different. Warmer, smaller, and... I sniff again... I smell vanilla and cedar. I'd know that scent anywhere. Cove's in the room.

I sit up and turn on the lamp next to the bed. He's on the sofa in front of the fireplace, head down, his back turned to me.

"Cove," I whisper.

He sits in silence, motionless.

"I can't decide if I want to hit you or hug you," I say.

No answer. No movement. I'm suddenly worried. Maybe he's hurt, or worse, maybe they killed him. I stand and approach the sofa with caution.

"Cove?" I say in a soft voice.

He sits back and sighs, placing one hand on the sofa back, running his other hand through his hair.

"I'm sorry," I say, stepping closer. "Dayne told me how we were both set up."

He takes off his black oxford shoes and throws them against the wall. I jump back quickly. "I don't know whether to laugh or to cry that you just said that to me. You'll fucking listen to Dayne Rosen's words over mine," he says, his body language emanating anger. I take a second step back as he continues to speak. "You promised you'd remember not to listen to any words exchanged in that office. You said you'd remember that I loved you."

"Oh, hell no. Don't you dare turn this around on me," I say, walking toward him. "How could you tape me, us, our first time and not tell me?" I stop in front of him and he turns away. "Look at me!" I shout. He turns, his eyes glare and his nostrils flare. He has two days of stubble on his face, a black eye, dried blood under his nose and on his suit. The same suit he had on in the office. Where has he been? Has he bathed, eaten, or slept since then? I close my eyes and shake my head, still in a fight with my heart. I want to run into his arms and comfort him, but my mind tells me I should slap him instead. I lower my voice and sit on the sofa. "I'm sorry. You're right, but so am I. You shouldn't have taped us, and you know it, but I should've trusted your actions and words in the office."

"I was trying to give you and everyone what they wanted."

"What about you? What is it that you want? You were trying to sell me to my dad... to the industry."

"I fucking said not to listen to what Paul and I said!" he shouts. "You know as well as I do that I can't have what I want. So I'm going to spend my life giving people what *they* want."

"Why didn't you tell me what you were doing?"

"It wouldn't have been the same if you knew. Not as passionate, not as real," he says, taking off his jacket and tie as he lowers his voice. "You'd think about the camera, how you sounded and looked when you came." He rolls his shirtsleeves and I notice a cut on his arm and more blood on his clothing. "It meant something to me, whether you believe it or not. I would've never given myself to another woman. No one's ever captured my heart like you, Sophia. And I've never felt so sick and broken because of it. I don't have the words to explain what you've done to me. I wanted that time with you to be about what we saw and felt in *that* moment. Nothing else."

"You could at least apologize. I'm sorry I didn't trust you in that office and about everything that we've gone through, but I'm not taking all the blame."

"I'm not sorry."

"What?" I question and lean forward on the sofa. "What did you just say?"

"You heard me. Fuck you if you think I'm sorry. I was in a perfect moment with the woman I love, and I'll never regret that time, even if this company has control of it now.

I can't change who I am and what I did. We were together and that's all I wanted. This fucking company is separate from my heart, but I still have a job to do. This is how I've spent half my life and I don't give a shit anymore that I recorded us. That was all them, not me."

"No, it wasn't. You made that decision, not my dad and the Rosens," I say harshly.

"No one gave me a choice, not you, not any of them!"

"You need to learn how to make your own choices!" I yell, standing. "So, you're really not sorry you gave that to my dad? You think they should market us? Me? Is that what you're saying?"

"All I care about is never feeling the way that I did when you walked out that door. I stayed by your side through all of this, and you turned on me in that room," he says. "Remember that night under the stars? You said you'd be right by my side. You said you wanted to be in that office to support me, no matter what I said to Paul or what I had to do. I haven't slept or been able to eat. Your father gave me a bottle of liquor and locked me in the fucking theater room with early NOVA movies playing on the screen. I wish they had killed me instead. Now I've stepped out of one hell and into another. Now I'm locked in a room with a woman who's ripped my heart in two, who hates me, and who wants me dead."

"That's not true. How could you say that? Why are you acting like such a shit?"

"See."

"Enough!" my dad silences us.

I jump and Cove throws his head back. "I was wrong, I'm in a whole other hell now."

"Both of you, in my office," he says, dressed in black

silk pajama bottoms and a black silk robe.

"Great!" I walk quickly to the door. "Get me the fuck out of this room." He grabs my arm and holds me close to him. "Let go," I demand in an unforgiving tone.

"You and I need to talk. Then I'll bring you back here until morning, which is only a few hours away." He looks at his watch. "Cove, now!"

Cove follows us out, his hands in his pockets and head down as he walks. We enter an open space at the end of the hall, just past my bedroom suite, and stop at a set of carved, wooden double doors. They reach the height of the ceiling. My dad pulls one side open and releases my arm, allowing me the freedom to step inside on my own.

It's his home office. The entire room is wood—the ceilings, floor, walls, bookshelves, desk, and a set of stairs leading to the third floor—all a mahogany-stained wood. There's a desktop computer and a laptop on his desk, as well as a second desktop on the table behind his chair. A painting of a female nude hangs above the second computer, and by the colors and style, I can tell it's one of Leondra's.

"Sit down, both of you."

Cove immediately takes a seat as I continue to scan the room. "What's upstairs?" I ask.

"Sit down."

"No. You need to let me out of this house. I'm your daughter and you're treating me like an animal!"

"If you do what I tell you, when I tell you, you'll be able to leave soon. I need to take care of some things first. I'm not sending you out into this world until everything's settled. Now sit down!"

I fall into the hard wooden chair next to Cove, as my dad leans against the front of his desk, taking a cigar out of a box. "So tell me kids, what's with all the fighting? I expected you guys to run into one another's arms after spending so much time alone, but now all you're giving me is something that should air on *Divorce Court*," he says, lighting a cigar. I turn away and look over at the stairs again. I wonder if I can outrun him? "It leads to my bedroom, not outside," he says. "Turn around and listen to me."

I raise my legs so my feet are resting on the chair. I wrap my arms around them and hold my ankles, trying to curl into a ball and disappear.

"Cove, you need to talk to your mother. She's been calling my cell and yours all night and I need her to stop. Check in with her so I can have a day of peace," he says, taking Cove's cell out of his robe pocket and tossing it in his lap. "Sophia," he says, turning to me. "Not a word comes out of your mouth, you understand? You're here because we need to talk, and that will happen after his phone call."

I place my head between my knees.

"Good." He looks back at Cove. "Tell her everything's okay, convince her you're fine, just like old times."

Cove looks at his cell but doesn't move. My dad walks around his desk and sits in his chair, typing something into his laptop. He closes it and puffs on his cigar, then places his feet up on the desk. I hear footsteps on the stone floor outside the office and within seconds, Dayne's by my dad's side in jeans and a t-shirt. My dad smiles and looks at his bare feet.

"What's the issue, Paul?"

"Sorry to get you out of bed. I need your gun."

"What, this gun?" He pulls out a semi-automatic pistol from the back of his jeans.

"Ah, the Glock this evening. Good choice." He takes it from him and points it at Cove. "Put it on speaker and call. Make it quick so we can get some sleep."

Cove calls and rests the cell on the arm of his chair. We wait for his mom to pick up.

"Cove! Sweetheart, where are you?" Leondra weeps. "Are you and Sophia okay?"

"Yes, everything's fine."

"Why haven't you called?"

My dad pulls the slide of the gun back and loads a round into the chamber. Cove looks directly at him then leans forward. He rests his arms on his legs and looks down at the floor. "I was busy. I'm sorry."

"Cove, what's wrong?"

"Everything's just like it usually is, no need to worry."

"That *is* what I'm worried about. Where are you?"

"I'm at Paul's. We're both at Paul's. I have some business to finish for him, but it shouldn't take long."

"Cove... are you alone?"

He's quiet and my dad stands.

"No, he's not," I say. "I'm here, Leondra." Dayne gives me an inquisitive look, and my dad slowly turns the gun on me. Really Dad?

"Sophia, is everything alright?"

"Yes," I respond in my cheeriest voice. "We've had a little argument, but we're okay... for now."

She laughs and sighs in relief. "Is that what's wrong? The two of you are in the middle of another fight? It's a sign of true love."

Cove laughs and shakes his head then turns away from me. My dad waves the gun to wrap things up.

"I'll try to call you soon, but don't worry so much if I don't. It's not like Paul has us locked up in a room somewhere, we're just busy."

Dayne immediately stands behind us and places his hands on Cove's shoulders, pulling him back into the chair. "That was a joke, by the way," he says.

"I know, sweetheart. Just do a better job at staying in touch with me, okay? Especially when you have issues in your love life. I want to help you... and you, too, Sophia."

"Give Lewis a big hug for me," I say.

"Always. Cove, your father wanted me to pass along a reminder to be respectful and kind to Sophia."

"No problem. And Mother?" He hesitates. My dad turns the gun back to him and places his index finger on the trigger. Cove swallows, looking into his eyes. "I love you."

My dad smiles and there's silence from Leondra's end. I hear a whimper that turns into a soft cry. "I love you too," she says before ending the call.

Cove tosses the cell on my dad's desk and exhales deeply.

"That wasn't so bad, was it?" My dad grins. "Dayne, take him back to the room and get him something to eat, I need to talk to my daughter. Cove, take a shower and put on some clean clothes. Clean yourself up."

He stands and leaves the room, not saying a word. Dayne closes the door behind them, leaving me alone with my dad. I turn and look directly into his eyes, searching for some hint of love coming from the stranger before me.

"Mera told me she's happy, which I find hard to

believe."

"Why? We treat her well."

"Why did you leave me that note in my loft, and why won't you allow us to be in contact with one another?"

"Two people together can do a lot more harm than one."

I roll my eyes and place my feet on the floor. "I'd like to leave, please," I say, trying a different approach.

"Where will you go if I let you out of this house?"

"Home, to St. Louis."

"Where will you live?" he asks, relighting his cigar. He takes two puffs and blows out a large cloud of smoke. "You no longer have access to your loft, and I've had Mera's place cleared and her things sent here. Where you gonna live, Kiddo?"

"I don't need your money."

He chuckles and swivels in his chair, blowing out another puff of smoke. "We have a gold mine here, thanks to Cove, words I never thought I'd say. But... Sophia, I need you to sign this form so I can release some information to our clients." He slides a piece of paper across his desk. "It says you were aware of all the times you were filmed and recorded, you're of legal age, and that you agree to receive a total of five percent of all profits from your site, no more. You'll be able to leave and live on your own as soon as we make some money and you get your share. Until then, I won't be sending you out on the streets."

"I have money in my bank account."

"No, you don't. You *had* money in your bank account."

"Leondra will let me stay with her."

He laughs and places his feet back on the desk, his hands behind his head. "No she won't. Not if I talk to her."

"I'll stay at a fucking shelter!" I yell. "You can use the fucking video, I don't care, but I don't want to be a prisoner!"

"Sign the form, Sophia," he says. "Sign it so we can all go to bed. Tomorrow will be a brand new day to discuss more details about your time here. Soon, you'll be able to roam the house. After that, when you have your money, you can leave."

I take the piece of paper and a pen off the top of his desk and read each sentence carefully. I place the point of the pen on the signature line and stop. "Tell me something first. Do you expect me to be in more videos? Do I have to do more, or are we just discussing the airplane video?"

"There may be more."

"How many? One? Five? A hundred?"

"A few. We'll see how it goes. But I don't think people will want to see much after the first one. That's the whopper. It will be our top video for a few weeks then fizzle out. We'll make a lot quickly and move on. So probably less than ten shots."

"With who?"

"Who the fuck do you think?" He sits up and slams his feet on the floor. "You may not believe that I care for you, but I do, I care for all my employees."

"I'm your daughter, Dad, not your fucking employee. Would you like me to say that again?"

"Miss Sophia Jameson, I don't really know you. We don't seem to know very much at all about one another."

"How can you say that?"

He ignores my question and takes another puff on his cigar. "I won't bring in random men for this. It's you and Cove."

"Well, if you haven't noticed, we hate each other."

He laughs. "If *you* haven't noticed, the two of you are so madly in love I want to puke every time I see the two of you together. You're just too young and inexperienced to realize it, both of you. Now play nice."

"I don't believe a word that comes out of your mouth. If that were the case, if this is over soon and I'll only be with one person, then what's with the fucking tattoo?"

"What tattoo?"

I pull my shirt neck to the side and he stares at the tat, his eyes narrowing. He takes out his cell and looks away only for a brief moment to place a call.

"I need you back in my office," he says, slamming the cell firmly onto his desk.

I lower my hand and my collar falls over the ink.

"You're right, Sophia, I'll use my own daughter for money, and the only thing I feel bad about is that I don't feel bad. You have my word that you can leave soon. When I say the time is right, you can move forward with your life and us with ours."

"And Cove?"

"Maybe."

"Dad... please. You have total control over a grown man."

"What do you want, Paul?" Dayne asks, entering the room. My dad and I stare at each other, neither one of us moving.

"Sign the form."

I sign it and throw it at him. It floats down to his desk and he smiles. "Dayne, I need you to do a couple of things," he says, keeping his eyes on me. "One, damage control with Devery. She called Sophia's phone twice today. Call her tomorrow and talk to her. Two, I need you to walk Sophia back to the room and make sure both her and Cove have breakfast in the morning."

"Done. Anything else?"

"Yeah," he says, still in possession of Dayne's gun. "Get your ass back in this office as soon as she's locked in her suite."

Dayne reaches his hand to me, but keeps his eyes on my dad. I stand and try to walk past him, but he grabs my arm. "Let's walk together, beautiful," he says, leading me down the hall. "Let me guess," he whispers. "You showed him the tat?"

"Let me guess," I whisper back. "The reason he thought you drugged me was because you told him I was out of control. Right? He didn't know about the tat. Hope you have fun," I say with a smirk as he opens the door and pushes me inside the bedroom suite. The door slams hard in my face and a breeze blows my hair back.

"Fucking bitch," he says from the other side, his shadow under the door disappearing, headed to my dad's office.

Seventeen

COVE LIES ON the sofa on his stomach. His shirt and socks are in a pile on the floor next to him, his dark eyes reflecting the flickering flames in the fireplace. I notice that his suitcases are by the desk next to mine, and a white ceramic plate full of crumbs is on the coffee table.

"Cove, I'm sorry." I walk toward him.

"Don't," he says, raising his hand for me to stop. "I don't need you to comfort me."

He closes his eyes and hides his face with his arm when I sit on the floor next to him. The smell of liquor and body odor overpowers his cologne. I pull his arm away to uncover his face.

"Please don't," he whispers.

My finger gently traces his black eye and swollen nose. "You're beautiful, Cove Everton," I say, trying to ease some of his pain.

"Yep, look where that's gotten me."

"I was talking about what's inside you." He keeps his eyes shut. "I know you tried, Babe."

"Don't call me that, Sophia."

I swallow hard and start over. "I understand that you did what you had to do."

"Do you?" He looks at me. "The fuck you do."

"I signed the agreement form for my dad."

He laughs and rolls on his back, placing a hand on his head. "So that means you understand? You signed a form and now you're just like me, right?"

"You know what? Screw you!" I stand and throw myself on the bed. "I hate you!"

"Then why'd you pick me from the menu? You could've had a nice clit lick from Larry."

"Oh my God. I can't believe I've spent the past two days upset over you. I can't believe I loved you!"

"Well I can't believe *I* loved you!" he shouts and sits up, his eyes glaring back at me. "A fucking Jameson, I should've known better."

"What? Why are you so angry with me? I don't understand why you're treating me like my dad treats me!" I shout, losing complete control. My body convulses and I fall back into a fit of tears.

That got him. The room is quiet except for sniffles and cries, his and mine.

I can hear my dad and Dayne in an argument down the hall. It sounds like a fistfight between the two. Furniture topples over and someone is thrown against a wall. I sit up and see that Cove is doing the same. We listen to the fight. It's worse than ours, powerful and violent.

"What happened when you left?" Cove asks.

I take a tissue off the side table and blow my nose. "I signed the contract and that was it," I respond, my heart telling me not to tell Cove about the tattoo. Not now.

We listen and wait for them to stop. It sounds like the entire office is being destroyed. Then, in an instant, it ends.

Footsteps approach the bedroom suite. A shadow appears under the door. Cove places a finger to his mouth to stay quiet. It sounds like Dayne, he's panting and I can sense his hand is on the handle. His fist pounds the door, sending Cove to his feet.

Five seconds, ten seconds, finally, the shadow vanishes and we're left alone.

Cove paces in front of the fireplace with his hands in his pockets. "I *don't* treat you like Paul treats you," he says. "I'm not like him."

"Oh no? Are you sure?" I ask. "Neither one of you respects me or listens to me. You're both so caught up in the business that you don't care who you hurt, including the people closest to you. He'll market me because of you. The first time I've ever showed love for another person will be sold for people to jerk off to, and that's because of the two of you. You're just like him."

Cove rushes over to me. "I'm *not* like Paul Jameson!" he shouts, grabbing my shoulders, his face in a rage like he wants to shake those words away. I howl when he presses against the tattoo.

"Oww! You're hurting me!"

He steps back and lowers his arms, appalled by his actions. "I barely touched you. I wasn't going to hurt you," he says.

I fall to the floor and curl into a fetal position, my heart cold and lifeless. "You *have* hurt me."

"Sophia, hey," he says softly. "I'm not like Paul. Don't

think of me that way."

I sob from the events of the past three days, from being struck down by every person I know and love. He lowers next to me and runs his hand along my body. "Get up, please. I can't stand to see you like this." He places his hands under my body and lifts.

"Aaew!" I cry.

"Jesus, Sophia. What's wrong with you? Are you hurt?" he asks, placing me back on the floor. He circles me, at a loss as to what to do. "Get up," he pleads in a louder voice. "Don't fool around anymore, get up."

My arms shake as I lift my body. I pull my shirt over my head and bow down, embarrassed by my own last name that's inked on my body.

"Fuck!" He slams his fist into the wall. "Fucking Paul. Goddamn you! This is your daughter, your own daughter," he yells as I curl back into a ball. He falls to the floor, wrapping his arms around me. "I'm sorry, Sophia. I'm so sorry," he whispers. "I didn't mean for this, for any of this to happen to you. I didn't know it was going to get this bad."

This is it, my nervous breakdown. I felt it coming yesterday, but Mera and I drank it away. Only now, I'm fragile from this entire experience, and my heart and mind have collapsed.

"Soph, please say something." I'm too upset to answer him. I just whimper and put my hands over my face. "I really thought I had it this time. That I could make something work, make Paul happy, but I knew I was in trouble when he said he didn't think he would make enough of a profit for an exchange." He lies alongside me. "I saw you explode in a fury. I figured you weren't ever going to speak to me again after seeing the video, so I said shit to get you out of the room. I said stupid shit, like he should market you, to piss him off, because I was mad at everyone. I spoke out of anger and hatred..." I sniff and wipe the tears off my cheeks. He kisses the top of my head and holds me closer. "I also wanted you to hate me."

"Why?" I ask, looking into his eyes.

"I couldn't bear it. I was heartbroken, still am. I thought it would be easier to let you go if you hated me, that I wouldn't think about you as much or feel the pain that I started to feel when we woke up that morning in the hotel. But it didn't work. I'm a complete wreck without you. I don't know how to heal and make this pain go away."

"Cove, I don't hate you. I don't."

He attempts to pick me up again, slower, more carefully this time. He carries me to the bathroom and places me on the counter, then turns on the water to the shower. I scan his bruised body. His back has marks that look like he's been hit with a baseball bat. He's teary-eyed, filled with a sadness that shatters my spirit.

"You okay?" I whisper.

"No."

"What can I do?"

He unbuttons his pants and slides them off, then his boxers. He turns to me, semi-erect. His eyes focus on my tat, not my face, or breasts, not my hand reaching out for him, but the tat. His lips form a thin line.

"Cove?" I lower my hand.

"Hmm?"

"How hurt are you?"

More tears roll down his face as he shakes his head.

"I'm fine. A few cuts and bruises that will heal," he whispers. "My wounds will go away, that won't." He points to my shoulder.

"I'm sorry," I whisper.

"No, I am. I'm sorry we're in this moment. I've already gone through it with my father when I was twelve. What happened to you, this conversation, it's the same as what I experienced one night with him. My life has come full circle." He comes to me, putting his hands on the counter, one to each side of my thighs. "This can't be good. To relive the most traumatic day of my life has to be some sort of a sign. Something's off. Something's always wrong in this house, but this is different. I can feel death hanging in the air."

"Don't say that. What happened to you?"

"An entire day sitting drunk in the theater room watching myself on the screen being raped as a teenager didn't help to keep my sanity. But it's more than that. I hurt you. Everything I did and said was out of anger. And your words in that office... I would have rather been shot dead years ago. I won't go through that again. I'm terrified to touch you and start over because I know that in an instant you could turn on me and be gone."

"I'm not going anywhere. I'm not."

"You've said that before." He places his forehead against mine. "Sophia... I don't want anyone else. I need *you*. Don't say it unless you mean it."

He backs away and steps into the shower, placing his hands against the wall under the showerhead. Water glides down his body, the dried blood slowly washing away. "I love you," he whispers.

"Cove, what happened?"

"I just told you."

"No, the traumatic day with your dad. How did it end?"

He sucks in a quick breath then forces the air from his lungs, once, twice, before he begins.

"I was in the shower, exactly like I am now. Same position. He was by the sink, just like you. He said I'd realize the difference between Paul's world and love once I found someone I had feelings for. He said he didn't want me to think that the industry was reality, and when I found someone special, I'd be able to move on. You're that person, Sophia." He pauses. "Maybe this is a sign for me to make a change. Everything's starting over, I'm back to day one, but this time I need to do something differently. If I have to relive the past, I won't allow it to take the same course it did when I was a kid. I'll make sure of it."

He turns and stares. The door to the shower is open and he holds out his hand for me to join him.

I step in and lather his back, careful not to put any pressure on his bruises. He flinches every so often as I wash his arms and legs. His eyes explore the ink on my shoulder, zoning out for a moment, but then he quickly pulls me to his chest. This is the embrace that we need. Our hearts unlock, overflowing with desire. We're unable to ignore the powerful love we both feel. I place my arms around his back and we kiss. Hot water streams down our faces as steam rises and conceals our bodies. His tongue chases mine and we dance inside one another's mouths.

I hope he's okay. I want him to know that I love him. He has to feel it. He must know.

I melt as he nibbles my earlobe, tugging, kissing, and licking my skin. "Sophia," he whispers in my ear. "Can you hear me?" His words are barely audible.

"Yes," I whisper back.

"The sound of the water should help drown out my words," he says. "I want you to know that my mother's coming."

I kiss his neck to his ear. "How do you know?" I ask in my smallest voice. I wrap my legs around his hips and my arms around his neck. Our lips connect in a fiery craze.

He whispers, "I told her I loved her. She always says it first. It's our code. If I say it before her, she knows something's wrong."

"That's why she started to cry?" I whisper.

"Yes."

"What's her plan?"

He kisses my chin. I throw my head back and smile. "Haven't a clue," he says. "It's out of my hands."

He sets me down and turns off the water. Gently, he peels the tape and takes the covering off my tattoo, throwing it in the trash. I'm wrapped in a towel, my heart melting when he smiles.

"Make love to me," I say. "I want you inside me."

"I'll do anything you want. But you know we're not alone."

"I know. Just tell me that you'll be with me because you want to be, and not because I placed an order for you from a menu."

"I'll be with you because I love you." He carries me to the bed, lays me down, and unfolds the top of the towel, exposing my breasts. "You're beautiful, my pretty little dove." His cock is firm as he crawls over me, planting kisses from my lips to my breasts.

"I love you," I whisper.

He opens the towel and uncovers me. The back of his hand brushes across my face and down my chest, ending at my swollen lips. He slides a finger inside, and another; his eyes closing with a deep exhale.

"I never thought I'd feel this again."

"Me either," I say.

"I'm talking about my heart, Sophia."

"So am I."

He smiles, positioning my ankles over his shoulders while kissing my knees and inner thighs. I moan in delight, the desire for him to fill me is overwhelming.

"Cove... please."

He holds his cock and dips between my inner lips. With one quick thrust, he fills me whole, and my insides come undone. I grip the sheets in pure ecstasy.

"You feel incredible," I say with a jagged breath. "My entire body just exploded, all because of you. Dominate me, Cove. Be the one who controls all of this. I'm yours."

He moves fast and hard, thrusting deep. I place my hands through his hair and grip the back of his neck, steering his mouth to mine. Our heated bodies slide in excited movements. I'm wild for him, unable to control the erotic sounds crawling out of my mouth. He lowers his groin over my clit and rubs quickly against it, the pressure growing my arousal.

"Cum for me," he says. "Do it now." He hammers relentlessly over me. "Do it."

I grab onto his arms and tilt my head back, my abdomen and chest tense.

"That's it, keep closing around me. Keep clutching my

dick. That'll make me cum, Baby."

"Cove!"

"Cum. Do it now," he demands.

I seize his arms as showers of pleasure race through my body.

"Fuck, Fuck, Sophia. I'm cumming with you," he says as he pulls out and jerks himself off. I whimper at his absence and place my hand to my clit to finish my release. His cum lands on my chest. He gasps at the gratification, falling over top of me with a huff and a smile. We inhale deeply, our pleasure ending with a passionate kiss.

A light enters his eyes, making me feel revived and happy, something I haven't experienced in days. "You okay?" he asks, brushing my hair off my face.

"I'm more than okay," I respond with a smile. "We're both okay."

He blushes and rolls over, placing his arm under his head, looking like the God that he is. I take the towel and wipe his cum off our stomachs. His body is amazingly toned. I just can't get enough of his features, his gorgeous dark hair and dark eyes. He's so beautiful.

He grins, catching me admiring him. "What are you thinking about?" he asks.

"That I'm lucky. That we're lucky."

He laughs. "I'd like to agree with you, but we *are* locked in a room, and Paul's house for that matter."

"Besides that. We'll make this work. Together, we're stronger than they think we are."

He places his hand behind my neck, guiding me closer for a kiss. "You're right. Besides all that, we are lucky," he says.

I take his hand in mine and put it over my heart as we both stare at the ceiling fan. "Hum for me," I request. "I've only heard rap music for two days and I'd like to hear something pretty as I fall asleep."

"Rap music can be pretty."

"Please?"

"I usually only hum when I'm nervous, but for you, I'll make an exception. Any requests?"

"Whatever you feel is right for the moment."

"You like John Legend?" He runs his hand through my hair.

"Mmm."

"I'll take that as a yes. 'All of Me' it is." He hums softly.

I yawn, closing my eyes. "Thank you," I whisper. "That's a sweet love song. When you finish, I'd like to hear Bruno Mars, David Gray, and Maroon 5."

I sense a smile on his face as he finds my demands playful. "Don't ever leave me, Sophia," he whispers. "Don't turn your back on me again. Please... just let me have your heart, forever."

We fall into a deep sleep, our hands and bodies tightly entwined. We're exhausted, sore, bruised, and beaten... but in love.

To continue reading The NOVA Trilogy, please purchase Sunset Rush (Book Three).

About the Author

Aven Jayce was born in Buffalo, NY. She received her undergraduate degree from SUNY Fredonia and her graduate degree from the University of Colorado. Now in her mid-forties, she resigned her position as a college professor to enjoy life as an author, wife, optimistic introvert, and loving mama.

Novels by Aven Jayce:

The NOVA Trilogy
Fallen Snow (Book One)
Desert Star (Book Two)
Sunset Rush (Book Three)
The Dark Scarlett
Jameson Hotel Series (Parts 1-6)
The Land of Rabbits: Long Shot Love Duet #1
The Lair of Jack: Long Shot Love Duet #2
Love Death Obsession

85793266R00158

Made in the USA
Lexington, KY
04 April 2018